Connor

By

Barbara Davidson-Miles

Barbara Davidson-Miles

ISBN: 1-4107-1094-7 (e-book)
ISBN: 1-4107-1095-5 (Paperback)
ISBN: 1-4107-1096-3 (Dust Jacket)

Library of Congress Control Number: 2003090033

This book is printed on acid free paper.

Printed in the United States of America
Bloomington, IN

1stBooks - rev. 04/04/03

Dedication

To my husband, Steve,
who has always believed in me.

Acknowledgments

I wish to thank Marilyn Weishaar, The Weisrevise, for her editing services, advice, and encouragement.

I would like to give special thanks to my niece, Kelly (Red Pen Publishing), for many hours of help and advice from the very beginning, when *Connor* was just an idea in my head. I am also grateful to her husband, Gary, for his insights into the world of geoenvironmental engineering.

Prologue

Mireya stared across the dinner table at her mother. Even at eight years old she recognized the signs. Anna Blackwood Richardson returned her daughter's gaze with glassy, unfocused eyes. There was no conversation. Periodically their butler, Mario, would glide into the room to refill the wine glasses, and then melt into the background again. Mireya's mother was not eating, just rearranging the food on her plate between glasses of wine.

Why didn't her father just tell Mario not to bring any more wine? She would never understand his lack of intervention when they both knew very well what was on the horizon. In a few weeks, Anna would isolate herself in her room, drinking and sleeping around the clock. In a month or so, Mireya's Native American nanny, Gina, would pack a bag for Anna, and Mario would drive her to a private rehab center in the Berkshires where she would remain for five or six weeks. This cycle had been a part of Mireya's life as long as she could remember; it would repeat itself until her mother's liver gave up the fight during Mireya's junior year in high school.

For now, it was the lack of conversation that vexed her. She wanted to tell her father all about the vegetable garden she and Gina had planted. She wanted to tell him how later that summer they could skip their weekly produce-buying journey to Haymarket Square, because she would be picking fresh vegetables from her garden every day. She had a lot to say, but was afraid to break the silence. So she remained quiet, internalizing her sadness, her anger, and her frustration. She sat with her family and ate her dinner alone.

She stared at her plate, contemplating how much bigger and tastier her garden-fresh green beans would be than the ones she had yet to finish. Hers would be bright green and slightly crunchy when she bit into them, not all soft and mushy like these. She pushed her beans into a row. They reminded her of rafts of logs lumberjacks floated down rivers to sawmills.

A small seed of panic sprouted somewhere in her core. Its voracious tentacles insinuated themselves throughout her being, constricting her heart and soul; gripping her as though she were in an ever-tightening vise. She lurched to her feet, knocking her chair over backwards. Clapping both hands over her ears, she screamed until she emptied her chest of air. Still the tentacles of panic refused to release her.

"S-N-E-A-K-E-R-S!" she screamed.

Her mother's eyes widened with surprise. Her father dropped his fork and stood up.

"S-N-E-A-K-E-R-S!"

Her father grasped her forearms and pulled her hands away from her ears. "What's wrong, Rey?"

"SNEAKERS IS SCREAMING!"

"What?" He stared into her eyes, trying to understand, unable to hide his alarm.

She pulled away from her father, one hand over her ear and the other clutching her throat. “IT HURTS! STOP IT!”

Panic’s grip began to ease, but as the tentacles withered, she was filled with a darkness that she sucked in like ink into her father’s old-fashioned fountain pen. Blackness, hopelessness, futility, misery, anguish; this was despair. This was an emotion far too powerful and far too dark for a child to embrace. She slipped to the floor in a dead faint.

“GINA! MARIO! DIAL 911!” Mireya’s father lifted her from the floor. Bewildered, he stared at her small, limp body.

They had been dining informally in the solarium of the mansion in Marblehead, Massachusetts, which was Mireya’s childhood home. “WHERE THE HELL IS EVERYBODY?” he shouted as he ran through a series of cavernous rooms toward the kitchen. Rey’s mother stood up and tried to follow but realized that she was too unstable to walk and sat back down.

The kitchen was deserted; the back door stood open. Through the open door he could see Gina, Mario, and the groundskeeper, Henry, standing in a circle looking at something on the ground. He ran out the door.

“WHAT THE HELL IS GOING ON HERE?” He ran to the group with every intention of sending them all packing but what he saw stopped him in his tracks. Mireya’s cat, Sneakers, was lying on the ground, dead, his throat torn open.

“Oh, my God! How did this happen?” he asked, unable to tear his eyes away from the mangled cat.

“The Nicholson’s Doberman got loose,” Henry said. “I saw him chase Sneakers across the front lawn and grab him. I ran after him with a shovel and he dropped the cat and took off, but it was too late.”

Mireya began to stir in her father’s arms. He remembered her screaming and clutching her throat. “I’m taking Rey to her room. Henry, would you be so kind as to dispose of the cat. I don’t want Rey to see this.”

“I’ll take care of it, sir.”

“Mario, call Rey’s pediatrician and tell him that she got very upset at the death of her cat and fainted. Find out when and where he wants to see her.”

Mario nodded and hurried back into the kitchen.

“Gina, you’d better come with me.” He turned and reentered the house.

He gently laid Mireya on her bed. Her eyes fluttered briefly, and she relaxed into a deep sleep.

“What happened to her?” Gina asked.

“I’m not sure,” Rey’s father replied. “Maybe you can make sense of it.” He related the story with all the accuracy and detachment of a lawyer giving a brief.

Gina sighed and walked slowly to Mireya’s bed. As was her custom each and every night, she lowered herself to one knee, bowed her head, and prayed softly.

"Your beautiful rays may color our faces;
being dyed in them, somewhere at an old age
we shall fall asleep old women."

He had watched this woman, who was of the Hopi tribe and as deeply spiritual as anyone he had ever met, pray over his daughter since her infancy. He was enormously grateful for her role in Mireya's life. Gina stood up and turned to him, "She needs to sleep and we need to talk."

Chapter l

Mireya stood on the top of Echo Cliffs and gazed out over what seemed an unending tract of land that was the Navajo Reservation. Arizona. Just what is it about Arizona? It's the sky. So blue. In all directions, horizon to horizon, an uninterrupted vast expanse of blue. Blue. The most excellent color. The color of the ocean, the color of heaven, the color of first place ribbons, the best kind of sno-cone, and those satin sashes in the Sound of Music. The color of life.

And what a blue. This sky redefines the color blue. This sky is bluer than a robin's egg, bluer than those suede shoes, a hyacinth macaw, Mimi Bobeck's eyelids, Dennis Rodman's hair (this week, anyway). This sky is bluer than that song by Janis Ian, bluer than the water in the blue grotto, bluer than the Blue Bayou. Is a bayou blue? This sky is bluer than Paul Newman's eyes…

"Rey!"

"What?" Startled, she jumped about a foot in the air.

"Earth to Rey. Were you in a trance? How long can you stare up at an empty sky?"

For a moment she stared blankly at him. "It's not empty."

"What do you mean?"

She pointed to the south.

"I don't see anything." He squinted into the sun as he stared in the direction Mireya was pointing. Slowly, he raised his binoculars. "Wait a minute. This could be her. Come on, Momma. Come on home. That is one…very…big…bird."

He dropped his binoculars and looked suspiciously at Mireya. "Wait. You weren't using your binoculars. You couldn't have seen her coming!"

She was staring at the sky again, the corners of her mouth turning up ever so slightly as a satisfied look settled over her face.

"I get it. Another Navajo cosmic connection. Whatever. Are you ready to go?" He held her climbing harness out to her.

As she took it, she marveled at people who actually enjoyed hanging off a cliff by a rope and a couple of carabiners. She failed to see the recreational value. The familiar brick was settling back in the pit of her stomach.

Mireya was a professional wildlife photographer and preferred to work alone, but for those times when she needed a partner, she felt fortunate to have Chet. He was good at his job and never required her to make conversation. He was happy to keep a running commentary going, while rarely expecting her to respond. He tolerated her frequent lapses into what he had come to refer as her personal zone. He went about his business until she returned, making no comment about her absence except for the occasional query about life in the ozone.

He was the mountain-climbing equivalent of a beach bum. He worked only when absolutely necessary, just enough to keep himself fed. Most of the time he was as an Outward Bound instructor and a free-lance mountain guide. His college degree in environmental science enabled him to occasionally hire on as a naturalist for various ecotourism companies.

He was an amateur photographer and never turned down an opportunity to work with Mireya. She was generous with her time and always willing to share her expertise.

He double-checked each piece of equipment as she strapped it on. The custom-made belt she hooked on last was one they designed together. It held all of her photographic equipment within easy reach. She walked to the edge of the cliff and looked out at the sky for the condor. Mireya knew she was out there, riding the thermals, just beyond the range of the human eye.

The California condor was extirpated from the environment in 1987, when the last of the wild birds were captured near the San Joaquin Valley. Extirpated. That's two syllables away from extinct. Condors had not graced the skies of Arizona since 1924. For nearly a decade condors existed only in zoos and breeding facilities until the first captive-bred juveniles were released from Arizona's Vermilion Cliffs in 1996.

Mireya was standing on the edge of Echo Cliffs, barely twenty miles southeast of the original release site, hoping to photograph the nest of the first pair of released condors to mate in the wild. Workers on the condor project had observed the courtship behavior of the pair and tracked them to this section of Echo cliffs, where they suspected the birds had a nesting site.

She would have to rappel about twenty feet down the face of the cliff, then traverse along an old pre-protected, sport climbing route running under a large overhang, which completely obscured any view from above.

Heavily used routes like this one was were frequently fitted with permanent anchors to facilitate the climbers and preserve the face of the cliff. In this case metal bolts had been hammered or shot into the rock with a bolt gun, each with a metal ring called a hanger attached.

Short of flying a helicopter up the cliffs, which would endanger the birds, there was no other way to observe the so-called nest. The condors do not build nests, but rather lay an egg right on the bare rock, usually in a crevice or small cave in the cliff.

Echo Cliffs were on Navajo Reservation land. Years ago this formation was popular with recreational and sport climbers who used it to practice climbing the overhang. After a fatal accident, the Navajo stopped issuing climbing permits to outsiders. Because Mireya's mother was full-blood Navajo and Mireya was registered with the Navajo Nation, she had little trouble getting a permit for her photographic excursion. This delighted the Peregrine Fund, the organization that financed the captive breeding program and the reintroduction of the condors. Mireya had worked with the Peregrine Fund twice before, once on a project photographing Peregrine falcons right here in Arizona. The other time she photographed the release of a captive-bred Harpy Eagle in Panama.

She envisioned the condor, soaring several thousand feet above the earth at speeds in excess of 55 miles per hour. On the wing it looked for all the world like the embodiment of grace and power. Unfortunately, as soon as it landed it looked like just another butt-ugly buzzard. A large buzzard, 25 pounds with a wingspan of more than nine feet, but a buzzard just the same. Condors were sacred to the Navajo, who believed they were communication links to the supernatural world. Mireya would defend to the end their right to a place in the natural world, but they just didn't have the same attraction for her as the slim, swift Peregrine falcon or the magnificently powerful Harpy eagle. She closed her eyes and let the strong thermal updraft lift her consciousness upward, in a slow spiral toward the condor…

"Radio check!" Chet's voice boomed over the voice-activated two-way radio headset she wore. Mireya jumped, once again jolted back to earth. She felt a hand on her shoulder.

"Stay with me, baby. It's a long way down, and you are not yet on belay."

"You're gonna kill me, Chet."

"Maybe so," he said grinning, "But not today."

He clipped a figure-eight descender onto her harness, stepped back, and waved bye-bye.

She was careful not to make eye contact with him as she backed over the rim of the cliff and leaned back into her harness. If he saw her eyes, he would see her fear, and nobody knew she was afraid of heights except her former nanny, now housekeeper, Gina.

Mireya's mother hired Gina, a full-blood Hopi woman, to be her nanny when she was just an infant. Gina knew as much as any human being could know about Mireya Richardson, and Mireya knew more about Gina Rizzo than any other human being she had ever met. That said a lot.

She thought of a prayer that Gina taught her to say when she felt she was in a dangerous situation.

I live, but I cannot live forever.
Only the great earth lives forever,
The great sun is the only living thing.

It was supposed to give her perspective on her mortality, on her place in a universe so much greater than herself. She thought it odd, yet strangely comforting.

"How does the protection look?" Chet's voice brought her focus back to the task at hand. She took a carabiner off her rack, placed it on the first bolt hanger, and clipped in.

"It looks old and rusty." She brushed away the dust on the old bolt and hoped she wouldn't need to rely on it.

"Great. You stay sharp. On belay."

"Again."

"On belay. You're good to go."

"OK." She unclipped her rappelling gear. "Take it up." She watched as the gear disappeared over the top of the cliff.

"Slack." She waited for him to feed out some of the line before she began to traverse the face of the cliff. Soon she was under the overhang and out of sight. She let out a small sigh; she liked it better knowing she was out of sight. If she were to have a problem, Chet wouldn't see.

The going didn't seem that tough. The challenge of this route was to climb up and over the overhang. She could still see some faint traces of chalk from those foolhardy souls who did attempt it. Thankfully, there was no reason for her to deal with that. She had only to move laterally under the overhang until she got around the first corner, a distance of a hundred feet or so. From there she should be able to get a good look at the nesting site.

She took a deep breath. There was no possibility that she would fall the three hundred feet to the ground because Chet was belaying her from above and she trusted him completely. The worst that could happen if the old protection failed was a swinging fall. Not that she couldn't be seriously injured that way, but she was less likely to die. She pushed the thought out of her mind and moved along the face of the rock, attaching carabiners to the bolts and clipping her rope into them as she went.

Twenty feet from the outcropping that marked a bend in the line of the cliffs, she came to a narrow ledge. She put her right foot out on it, cautiously testing its strength by shifting some of her weight. It seemed solid.

She slid her foot out a little farther, shifted all of her weight onto it, and stretched for a handhold that was just barely within her reach. Just as her fingers curled around a notch in the rock, part of the ledge under her right foot crumbled. She lost her footing. Her right hand grasped desperately at the wall, her fingertips clawing at the rock as she slipped, each leaving a thin trail of blood on the unforgiving stone.

For a moment, she dangled three hundred feet above the canyon floor, her left hand still wedged in a crevice. She reached up, located her previous handhold, found a new toehold and steadied herself, her eyes closed and her forehead resting against the stone.

Then it began.

She froze. She heard a voice over the radio, but it sounded far away, like she was hearing it underwater. Soon, the sound of her own heartbeat and respiration drowned out even that. A single drop of sweat trickled down her forehead to the bridge of her nose, where it came to rest hanging off the tip. She stared blankly at the rock, hearing only her increasingly rapid heartbeat and breathing.

She squeezed her eyes shut in a desperate effort to ward off a blackout. Her body sagged like lead against her arms, her forehead pressed against the rock. Her waning consciousness cried out against the encroaching darkness. Unable to speak, she mouthed the words, "Help me…"

Chapter 2

Soaring high above Echo Cliffs, the condor scanned the landscape looking for food. She had been feeding on the carcass of a dead lamb but was run off by a coyote, unsatisfied. She surveyed the sky, looking for circling turkey buzzards, which could signify a food source. She could ride the air currents for hours, rarely flapping her wings, expending little energy. She banked slightly and headed for the roadway, where animals of all kinds frequently ended their lives.

The condor wasn't sure at first what exactly it was that drew her attention. She turned her head and sighted in on a tiny figure clinging to the rock. She changed course, beginning a downward dive, directly at the now motionless climber. She was approaching at great speed, her enormous wings outstretched. Fifty, now sixty miles per hour, the huge bird closed the distance between it and the climber. At the last moment, she wheeled right, casting her immense shadow across the helpless human, the tremendous rush of displaced air blowing Mireya's hair into her face.

The condor continued around the bend in the cliff. She landed lightly on a wide ledge in front of a depression in the rock where her newly hatched chick was waiting expectantly, mouth open.

Chapter 3

Mireya opened her eyes, her face now relaxed. She nodded her head almost imperceptibly, a suggestion of a smile touching the corners of her mouth.

"Rey! What's goin on? Rey! Answer!"

"Sorry. I had a little problem with some loose rock, but I'm OK now." She looked down at her bleeding fingertips, raised them to her lips, and blew on them.

"Did you see the condor?"

"I did. I'm very close to the nest."

"I can't see shit with this overhang here."

"No kidding. If we could see the nest from up there, why would I be hanging off this damn rock?"

"Right. Can you see the nest?"

"Not yet."

"Then how do you know you're close?"

"I just know."

"Well, let's just pray there's an egg."

"No egg."

"No egg?"

"No egg."

"What do you mean, no egg? How do you know there's no egg?"

"No egg. There's a chick."

"A chick? A chick? How could you know there's a chick?"

"Slack." She waited for him to feed her some more line, then worked her way around the bend in the cliff.

"Rey? Come on, Rey. What about the chick?"

Mireya carefully edged herself around the outcropping that formed the bend in the cliff. She placed a carabiner on the last bolt she would need, clipped in her climbing rope, and looked down. There, sitting on a wide ledge, was the condor, and in a small depression in the face of the rock sat a newly hatched chick.

She took a spring-loaded camming anchor off her rack, placed it in a horizontal crack in the rock, and clipped it onto her harness.

"Come on, Rey. You're pissing me off. Are you sure there's a chick?"

"Absolutely sure."

"How can you be so sure?"

"Cause I'm looking at it."

"No way!"

"Way."

"Great! Don't forget to use two cams while you're photographing."

"Yes, mother."

"I mean it, Rey."

Mireya sighed loudly, pulled another cam off her rack, anchored it in the crack, and clipped it onto her harness. "I just clipped onto cam number two. Happy?"

"Good girl. Now take some good pics and get back up here. You woke me up so early this morning I didn't have any breakfast. I'm hungry."

"You're always hungry. I'm perfectly safe, anchored with two cams. Just take some granola bars out of my pack. You can eat while I photograph."

"Dream on. You're on belay until you're back up top. Just take the pictures."

"Whatever you say."

Chet's shoulders slumped and his chin dropped to his chest as he shook his head. The only time he ever got his way with Mireya was in obvious no-brainer situations like this one. Normally, she patiently listened to anything he had to say, nodded her head, and then went about her business exactly as she had already planned. He had to admit, though, her plans usually worked out.

Mireya closed her eyes, took a few deep breaths, and leaned back into the harness. She knew Chet would never let her off belay for any reason. The camming anchors were rock solid, and with Chet as a back up some of her anxiety began to dissipate. She shot three rolls of film using a variety of lenses and filters. The chick was even more ugly than its mother (if that was possible), but he or she would go down in history as the first condor to hatch in the wild since the species was reintroduced. Mireya believed that it was a momentous event. She was sure that *National Wildlife* magazine would jump at the chance to publish her article and pictures.

As she looked down at the condor feeding her chick, she switched off her two-way radio and relaxed in her harness.

The condor turned away from her chick and stared up at Mireya.

A ritual verse came to mind, and Mireya began to recite:

Over the prairie flits, in ever widening circles,
the shadow of a bird as I walk.
Upward turn my eyes,
Kawas looks upon me,
she turns with flapping wings, and far away she flies.

"Thank you, condor mother."

The condor stared back at her with unblinking eyes.

Mireya disengaged the camming anchors and hooked them back onto her rack. She unclipped her last carabiner and began to work her way back around the outcropping, removing and racking her protection as she went. She made it back to the spot where she had nearly fallen without incident.

"Up rope." Most of the slack in the rope disappeared.

She took a deep breath, stretched her foot past the crumbled section of ledge, hopped across it, and searched for a solid handhold with her left hand. For a moment it seemed as though she had made it past the danger zone. She exhaled. How long had she been holding her breath? As she stretched her left foot for another toehold, the rock under her left hand let go.

"TENSION!"

The line jerked tight as the first bolt and hanger in her protection broke her fall. As she grasped at the rock, she heard it: a sickening ping as the old bolt broke, sending her downward. There was another ping as the second bolt failed immediately. As her weight hit the third bolt she was swinging at the end of the rope, which dislodged a great deal of debris as it dragged along the cliff wall. She swung into a shrub growing out of a crack in the cliff wall and grabbed on.

She took a camming anchor off her rack, shoved it into the crack, and clipped it onto her harness. Relief and nervous exhaustion simultaneously drained the color from her face. She slumped into her harness and shook her head.

"All this for a picture of a buzzard."

Chapter 4

The late afternoon sun warmed Mireya's face, as well as the grass on which she lay. It felt good to be home.

She had taken a red-eye flight from Phoenix to Boston, arriving at Logan International at seven o'clock this morning. Chet had wanted to take her to the emergency room in Flagstaff after her fall, but Mireya didn't think the scrapes and bruises she sustained warranted that much of her time. Instead she used the time to get her film developed. The pictures of the condor chick exceeded her expectations, and as always, when her assignment was finished she could think of little else but home.

She opened her eyes ever so slightly and watched the river through the veil of her eyelashes. The Harvard women's crew team was practicing on the Charles. The sleek, needle-like shells skimmed over the river's surface like a collection of water bugs, propelled by spider-thin legs working in perfect unison.

She had just finished her run, circumnavigating the three major cemeteries of Cambridge. This was her favorite spot for a cool-down contemplation. Today's meditation centered on the crew team. Precision, timing, strength, teamwork. She admired the qualities upon which a successful team was built, although she herself had rowed single sculls for the Harvard team. She preferred to challenge the river one-on-one.

Off in the distance a rookie caught a major crab, throwing her teammates' timing into chaos. Simultaneous shouts and laughter erupted from the affected and neighboring boats, but soon the coxswains restored order and the metronome-like strokes resumed. Mireya imagined a scarlet-faced rookie aggressively pulling in perfect synchrony with her teammates, determined not to repeat the mistake.

A small wave of nostalgia washed over her as she followed the progress of the group flying down the Charles. Her years on the crew team at Harvard were the only time in her life where she felt she was truly part of a group, part of a team. Although she refused to row anything but singles, she won so many races she was elected team captain her senior year. Elected by the other members of the team, chosen by her peers. It had come as a complete surprise, but she had to admit that it was a good feeling, though one she had never sought to duplicate.

She still kept in touch with a few friends from those days. They would send Christmas cards and the occasional note via e-mail. They forwarded jokes and computer virus alerts, and they monitored her web page. Occasionally there would be a congratulatory phone call when one of them saw a photograph of hers published in a magazine.

One of these friends became a hotshot divorce lawyer in Palm Beach, Florida. One traded her career as a concert violinist for a husband and family, and now spent most of her time driving a minivan full of kids from one activity to another. One was teaching special needs and exceptional children at a private school in upstate New York.

Mireya reflected on her own life, which seemed to be a perpetual quest to save one endangered species or another. She spent hours doing research in libraries, or on the Internet, and then at a moment's notice could be hanging off a cliff taking pictures of a buzzard, or slogging through a swamp in search of one of Florida's fifty remaining panthers.

The conventional lives of the lawyer, the soccer mom, and the teacher were as alien to her as lipstick to a chicken. When Mireya turned down her lawyer friend's invitation to a vacation in south Florida for about the tenth time, she said that Mireya should stop looking at life through the lens of her camera and actually experience it for a change.

Was that really how she lived?

Probably.

She was jolted from her thoughts as she simultaneously felt and heard something slicing through the air inches above her head. She sat bolt upright just in time to be knocked flat by a large chocolate Labrador retriever in hot pursuit of a Frisbee.

It was a righteous shot to the solar plexus, and she lay face down on the grass, completely winded. As she hauled herself up on hands and knees, futilely gulping air like a fish out of water, she noticed the panic-stricken owner of the dog running toward her. Obviously a student, he wore a Harvard rugby shirt, sweat shorts, and mismatched athletic socks.

He literally dove onto the ground next to Mireya and looked at her through a mop of curly hair long overdue for shearing. The intensity of his concern would have made her laugh if she were able to draw a breath.

"I'm so sorry! I didn't even look before I threw it. This is all my fault. Oh, God, it sounds like you're choking. You can't breathe! I should call an ambulance…"

Mireya held up her left index finger, signaling for him to wait. She would be breathing again in just a minute if she could relax and wait it out. She rocked back against her heels and sat up straight. At that moment the exuberant Labrador galloped back with the Frisbee in his mouth and headed straight for Mireya, knocking her over backward. The dog dropped the Frisbee and firmly planted itself on Mireya's chest, covering her face with dog slobber kisses.

"Bear! No! Bad dog! No! Bear! Get off!" With great difficulty, the young man hauled the dog off Mireya, collapsing onto the ground with a clueless but happy Bear wriggling in his lap.

"Geez, I'm so sorry. Are you OK?"

Mireya struggled into an upright position again, wiping her face on her sleeve, breathing a little easier.

"That's quite a dog," she wheezed.

"It was my fault. I didn't look where I was throwing, and Bear is a little deranged when it comes to his toys."

"No harm done." Mireya stared at Bear, who was looking longingly at the Frisbee on the ground just a few feet away.

"He likes the red one better."

"What?"

"The red Frisbee. He likes it better than this one."

"How did you know he has a red one?"

Mireya stood up, averting her eyes in the direction of the river. "Well, I…I think I've seen you here before."

"Oh. Yeah, well, he lost the red one. I can't find it anywhere."

Mireya smiled to herself as she began to walk away. She paused, looked back over her shoulder and said, "Look behind the couch."

The student released the dog, a confused look on his face. "We have three couches in the frat house."

"The plaid one," Mireya replied, still walking.

The student stood up, now completely baffled. "Do I know you?"

Mireya raised her hand in a wave and kept walking.

Chapter 5

Mireya yawned uncontrollably, stretched, and leaned back in her chair, stopping just before the point of no return. A few degrees more and she would be lying flat on her back in the middle of her office floor. She should probably have the chair repaired, but she inherited it from her father that way and because there was nobody but her to sit in it, it never climbed very high on her to-do list.

She loved her chair. It was big, squishy, and leather, with that barely detectable earthy smell that lingers just below your subconscious. It was the color her father described as ox blood and looked totally out of place in her snug little office.

A chair like this belonged behind the desk of the chairman of the board. Her father had not been a chairman of the board, but he *had* been the senior partner in his own law firm, and his chair had been completely at home behind his huge antique mahogany desk. His offices hadn't been in the chic, sterile concrete and glass buildings of the financial district, but in a restored nineteenth century brick building near Faneuil Hall. She could close her eyes and visualize the cherry-paneled, book-lined walls, oriental rugs, and hardwood floors that creaked softly as she walked across them.

She yawned again. The nap she took this afternoon was not enough to make up for the sleepless night she spent on the plane. She tried to focus her attention back to the unfinished manuscript on her desk. Should she make coffee or pack it in for the night? It was barely eight o'clock, and as a lifelong night owl, she always seemed to find something important enough to occupy her until the wee hours. She should really drink some herb tea and go to bed. She loved coffee, but caffeine was definitely not her friend.

As she swiveled her chair around to face the door, which led to the living room, which led to the front hall, which led to the kitchen, wherein lived the coffeemaker, the phone rang. It was the Lost Friends message center. She had a separate phone line installed to handle the calls that came in to her part-time business, which she called, Lost Friends Pet Finders.

She swiveled back to her desk, shoved off with both feet, and rolled the chair smoothly across the room to the answering machine. She picked up a notebook and a pen and waited for the machine to intercept the call. After the third ring she heard her own voice.

"Thank you for calling Lost Friends Pet Finders. We understand how important your pet is to you, and we're here to help. Our recovery rate exceeds eighty-five percent. Please leave your name, phone number, and the circumstances of your pet's disappearance after the tone. We'll return your call as soon as possible. Our payment terms are fifty dollars down, and fifty dollars when you recover your pet, alive or deceased. We accept Visa or MasterCard. We look forward to helping reunite you with your pet."

The end of the message was followed by the beep and the inevitable pause that ensued as the prospective clients quelled their last-minute doubts as to whether they could actually bring themselves to buy into the concept of the service she provided. She could feel their skepticism in those empty seconds. She smiled broadly and leaned back recklessly in her chair. She mouthed the words "three, two, one" and pointed at the machine.

As if on cue, a hesitant voice with a pronounced southern accent came from the machine.

> *"This is Delia Wallace from Atlanta. That's Atlanta, Georgia. I'm callin to tell y'all about my cat, Oprah. She's normally an indoor cat, but she, ah...got out the door when some deliverymen were bringin in my new refrigerator. I tried to go after her but, ah...they was blockin the door with the fridge and by the time I could get myself out the door, she was gone. I've looked just about every place I can think of, and I even offered a twenty-dollar reward to the kids on my street, but she's been missin almost two days now, and I'm gettin scared. I hope you can help me. My number is (404) 555-1289."*

Mireya sat up, dropped the notebook and pen in her lap, picked up the phone, and dialed the number.

"Hello."

"Hello. This is Mireya from Lost Friends returning your call."

"Why, thank you for gettin back to me so quick. I hope you can help me."

"Why don't you start by telling me a little about your cat?"

"Well now, Oprah, she be four years old next month. She's spayed, female of course, and she's pretty timid around people she don't know. She's mostly black with four white socks and a little white spot on her nose. She won't eat nothin but Sheba cat food that come in those fancy little cans. I guess she got expensive taste. An if I don't buy Fresh Step cat litter, she do her business in my plant pots. Nasty. Lordy lord, I do get so angry at her sometimes. Like the time I went on vacation and I got my neighbor Louise Franklin to come over and feed her every day instead of boardin her out. I gets back and didn't she scratch a big hole in my livin room sofa just to spite me. And then there was the time…"

"Excuse me, Ms. Wallace…" Mireya was stifling a giggle.

"Delia, please, all my friends call me Delia."

"Delia. Does Oprah have short or long hair?"

"Short hair. And she's got kind of a weight problem. Serves me right by namin her Oprah, but she was such a pretty kitten and that's my favorite show. The vet says I should have her on a diet, but if I feeds her that special Science Diet food he gave me she won't eat at all. And if I give her less food she follows me around all the damn day yowlin and carryin on somethin fierce. That cat can be some aggravatin, I'm tellin you what. One time…"

"Whoa, Delia." Mireya covered the phone as she snorted out a laugh that wouldn't be stifled. She bit her lip, regained her composure, and continued.

"I think I have a pretty good sense of your cat now, and I understand why you want her back so badly. She sounds like quite the personality."

"Lord, yes. I 'bout died of loneliness these last few days without her, precious thing."

"Did you understand my payment terms?"

"Ah…yes. I have a MasterCard."

"I'm ready for your number now, followed by the expiration date." Mireya wrote the number down as Delia read it off.

"That be all you need to know?"

"That should do it. I'll call you as soon as I have some information. I'm going to start working on it right now." She knew that comment always encouraged the client to get off the phone. Laughing, she put the phone down, entered the number into the credit card machine, and waited for the card to be approved. When the purchase authorization came through she swiveled her chair around again.

She closed her eyes and took a few minutes to relax, focusing herself inward until her mind went gray. Blank was the word that some people used, but it didn't describe her frame of mind. Her mind went gray, not blank and harsh like a white sheet of paper, but gray, soft and gray like twilight or dawn. Soft and gray like standing on the beach in the fog, like flying through clouds without a plane. She was there now, in her own Twilight Zone. She whispered, "Oprah…"

Slowly, an image began to form in her mind. It gradually became clear, much like an old downloaded image from the Internet. She was looking at a large vegetable garden, as viewed from a high vantage point. There was a row of beautiful rose bushes along one side, some red and some yellow. A wooden split rail fence separated the garden from the road, and a blue tractor was parked nearby. This image began to fade and was replaced by another, a running horse that seemed to be made from copper or brass.

As soon as Mireya opened her eyes, she began to scribble notes about what she'd seen. She read over them once or twice to be sure she recorded everything accurately, then picked up the phone and dialed Delia's number.

"Hello."

"Delia? This is Mireya. I have some information on the location of your cat."

"Lord have mercy."

"Delia. You should get a pencil and paper so you can write down what I tell you. It's so easy for the details to get confused."

"I got somethin right here on my table."

"Good. Oprah is in a very high place like a tree, but more likely a roof. She's looking down at a large vegetable garden with a row of rose bushes along one edge. Some are red and some are yellow. There's a split-rail fence along the road and a blue tractor parked nearby. She also sees a metal figure of a running horse, probably made from copper or brass. I think it might be a weathervane."

There was silence on the line. Mireya supposed that Delia was still writing.

"Did you get all that, Delia?"

"I'm writin it all, but I think I already know where she's at."

"Really? That's great."

"The Casperson's farm is only about a half mile from here. They have a garden with beautiful roses, and a big old barn. It must be three stories tall, and I'm pretty sure it has a weathervane!"

"Why don't you go on down there and check out the roof? Please call back and leave a message for me if you find her."

"I will, and I can't thank you enough. I'd be lost without my Oprah."

"You're very welcome. I hope everything works out. It's been a pleasure talking with you."

Mireya put the receiver back on its cradle. She backpedaled the chair across the room again and swiveled around to face the desk. She picked up the unfinished, untitled condor manuscript and set it aside. She opened the desk drawer and took out another manuscript-in-progress: "The Plight of the Piping Plover." She took the first of eight boxes of slides out of the drawer, opened it, and dropped the first slide into her desktop viewer. One by one she went through them all, hoping to find a gem in there that she had missed the first twenty times she looked at them. She took out the prints that she made from the six best slides and spread them out on the desk. No matter how hard she looked at them, they just weren't good enough.

Chapter 6

Gary Coakley wiped the steam away from the center of the mirror and leaned closer. He had replaced the heavy gold-handled Nieman Marcus shaver and the old-fashioned mug-and-brush style imported English shave cream with a can of Barbasol and a fifteen-cent disposable Bic.

He never had the heart to tell his wife it's what he preferred to use, since she bought him the set as a Christmas gift the first year they were married and dutifully stuffed his stocking with two refills of the sandalwood-scented shave cream every year thereafter. He got a much better shave with the Bic, but he loved the way she would press her cheek against his every morning in the kitchen and breathe in his scent. Almost five years had passed, and he could still feel the brush of her eyelashes against his face and the way her breath would make the little hairs on his neck stand at attention.

Life was a collection of trade-offs. The Nieman Marcus kit was now carefully stored in the back of his drawer, next to the Santa Claus tie he hated and four pairs of unworn argyle socks.

Right now he didn't much care what he was shaving with, he just wanted to be able to see what he was doing. Damn. When was he going to find the time to fix the exhaust fan in this bathroom? He wiped the steam off the mirror again and turned the other cheek. He would have to hire someone to do it, which seemed like such a waste of money when he could easily do the job himself in one Saturday afternoon. It's just that he couldn't bear to be working on the house when he could be spending that time with his eight-year-old daughter.

Last month she started playing soccer in a league and their games were always on Saturdays. Another trade-off.

He walked to the kitchen following the heavenly smell of brewing coffee. His housekeeper, Mrs. Matthews, hustled toward him brandishing a kitchen towel.

"You've got shaving cream all over your ear, Mr. Coakley," she said with a charming trace of an Irish accent. She grasped his jaw with her left hand, turned his head to the side, and wiped his ear clean.

"Thanks. I'm no architect, but why would you design a bathroom with no window? It makes no sense."

"All that humidity is no good for the wallpaper. You should get that fan fixed," she said as she handed him a cup of coffee.

"I know. What's the name of that handyman you met at the senior center?"

"Ahh…Gonzales, I think. Bob, maybe."

"Do you think you could call him and see if he can fix it sometime soon?"

"Sure. He did some painting for my neighbor. She'll have his number. She thought he was a good worker."

"That's great, thanks." He turned toward the door. "SANDRA! ARE YOU TAKING YOUR PUPPY OUT?"

Sandra appeared in the doorway, fully dressed, leash in hand. "You must be psycho, Gary. You read my mind!"

Gary tried unsuccessfully to suppress the huge smile that thwarted his attempt at being stern. "That's PSYCHIC, not psycho. Psycho means crazy." He pointed at his head and made a few circles with his index finger. "And what did I say about that Gary business? There are about a million guys in the world named Gary, but I'm the only one who is your father."

"OK, Dad," she shrugged and turned to leave.

He followed her to the front hall where her three-month-old beagle puppy was scratching and whining in his crate. She opened the door, scooped the puppy up in her arms, and carried him out the front door. She hopped down the four cement steps and gently put him down on the grass next to the front walk. He immediately began to pee.

Gary had to smile. That puppy was so excited to see Sandra in the morning, if she let him run out of his crate, what was watering the lawn right now would be all over the front hall floor.

He sat on the top step, put his coffee down, and called Sandra over to him so that they were talking more or less eye-to-eye. "Sandra, you remember that I'm going out of town for a few days?"

She nodded.

"I want you to remember that this puppy is a big responsibility. You agreed to be responsible for him when we got him. You have to take him for a walk around the playground every morning before school and every afternoon when you get home. Mrs. Matthews is NOT going to do this for you. Understood?"

"Yeah, I promise." Sandra put her arms around her father's neck and hugged him. Gary embraced her as tightly as he could without suffocating her.

Finished with his business, the puppy ran up the steps and began jumping up against Gary's back.

"I'm gonna miss you, Dad."

"Me, too."

"Are you gonna call me before I go to bed?"

"Of course I will. I always do, don't I?"

"Did I tell you I'm changing Scooby's name?"

"No," he laughed. "To what?"

"Instead of Scooby-Doo, I'm going to call him Scooby-Don't. That's all we ever say to him, anyway."

"OK." He laughed again. "I'll buy that. You'd better get going so you aren't late for school. I'll be home before you know it."

She turned, ran down the walk and skipped onto the sidewalk, the puppy bouncing along beside her on his leash.

"Bye, Dad! Come on, Scooby!"

Gary picked up the still-warm cup of coffee and cradled it in both hands as he watched the carefree pair until they reached the end of the street and disappeared through the gates to the playground.

Chapter 7

Gary drummed his fingers on the steering wheel. He was less than a half mile from his office, and he was going nowhere because the entire Downtown Crossing area, which precedes the financial district, was gridlocked. This was one of the many prices he paid for working and driving in Boston.

Sometimes he missed the old days when he was just starting out with the firm. He used to take the "T," as Bostonians fondly called the Massachusetts Transit Authority (or the "fucking T" when feelings were less fond). His wife would drop him off at the Chestnut Hill Station and he would take the Green Line all the way to Government Center, then the Blue Line to State Street. From there it was just a short walk to the Hawthorne & Associates building, which was located on the outskirts of the financial district.

Back then the cost of parking in the city was prohibitive on his starting salary, and besides, they only had one car. Now he was one of the associates, and as part of his compensation received a free parking spot in the small garage under the building. He didn't have to buy a "T" pass anymore, but occasionally he had to sit in traffic for unreasonable periods of time. Yet another of life's trade-offs.

He looked at his watch and decided to call his secretary. There was a possibility that he would miss the staff meeting.

"Hawthorne & Associates, Gary Coakley's office, may I help you?"

"Joan, it's me."

"Are you sitting in that snarled up mess out there?"

"I most certainly am."

"I guess I should thank you for not paying me enough to be able to afford parking around here."

"Quit. Tell Blake I might miss some of the meeting. I'll give my presentation at the end."

"He's not in yet either so the meeting will probably be delayed."

"I'd like to say that I'm on my way or I'll be right along, but you know how that goes."

"Yes, indeed. See you whenever."

"Right."

He managed to crawl about another half block while talking on the phone. He had a 5:15 p.m. flight out of Logan, and if this was any indication of what rush hour traffic would be like this afternoon, the Blue Line was looking like a better choice than a taxi.

He picked up his travel mug and reflexively put it to his lips before realizing that it was long since empty. The end of his five-mile drive and the bottom of his mug usually coincided. He looked at the old insulated mug, turning it over and over in his hand. The familiar feel brought back a rush of memories.

In the early days of his marriage, he had been unable to tear himself out of bed in the morning. On many occasions he and his wife ran out the door, his hair still wet from the shower and her nightgown tucked into a pair of sweat pants. They would make it to the "T" just as it pulled into the station. He would jump out of the car and run for it, briefcase in hand, the way O.J. Simpson ran through airports in the old Hertz commercials.

Each time he lamented not having a cup of coffee. On his next birthday, his wife gave him this travel mug. She told him that now he could oversleep and still have a cup of coffee in the morning. She had bought it at the Sharper Image store in Copley Place and told him it was considered state-of-the-art. As an engineer, he couldn't really see that it represented any major breakthroughs in the technology of insulation, but it looked the part.

"This is very thoughtful, honey," he remembered saying with genuine sincerity, "but where am I going to get the coffee to put in it if I don't get up earlier?"

"I've got that covered," she said and handed him a large, beautifully wrapped box containing an electric coffeemaker complete with timer. He remembered smiling at the term used for it in the owner's manual: automatic brewstarter. They could set it up the night before and program it to have coffee ready and waiting for his dash out the door the next morning.

So many memories, good memories, hiding just out of sight behind a coffee mug. He missed his wife, and being married. He wasn't much for introspection, self-discovery, or any of that other touchy-feely crap, but he was very aware, even before he exited the church with his bride on his arm, that he was a man who was well suited for that kind of commitment.

He inched his way to the end of the block and turned right onto a side street, hoping to thread his way around the traffic jam. He soon found out he wasn't the only one who had that idea, but after crawling another block, traffic began to ease, and twenty minutes later he was rolling into his parking garage.

A few minutes later he breezed into his office. He grabbed a stack of thick files marked "Sund Oil" and his "#1 Dad" coffee mug off his desk and made a quick detour into the little kitchen where the secretaries made coffee.

He could have told Joan to bring him a cup in the meeting, but he never could get comfortable making those kinds of requests, and besides, it would only take him a second. Fortunately, someone had just made a fresh pot. As he began to pour, he heard a voice behind him.

"Hey, Gary! Glad you finally made it in."

It was Natalie, the newest, youngest, and by far the hottest secretary in the building. He turned to smile at her. "Natalie, good…aaah! SHIT!" He poured hot coffee on his hand, jumped back, and dropped the mug on the floor. It smashed into hundreds of little pieces, splattering coffee all over his pants.

"Did you burn yourself? Oh, no! That was your Father's Day mug," Natalie said, looking at the coffee and bits of ceramic all over the floor.

As she bent down and began picking up the biggest pieces of the mug, Joan entered the room.

"Just leave that, Natalie. I'll call the custodian."

Natalie stood and handed the pieces of ceramic to Gary. “Sorry about your mug. I think it’s beyond help.” Her hand remained in contact with his at least a full second longer than was necessary.

“Thanks. I can’t believe how clumsy I am sometimes.” Gary’s face was scarlet.

Joan rolled her eyes as Natalie smoothed her incredibly short skirt, tossed her hair, and strutted out.

“OK. Let’s do some damage control.” Joan took a small bottle of club soda from the refrigerator. “Put your foot up on this chair.” When he complied, she began to remove the larger coffee stains with the club soda and a towel.

He looked down at what was left of the mug that his daughter had given him.

“Don’t worry about that. I’m pretty sure that I can find a replacement. I know where she bought it.”

“Thanks. I’d hate to have to tell her that I broke it. What would I do without you, Joan?”

“Take good care of me at bonus time and you won’t have to find out.” She finished treating the spots on his second pant leg and stood up. “You’d better get to your meeting. I’ll bring you a cup of coffee in a few minutes, after I call the janitor.”

“How long have you worked for me, Joan?”

“Ten years come September.”

“And have I ever not recommended you for the maximum raise and bonus?”

“Not so far, but an old girl like me can’t afford to get careless.”

Gary just shook his head and left the room. He was still smiling when he entered the meeting and dropped into the closest empty seat at the conference table.

Blake Hawthorne, president and founder of the company, paused in mid-sentence.

“Gary. Glad you finally made it.”

“Did I miss anything important? Juicy gossip about the Big Dig or any other major happenings from you bridge-and-tunnel builders?”

“Afraid not. It’s just another Monday. But since you’re here, I might as well turn the meeting over to you.” Blake turned a page in his portfolio.

Turning back to the others, Blake said, “Our newest contract is with Sund Oil. They’re looking to acquire property on which to build a refinery and have hired us to do an environmental site assessment. Since Minnesota is near the old stomping ground of our esteemed head of geo-environmental, I’ve given him the project. Gary? You want to bring us up to speed?”

“Why not,” Gary said and walked to a large map of Minnesota that Joan had hung on the wall that morning. He took a pen out of his pocket and used it as a pointer.

“This project, though large, looks pretty straightforward. The 3,500-acre parcel in question is about an hour’s drive north of Duluth, on the west coast of Lake Superior between the towns of Castle Danger and Beaver Bay.

“The owner, Nelson Paquette, lives in Manhattan and inherited the land from his father who bought it in 1934 with the intention of mining it for iron. Though there were other iron mines in the general vicinity, he was never able to find any economically significant deposits on this parcel. Instead of mining it, he sold off most of the accessible timber to Georgia Pacific in the '50s and later sold about half of the lake frontage to developers, but he held on to the section with the largest deep cove.

"I've completed my map review of the U.S. Geological Survey topographicals, U.S. Department of Agriculture soil survey maps and state bedrock maps, and find nothing remarkable. In developing the site history, I've had conversations with the town employees of both Castle Danger and Beaver Bay, as well as the local fire marshall and the folks at the county Department of Public Works, and found nothing unusual there.

"I've contacted a firm in Duluth that's going to send out a team of surveyors next week. I'm flying out there tonight so I can start the on-site inspection tomorrow. If all goes well, we should be able to wrap this up by the end of the month."

He picked up the coffee that Joan had quietly slipped in and set in front of him. "Questions?"

The room was silent. In truth, the bridge-and-tunnel builders, as Gary liked to call them, usually all but fell asleep when the Department of Geo-environmental Engineering gave its presentations.

"When will you be back, Gary?" Blake asked.

"It's a huge site, but I'm hoping that if I use all the available daylight I'll be able to fly home on Friday."

"Great. That's it for today. Bill, don't forget I need the preliminary proposal for the Millbury overpass by the end of the week."

As the engineers rose and began to leave, a young intern from Northeastern University walked up behind Gary and slapped him on the back. "Another walk in the big woods for the Eagle Scout, Gary? As usual, you get the trips to the really hot spots. Although, Beaver Bay may have some possibilities." He shot Gary a suggestive and knowing look.

Gary turned and thrust the entire stack of files he was carrying into the center of the young man's chest. "Mark, you get to visit the basement. It's a real hot spot, too. I want all these filed, as well as all the maps in my office, and the box of files next to Joan's desk. Now would be a good time."

Gary walked away smiling.

Chapter 8

Norman Sears put the receiver back on its cradle. This was good news. This was very good news. Why was it that he had this feeling of impending doom? He was not a believer in premonitions or intuitions, but he could not shake the feeling that this dog would never hunt.

He eased open the door to his boss's office. Nelson Paquette was sitting with his back to Norman, looking out through a wall of glass on what was left of lower Manhattan. When the dot-com market went sour, they were forced to give up their prestigious office space in One World Trade Center, lay off almost all their staff, and move to a much smaller sublet space at 55 Water Street. After 9/11, the move turned out to be the silver lining in the dark cloud that had enveloped Paquette Investments for the last eighteen months.

Now it seemed Paquette thought he was charmed. They would pull off one last huge deal and retire. Right. Norman had few illusions about his account at the First Cosmic Bank of Luck, Inc. His account was long overdrawn and his credit rating in the cellar. He used to tell people that he never complained about bad luck because if it weren't for bad luck he wouldn't have any luck at all. That line always got him a laugh, but he wasn't laughing now.

"Mr. Paquette."

Paquette slowly swiveled his chair to face Norman.

"Our source at Hawthorne says that the preliminary site history went smoothly, the surveyors have been hired, and the engineer is flying out to start the on-site visual inspection tomorrow. He says that everything could be wrapped up by the end of the month."

Paquette nodded, and slowly swiveled his chair back to face the window.

Chapter 9

Al Sullivan stepped out of his kitchen onto the cement breezeway at the side of his house. A heavy mist was being whipped around by a gusty wind. He flipped up the hood on his New England Patriots sweatshirt and turned his back to the wind so that he could zip it up.

"Mother-in-law rain," he muttered. Not enough rain to be beneficial in any way, just enough to be a total nuisance. The best thing about retirement was that on days like this he didn't have to put on his uniform, drive to South Boston, and carry a mailbag up and down the city streets. He was going to walk down his driveway, collect his own mail, finish reading the *Boston Globe*, and spend the rest of the day watching ESPN. If he was not mistaken, the Red Sox were playing Baltimore this afternoon. Life was good.

As he opened his mailbox, he noticed that one of the numbers was missing. Instead of 1226, it was now 12 6. There was no point in trying to stick another one on in the rain. He would add it to his job list. Somehow he never got to the end of his list, not because he had too much to do but because he and Connor were addicted to the sports channel. To be more accurate, he was addicted to the sports channel, and Connor was addicted to the couch and the junk food—the wide variety of munchies that just had to accompany any good (or bad) sporting event.

Thinking of Connor made him wonder where he was hiding out.

"Connor!...Connor!...Come on boy!" Al looked up and down the street.

"Connor?...Here boy!"

An aging but energetic golden retriever came running from behind the neighbor's house. He lumbered up to his owner and jumped up on him, his paws almost reaching Al's shoulders. The dog's tail wagged so hard his whole body swayed from side to side.

"So there you are," Al said. "Have you been mooching off the neighbors this morning?"

If possible, the dog's tail wagged even harder.

"Are you a good boy?" Al put his hand in his pocket, and the dog hopped up and down on his hind legs in anticipation.

"OK. Here you go." He pulled a Milk Bone out of his pocket and gave it to Connor. "Let's go inside."

Once inside, Connor trotted to the middle of the kitchen floor and shook from head to toe, sending tiny drops of water everywhere.

"Is it remotely possible that you would EVER learn to do that outside?" Al shook his head and slipped his feet out of his loafers and into his fleece-lined moccasins. He peeled off his sweatshirt and hung it on a peg by the door. Connor curled up on the living room rug with his head facing the kitchen so he could watch Al as he went to the closet, took out a sponge mop, dampened it in the sink, and wiped up the dirty drops of water that Connor deposited all over the floor. He returned the mop to its closet, picked the mail up off the counter, and tiptoed around the wet floor to the kitchen table.

The table, with its gray, marbleized Formica top and tubular steel-framed chairs with padded seats and backs covered in matching vinyl (except for the ripped parts, which were cleverly repaired with gray duct tape) was described by his granddaughter as being very chic '50s art deco.

In reality it was just a kitchen set they bought after he and his wife moved into the house in 1951. His granddaughter wanted it for her college apartment, but he liked it just fine right where it was. He'd eaten breakfast and dinner in this kitchen, seated at this table, for fifty years. In fact, just about every piece of furniture in the house was from the same era. He had a new, digital, Sony color television with a thirty-five-inch screen, and a new La-Z-Boy recliner, but all the other upholstered furniture had been through several sets of slipcovers. He saw no reason to replace anything that still served its function.

As he sat down, he heard the familiar "whoosh" as some of the air escaped from the padded seat.

"Well now, let's see what kinda garbage the mail carrier left us today." Mail carrier. That's a laugh. This guy drove around in a red, white, and blue jeep stuffing mail in curbside boxes from the comfort of a vehicle. He didn't have to beef a heavy mailbag up everyone's front steps and deposit the mail through the slot in the front door. He didn't have to trudge through the snow in sub-zero temperatures. In fact, if the town snowplow left a bank in front of Al's mailbox, the mail carrier would drive right by until Al shoveled it out.

"Mail carrier my ass," Al muttered. As he picked up the first piece of mail, Connor ran into the kitchen and sat by his side, his attention riveted on Al.

"First item: from the Society for the Ethical Treatment of Animals. These turkeys would think I'm exploiting you, boy, so I ain't even gonna open it. Here. Why don't you file this for me?" He handed the unopened envelope to Connor, who took it in his mouth, trotted across the kitchen floor to the open closet, and dropped it in the recycle bin, just inside the door.

When the dog returned to his post next to the table, Al picked up the next piece of mail.

"Next item: our phone bill. Guess I'd better hang on to that." He set the envelope off to the side.

"Next item: our Social Security check. Well, considerin how much we both like to eat, I guess I'd better hang on to this one, too." He placed the envelope on top of the phone bill.

"Next: a card from Jiffy Lube. They would like to give me five dollars off their signature service. Very generous, but I change my own oil, thanks just the same. Here, boy." He gave the card to Connor, who dutifully took it to the recycle bin.

"Next: Here's something from Medicare. Totally run by turkeys, but I guess I'd better hang on to it." He put it with the phone bill and his check.

"Next: Oh here's a good one. 'You may have already won a million dollars.' And all I gotta do is buy a bunch of useless magazines. Well, the world is FULL of turkeys, but not me. I'll let you handle this." He gave the envelope to Connor who trotted it to the recycle bin and returned to sit next to Al, looking up at him expectantly. Al held up both hands, palms open, to show Connor that they were empty.

"That's it for today!"

Connor immediately jumped up on Al, who was like a sitting duck, turning his face away in a halfhearted attempt to avoid the onslaught of dog kisses.

"OK! OK! Wait!" Al held up his index finger and the dog backed off a few inches, panting, his tongue hanging out one side of his mouth. As he looked into Connor's adoring eyes, he saw nothing but loyalty, trust, and unconditional love. He wondered what it would be like to be so completely happy. Connor's face was graying slightly, and Al worried a little about his dog's advancing age. He'd read that the large breeds tend to have shorter life expectancies. He reached into his pocket and slowly extracted another Milk Bone. He held it up in front of Connor, who took the treat gently, crunched it twice and swallowed it.

Al put both arms around his dog and hugged him close.

"Good boy," he whispered. "I love you, too."

Chapter 10

Mireya rose with the sun and a plan. She had opted to go to bed early the night before, her disappointment in her slides of the Piping Plovers precluding any productive work on either of her manuscripts. She would attack this problem head on.

WBZ was predicting good weather for Cape Cod for the next few days; she would drive out there and get some new pictures. She loved the Cape, and May was still off-season so she would have no trouble getting a room. The beaches where the little plovers liked to lay their eggs would be deserted for the most part.

She walked into her closet, which wasn't a closet at all. Her contractor had convinced her to convert the small bedroom, which had probably once been a nursery adjoining the master bedroom, into a walk-in closet/dressing room. This would be a dream closet for someone who was a shopper or a clotheshorse, but Mireya barely had it half full.

The morning sun streamed in through both windows, making lights unnecessary. She yawned and stretched away some of the cobwebs leftover from her dreams, whatever they may have been, and began to fill a suitcase with enough clothes for a three-day field trip. She dressed in camouflage cargo pants, lightweight hiking shoes, and a long sleeve T-shirt.

She carried her suitcase downstairs and dropped it next to the side door in the kitchen, then proceeded directly to the coffeemaker. She always set the coffee up the night before so she wouldn't have to wait those extra few minutes for her morning fix; she could barely function without that first cup. She flipped the switch, and in moments the room began to fill up with the intoxicating smell of brewing coffee.

Coffee was one of the few things she was particular about. It had to be hot and fresh. If the coffee sat on the warming plate for an hour, she would throw it away and start over.

Her machine had an automatic timer function, but she didn't have a schedule that got her up at the same time every morning so it went unused. If she slept past seven-thirty, Gina would arrive and deliver a cup to her bedroom when she was ready to get up. Now THAT was her definition of luxury. Waking up to a great cup of coffee and having an hour to read the newspaper, undisturbed, were two of life's greatest joys.

This morning while she waited, she went back to the living room to check on her parakeets. "Hey, Thelma. Hey, Louise. How's life in the big cage? Look how dirty you got your drinking water. You want to take a bath? OK, I'll fill your tub, too." She carried the water dish and the birdbath back to the kitchen.

As Mireya washed the parakeets' dishes in the sink and refilled them, Gina came through the door.

"Where are you off to?" Gina asked, noticing the suitcase next to the door and the pile of photographic equipment on the kitchen table.

"The Cape," Mireya said as she took the water back to the birds.

"What are you photographing this time?"

"Plovers again."

Mireya returned to the kitchen and took the cup of coffee Gina had poured.

"What's wrong with all the beautiful pictures you took last time?"

"Not good enough."

"You must be kidding."

Mireya shook her head and pointed to a copy of *National Wildlife* that was on the table.

"Going for the cover again?" Gina asked.

Mireya nodded. "Something has to be done to raise public awareness."

"How long will you be gone?"

Mireya started checking the photographic equipment and packing it in her backpack.

"Let me see…It's Tuesday. I'm heading down to Scituate this morning, then I'll drive to Wellfleet later on this afternoon. If all goes well I should be back Thursday night. Sooner if I get lucky." She continued to pack up an assortment of lenses and filters. She zipped up the backpack and started to lift it off the table. As if suddenly changing her mind, she let the pack drop back on the table and leaned against it, shoulders slumped, eyes down. She sighed.

"You're discouraged," Gina said quietly.

Mireya continued to stare down at her pack.

"In beauty it is done, in harmony it is written." Gina recited softly.

Mireya looked up, directly into Gina's eyes. *"In beauty and harmony it shall so be finished."*

Gina smiled.

Mireya picked up her backpack and suitcase and left the house.

Chapter 11

Gary squashed his jacket into the crowded overhead compartment and slid his briefcase under the seat. He was the last one to board the plane and considered himself lucky to have made it.

He should have listened to his subconscious and taken the Blue Line to the airport as he originally intended. Instead, when traffic appeared normal at three o'clock, he called a cab. He believed he could get to Logan ahead of rush hour. How could he have known a fender bender would tie up traffic in the Callahan tunnel for almost an hour?

With heightened airport security measures in full effect, it was a miracle he was allowed to board at all. He buckled his seat belt, stretched his long legs out into the aisle, and closed his eyes while the plane taxied out to the runway and took off.

Gary dozed in his seat until the flight attendants arrived with the beverage cart. He ordered a glass of V8 juice. If he were going to finish this on-site inspection in time to return home Friday night he needed a efficient plan. He dug his topographical map out of his briefcase and spread it out on his tray table, careful not to set the V8 on top of it.

The seven hundred or eight hundred acres closest to Lake Superior were fairly level and contained a large pond or lake, probably covering a hundred or more acres. There were at least three major tributary streams feeding into the lake and one large outlet leading to Lake Superior. In effect, the entire parcel was a watershed for this unnamed lake and Lake Superior.

He reached into the zipper pocket of his briefcase for his compass/protractor. Damn! Airport security took it from him when they searched his carry-on luggage. He wondered just how a guy was supposed to hold up a plane with a compass/protractor. Seriously, if you were to stab a person, say fifty or a hundred times with the pointy end, it would still probably take a month for the victim to bleed to death. And that was assuming that he or she was a hemophiliac and couldn't produce a clot at the site of the wound. They took his compass/protractor, but let another guy onto a plane wearing shoe bombs. Go figure. Well, at least they gave him back his pencil.

He decided to keep it simple He would start at the edge of Lake Superior and work his way west. He hoped he would get the four-wheel drive rental vehicle he'd requested, because some of these old logging roads were likely to be in pretty rough condition.

He studied the bedrock and soil survey maps all the way to Chicago. Obviously, Paquette-the-elder had not done his homework or he would never have expected to find significant iron deposits on this parcel. Anyway, that would just make his job easier. An old logging site was a lot simpler to evaluate than a major mining operation.

He had an hour to kill at O'Hare International Airport before boarding his connecting flight to Duluth. He stopped at a small shop that sold a lot of stuffed animals and found a great Snoopy dog wearing a Chicago Bears hat, matching scarf, and carrying a football under his arm. He bought it for Sandra's collection. She must have at least twenty Snoopies in her room. He was amazed that she named her puppy Scooby-Doo, or Don't as the case may be.

He was relieved to find the keys to a Jeep Cherokee waiting for him at the rental counter in the Duluth airport. Now if he could just find a way to stay awake for the fifty-mile drive to Castle Danger he could call it a day. He was by nature a morning person, so he felt fortunate to find a Dunkin' Donuts with a drive through on his way out of town. He bought a large coffee, and headed north on Route 61. If all went well, he could be checked into his hotel and asleep by midnight.

The Lakeview Inn turned out not to be an inn at all, but a shabby, one-story motel. There was also absolutely no view of the lake, unless you crossed the road and cut through the stand of trees on the other side. He was too tired to care. He brushed his teeth, undressed, climbed under the covers, and was immediately asleep with cobwebs hanging above his bed and musty dreams filling his head.

Chapter 12

He tried to shut out the irritating noise that filtered down to his subconscious but it refused to subside. It was two noises. One seemed like it was coming from inside his head, the other from far away. Was there an echo? He wanted them both to go away. He took a couple of steps in the direction of conscious thought, but was still deep within the disorienting depths of prematurely terminated sleep. He flailed an arm in the direction of the telephone, managed to grasp the receiver, but as he pulled it across the bed and put it to his head, upside down, he dragged the base unit off the nightstand and onto the floor. The irritating noises persisted, and he chucked the receiver onto the floor with the rest of the phone.

Grudgingly, he climbed a few more rungs up the ladder to consciousness, enabling him to open his right eye just a crack. He had no idea where he was. He took it up a few more notches and was able to roll over and open both eyes. OK, so the noise inside his head was actually his alarm watch. He had been sleeping on his left side with his wrist under his head. The other noise was his travel alarm, set up on the dresser on the other side of the room.

He covered his face with both hands and took a deep breath. At the moment he had to pee like a racehorse. Then he remembered the giant cup of Dunkin' Donuts coffee he consumed on the way to this lousy motel.

"Oh, God." He rolled over on his side and sat on the edge of the bed, his elbows on his knees and his hands still covering his face.

"OK." He moved his hands from his face, slapped his knees and transferred his weight onto his feet only to find out that his back was so stiff he couldn't stand up straight. This could no doubt be attributed to the sagging, musty motel mattress. He started walking toward the bathroom hunched over and gradually became more erect. He walked slowly, working out a few of the kinks with each step.

After two ibuprofen and a hot shower, he was feeling more like himself. He was ready to start his day by hunting up some coffee and breakfast. It was a crystal clear Minnesota morning and once outside, he filled his grateful lungs with the cool onshore breeze. In the distance he thought he could hear the faint sound of waves lapping against the shore.

On his way to the motel office he noticed that his car was the only one in the lot. Small wonder. Although there was no old house on the hill behind the motel, and the office clerk was an overweight teenage girl with bad skin and a nose ring, there was a buck's head complete with antlers mounted over the fireplace and the whole scene had a distinct Batesian quality. Fortunately, his shower had a glass door, not a curtain.

"I smell coffee! Is there a coffeemaker in here?" Gary smiled as he walked through the door. The clerk looked up from her copy of

Entertainment Weekly, moved the earpiece from her headphones off her left ear to a spot just behind it, and stared blankly back at him.

"Where's the closest coffee?" Gary asked again.

The clerk took a large Styrofoam cup from behind the computer, set it on the counter in front of Gary, and turned it around so that Gary could read the words "Beanie Gourmet."

"Great. And where do I have to go to buy a cup?"

"About a half mile south. The Mobil station."

"Thank you." Gary smiled at the clerk again, who had already replaced her earpiece and resumed reading her magazine.

"And you have a nice day, too," he said to the oblivious teen.

The Mobil station had two pumps, a one-bay garage, and a one-room convenience store. As far as he could tell, a guy who looked like he could have retired twenty years ago was holding down the fort on all of them. Gary parked in front of the store and got out. The ancient proprietor walked out from behind a Chevy Malibu, wiping his hands on a towel that was so saturated with grease it was the color of asphalt.

"Help you?" he asked.

"I'm looking for a cup of coffee and something to eat."

"I can help you out with the coffee, and we got doughnuts and muffins. No cinnamon buns this morning. If you want breakfast, you'll have to go into town."

"This will do just fine. What kind of doughnuts are they? They're small."

"Plain. Rolled in cinnamon sugar. The wife fries up about three or four dozen every morning."

"These were homemade this morning?" Gary began to salivate.

"Yup."

"I'll take a half dozen."

"Just help yourself," he handed Gary a small paper bag. "Your paws are cleaner than mine. Help yourself to the coffee, too. We got four kinds."

"Thanks." Gary loaded six still slightly warm doughnuts into the bag. "She make the muffins, too?"

The owner nodded, and Gary selected two blueberry muffins. He filled a cup with Beanie Gourmet Breakfast Blend and set everything on the counter. He thought about hiking around in the woods all day and decided to pick up some snacks in case he didn't break for lunch.

"That'll be $15.50."

Gary handed the man a twenty-dollar bill and ate one of the doughnuts while he waited for change. It struck him that if this woman had a mind to, she could put Krispy Kreme out of business.

"This is the best doughnut I ever ate," Gary said as he bit a second one in half.

"I'll tell her you said so."

"Do you know how far up the road it is to the large parcel of land owned by Nelson Paquette? I'm looking for the main logging road that goes up by the lake."

"Paquette. Now there's a name I ain't heard in a while." He studied Gary for a few seconds and then said, "You'll run into that about three miles north of here."

"Thanks," Gary said as he pocketed his change and picked his coffee and doughnuts up off the counter. "Is there a place to get lunch or dinner up that way?"

"If you're a guy who likes homemade, you might want to try the Brown Bear. It's a little diner run by a friend of mine about a mile and a half north of Paquette's logging road."

"Thanks again," Gary said on his way out the door. "I'll probably be back tomorrow morning for some more of these." He held up the bag.

The old man nodded and waved.

Gary had no trouble finding the logging road, and was immediately glad he'd had the foresight to rent a vehicle with off-road capabilities. It was obvious that nobody had been this way for a long time. The road was so overgrown in places he thought he might have to abort and find a place to buy some lopping shears and a saw. Eventually, a fallen tree halted his progress. He was close enough to hike to the lake. He could clear this tomorrow when he returned with the proper tools.

He opened the tailgate of the Jeep and unzipped his backpack to check the contents. He had his binoculars, a compass, a Swiss army knife, a first aid kit, a rain poncho, matches, a roll of duct tape, a length of rope, four single use cameras, his maps, a few extra pairs of socks, and his Teva sandals. He put the compass and the knife in his pocket, the binoculars around his neck, and set the sandals aside in case he needed to get out of his boots at the end of the day. He packed the things he bought at the convenience store, two large bottles of water, a handful of Slim Jims, two giant Snickers bars, and two bags of chips into the backpack. The doughnuts and muffins were long gone. He slung the pack over his shoulder, hopped over the downed tree, and hiked off in the direction of the lake.

Chapter 13

He had traversed most of the logging roads on the eastern part of the parcel and had hiked halfway around the lake. He wasn't looking for anything in particular, just anything in general that was unusual or out of place. Anything that might signify a potential problem or risk for the client, and escalate the geo-environmental study to the very expensive Phase II level would probably kill the deal because this was just one of several sites under consideration.

The shadows on the surface of the lake were like elongated caricatures of the trees behind him, foretelling the demise of another day, perfect though it had been. He sat on a rock on the western edge of the lake and let the late afternoon sun warm him as he polished off the last of his Slim Jims. Tired and still hungry, he decided to finish his hike around the lake and call it a day.

He jumped down off the rock and grabbed his pack. It slid a few inches down the hill behind the rock and then stopped, hung up on something. He gave it a good tug, but it wouldn't budge. He climbed back up on the rock and discovered that one of the straps was hooked around the stump of a broken sapling. He cleared the dead leaves from around the stump and realized that it wasn't broken at all. The stump bore the telltale marks of beavers at work.

He smiled. He thought that if you excluded ants, beavers were the undisputed engineers of the animal kingdom. In Wisconsin, where he went to graduate school, beavers would dam up large streams so rapidly and efficiently town officials used dynamite to remove them.

A remote lake of this size could support a huge beaver population, although he had not yet seen any signs of a colony. A quick look around by the water's edge revealed a few more trees that had been felled by beavers, but nothing indicating recent activity. In fact, the tree stumps in question were so rotted he guessed that it had been years since the beavers had been there. He decided to stay close to the edge of the lake and look for their lodge.

The going was painfully slow. He fought a tangle of undergrowth, and the ground was a jumble of slippery moss-covered rocks. After struggling for twenty minutes he arrived at the third and last significant tributary stream. It was still swollen from the spring rains, but it wasn't very wide and he managed to cross without getting his feet wet.

Another difficult ten or fifteen minutes passed, and the lakeshore turned outward, forming a huge cove on the southwest end of the lake. He stepped out of the brush and onto a large flat rock just a few feet into the water. As he stood there in silence, he was relatively sure that he was looking at one of the largest beaver lodges in the history of the world. The cove was easily the size of a football field, and the lodge occupied at least half of it. He could only imagine what it looked like from under the water.

On the other side of the cove, a large pine tree had fallen into the water. It looked like it was still partially attached at the base and extended about thirty or forty feet out into the lake. He hiked around to the other side of the cove to see if it could provide a better vantage point. On closer inspection, the tree was actually uprooted, although the roots on the bottom third of the tree were still attached and the tree was not yet completely dead. He took one of the disposable cameras out of his pack, climbed up on the trunk of the tree, and jumped up and down a few times to check its stability. It seemed solid enough so he dropped his pack and walked out along the trunk to get a better look and take some pictures.

The colony was not actually one huge lodge, but many large lodges adjoining one another like an enormous beaver condominium complex. He took some pictures and regretted for the first time that he didn't have a more sophisticated camera. He finished the roll, pocketed the camera, and stared out at what he thought was a true feat of engineering. If those Boston Big Dig contractors worked as efficiently and diligently as these beavers, that project would have been finished years ahead of schedule instead of lagging years behind.

As he stared out over the peaceful cove, the absolute quiet that he was enjoying slowly raised a red flag. It was just about twilight. He should be seeing some activity from the largely nocturnal beavers. They were shy animals, but not only had he not seen or heard an actual beaver in the water, he had seen no signs of recent beaver activity anywhere on the shore. He raised his binoculars and took a closer look at the lodges.

At first everything appeared normal. Then he noticed a hole in the roof of one of the lodges. As he scrutinized each of the tepee-shaped dwellings, he began to notice that many were in a state of disrepair. Then it hit him: This colony had been abandoned. He lowered his binoculars in disbelief. What could have happened to a colony this size in such a remote location? Food was plentiful, trapping was illegal, and natural predators seemed an unlikely cause. He was mystified.

The sun was setting, and if he didn't get going he would be trying to find his car in the dark. He would give this some thought and have another look tomorrow.

As he turned to make his way back to the shore, his left foot slipped off the wet trunk and he lost his balance. He pitched forward, then pivoted on his right foot, arms windmilling wildly for what seemed like an eternity in a futile attempt to avoid the inevitable. When gravity finally won out, he pushed off with his right foot so at least he would enter the water feet first.

"SHIT! I can't believe this!" he shouted to the nonexistent beaver population. The chilly lake water was about six inches below waist level. He didn't care that he got his shorts wet, but he knew that his boots would never dry out before morning.

"Shit! Shit! Shit!" He slogged his way out of the lake. On the shore, he sat on the fallen tree and took off his boots. He poured the water out of them and put on his extra dry socks. They wouldn't be dry for long. The last light of day was rapidly fading. He shouldered his pack and double-timed it back to his car.

Chapter 14

Gary navigated the last fifteen minutes with a compass and a flashlight. The last remnants of daylight disappeared just before he found the main logging road where he'd left his car. His sense of humor returned when he traded his soggy boots for another pair of dry socks and his Teva sandals. He could just imagine how his daughter would laugh when he recounted his latest misadventure. He changed from his wet shorts to a pair of sweatpants and decided to go directly to dinner.

He continued north on Route 61, looking for the diner the gas station owner had recommended. He had gone a little more than a mile when he found it. As he pulled into the parking lot, he hoped the food wasn't as bad as the place looked. He thought about those homemade doughnuts and decided not to judge the contents by the wrapper. Maybe the cook was a closet gourmet. Besides, he was too hungry to go looking for alternatives.

The diner was a one-story wooden structure with a flat roof and a couple of crumbling cement steps leading to the front door. At one point it probably wore a coat of brown paint, but it was so faded and weathered it was hard to be certain. The windows emitted a yellowish glow as light struggled to pass through glass coated with grime accumulated over many years. Above the door a wooden sign identified the structure as the Brown Bear.

Opening the door, Gary found a long counter with the traditional stools, and four small tables against the front wall, two of which were occupied. He took a seat at the counter.

An old-timer who looked like a contemporary of the gas station proprietor sauntered over to Gary.

"What'll it be?" he asked Gary, who was studying the menu posted on a blackboard.

"Ahh…Any recommendations?"

"How adventurous are you?"

"Tonight? Not very."

"In that case, I'd go with the fried chicken. It's pretty safe."

"Sounds good."

"You want fries with that?"

"Why not."

The old-timer started to walk away, then turned back. "Cole slaw?"

"You make it?" Gary asked.

"Indeed I did."

"OK."

"Something to drink?"

"Beer?"

"You got it." The old-timer sauntered into the kitchen.

Gary swiveled on his stool and looked around the shabby interior of the diner. His eyes wandered over walls covered in memorabilia.

There were many old photographs, mostly of proud fishermen with their catches, as well as some pictures of Little League teams from long ago, wearing T-shirts most likely provided by their sponsor, The Brown Trout. There were a couple of fishing rods, an old lure-covered hat sandwiched between two pieces of glass in a homemade frame along with a picture of a happy looking fellow wearing the hat, no doubt its owner. His eyes shifted to a couple of plaques—one from a fishing derby and one from the Lake County Fair Fried Chicken Cook-off. He hoped that was a good omen.

When his eyes came to rest on an old faded wooden sign, he paused. A picture of a large fish occupied the center of the sign. A small cartoon drawing in the lower right corner looked remarkably like a young version of the old-timer who took his order. Across the top of the sign, bold letters spelled out what was undoubtedly the name of an establishment as well as the name of the fish, "THE BROWN TROUT."

Chapter 15

"THE BROWN TROUT." To what did that refer, besides the obvious fish depicted below it? Was it a former, or perhaps a failed business owned by the same proprietor? Was it the name of this diner under a previous ownership? If so, how would he explain the caricature of the old guy that waited on him? Maybe he sold out to someone else and now only works here.

Gary stared intently at the sign as if waiting for the fish to turn its head and give him the answer like one of those ridiculous singing fish plaques that were all the rage a few years ago. As a matter of fact, there was one of those hanging on the wall just left of the entrance to the kitchen. Why would someone change the name from trout to bear when almost everything in the place had something to do with fishing? It's really odd…

"You look hungry," the old-timer said as he set a bowl of pretzels and a beer down in front of Gary. "Keep you busy while you're waitin on your dinner."

"Thanks." Gary grabbed a handful of pretzels and popped a few in his mouth.

"Say," Gary said as the old man began to walk away, "what's that sign on the wall? Did the name of this place change with new ownership or something?

"Naw. In the old days there was a lot more activity in these parts. There were two or three mining camps in the county and a lot more people in town. Me and a bunch of buddies would go up to the lake on Paquette's land, Pine Lake we called it. Real original name." The old man shook his head, a look of disgust and disappointment on his face.

"Anyway, we used to catch the biggest brown trout you ever seen. Those were the days. When I opened this place, and I *am* the original owner, I named it The Brown Trout. Yeah. Those were the days all right."

"So why change the name? Don't you go fishing up there anymore?"

"No point. Ain't no more brown trout, or any other fish neither. Power plant boys seen to that. Them and their damn dump trucks. We call it Pine Point Lake now."

"I didn't know there was a power plant around here." Gary's tone remained casual, although another red flag was starting to rise.

"Been closed for years. Property was bought by a Duluth outfit that recycles scrap metal."

"So what did they do to the lake?" Gary asked as he took another handful of pretzels.

"You ask a lot of questions," the old-timer said, a hint of suspicion coloring his demeanor. "You look like a city guy. What are you doin around here?"

"Gary Coakley. I'm an engineer with a Boston firm, Hawthorne & Associates. We've been hired to do the environmental site assessment on the Paquette property for a potential buyer." Gary stood up and held out his hand.

"That so?" the old man replied as accepted the handshake.

Gary nodded his head and took a sip of his beer.

"Gus Larson."

"Pleased to meet you. So what did the power plant do to the fish?"

"Ancient history. I gotta see to your dinner." He returned to the kitchen, while Gary sat contemplating a sea of warning flags that waved behind his every thought.

Chapter 16

Mireya was lying on the sand, absolutely still, carefully controlling even her rate of breathing. She was much too close to the nest. She would have only one chance at this shot because the sound of the shutter and motor drive would probably frighten the plover when she eventually came into view. She could see four eggs in the sand, perfectly camouflaged. Damn! Something was biting the back of her leg, and she didn't dare to move. Why hadn't she stayed in her long pants? There was always a breeze out here on Great Island, and the sand was not as warm as the afternoon sun would have you imagine.

The mother plover was just six inches from the nest now, partially obscured by a clump of grass. *O-o-o-o-w-w!* This was some form of bug torture, but she was Mireya Richardson, ultimate stalker of nature. Relentlessly patient, superhumanly focused, she would lie here motionless as long as was necessary to capture an image of this precious, fragile species in such dire need of protection. She was on a quest, and the cover of *National Wildlife* was her holy grail. Still, she wished the bird would hurry up and move into her viewfinder so that she could sit up and swat whatever it was that was biting the crap out of her left thigh.

Here she comes…just two steps away from cover girl status. Mireya held her breath. Come on…one more step. The light was perfect; the background was perfect. She made an imperceptible adjustment of the focus. Gotcha! She depressed the shutter, and the tiny plover flew away. She smacked the back of her thigh and sat up. There were a few shots left on the roll so she took some pictures of the eggs in the sand to finish up and began packing her equipment. She was a way from Jeremy Point, the tip of Great Island, but it would still take her well over an hour to hike back to her car.

When she had retreated a safe distance from the nest, she sat down in the sand and opened the refrigerated compartment of her backpack. The ice packs were still relatively cool, and she took a long drink from her water bottle. Her stomach reminded her that she hadn't eaten anything since breakfast, so she decided to take an inventory of her snacks. She had a Granny Smith apple, three granola bars, a raspberry yogurt, and a small bag of Craisins, those little dried cranberries that were tart and sweet at the same time. She opted for the yogurt, and marveled at how cleverly a disposable spoon had been built into the cover. Leave it to Gina to put exactly the right things into her pack.

As she ate her yogurt, she reflected on the relative success of her day. In Scituate she got some great action shots of a "smart" crow harassing a plover while standing on the top of its exclosure, a wire structure designed to allow the plovers to move in and out freely while keeping predators such as crows and skunks out. Crows have been known to kill adult plovers by grabbing them when they fly up near the top of their exclosure. Mireya intervened and chased the crow away at the expense of some very publishable pictures of the poor plover's unusual demise. The best shot of the afternoon was the last one she took, but it was just a single shot, and for it to be cover quality would be quite a stroke of luck.

She looked back along Great Island toward Jeremy Point. If she didn't let her eyes stray across Wellfleet Harbor, she could imagine that this pristine stretch of beach, a sandbar that at high tide would be submerged in some places and barely fifty feet across in others, was untouched by the hand of man. She could imagine that it was a habitat subject only to the trials of Mother Nature and unaffected by the pressures of commercial, residential, and recreational development. In reality, even here nests and chicks are sometimes crushed by ever-increasing foot traffic, and excessive disturbances cause parent birds to abandon their nests. Are there any truly wild habitats left in the world? So few came to mind. She shook her head and covered her face with her hands.

As stewards of the earth, solely responsible for the health and well being of the planet, the human race was a miserable failure. She had to stop taking the failure of her species so personally and just do what she did best, one picture at a time. Anything else would land her back in a shrink's office.

She stood up, hoisted her pack onto her back and started the hike to the parking lot, scratching a huge welt on the back of her left leg.

Chapter 17

Mireya drove straight to the Bowl & Baguette, her favorite sandwich shop in Wellfleet. They weren't open very late this time of year, and she didn't want to miss an opportunity to have dinner there.

The restaurant was named for the two most popular kinds of bread they baked. One was a round loaf that could be scooped out and used as a bowl for the homemade soups they always offered, and the other was a classic French loaf they used for most of their sandwiches. The owners, Marta and Ralph, were fellow eco-activists and served as volunteer monitors for the Massachusetts Piping Plover Census, a program sponsored by the Division of Fisheries and Wildlife.

A light rain began to fall as she pulled up in front of the restaurant. She would never luck out with a parking place like this during the summer months.

As she walked through the door she was hit by the overpowering smell of freshly baked bread. Bread. The ultimate comfort food. Nothing could satisfy the soul like a hot loaf of bread. It could enhance any food it accompanied, or stand alone, a meal in itself. More important, if you were a lover of butter, the real thing, cholesterol and all, there was no better delivery system than a slice of hot bread. A more perfect pairing could not be found in the entire gastronomical experience. In fact…

"Rey!"

Mireya suddenly realized that Marta was waving at her from across the room. She felt her face flush scarlet as she realized that she had zoned out in the doorway. She raised her hand in a sheepish attempt to return the greeting.

"Is something wrong, Rey? Are you OK?" Marta asked as she swept across the room in Mireya's direction.

Mireya raised her hand a little higher and extended her palm toward Marta as a signal for her to stop.

"I'm fine except being hit with the smell of that bread nearly rendered me catatonic. I'm starving."

"Ralph just took a batch of baguettes out of the oven. Sit anywhere you like, and I'll be right over." Marta disappeared into the kitchen, laughing. A moment later she heard Ralph join in.

The shop was half empty, and Mireya immediately went to her favorite spot, a small round table in the corner, next to the front window. It had two chairs, but she could not imagine that two place settings would fit on it. Table for one. She looked out the window at the rain that was coming down much harder now and accompanied by a gusty wind. She wanted to go back out to Jeremy Point in the morning so she hoped it was just a passing squall.

Marta emerged from the kitchen, delivered sandwiches to a table on the other side of the room, and returned to sit at Mireya's table. "What brings you out here this time?"

"Same thing."

"More pictures of plovers? George said your last ones were good."

"Not good enough."

"Really?"

Mireya shook her head. "I need a cover shot."

"Cover? You're going to get our little plovers on the cover of *National Wildlife*?"

"Gonna try."

"You are the best, Rey. Hey, we have your favorite soup today."

"The lentil?"

"Right. You want a bread bowl with that?"

Mireya nodded.

"We have some beautiful jumbo shrimp today. You want a shrimp Caesar to go with the soup?"

"You read my mind."

"You want water? Or maybe something hot to drink?"

"Just water."

"With bubbles, right?"

"Right."

"OK. I'll be right back."

Mireya smiled at her as she left, then turned her attention back to the rain. She should ask Marta about the forecast. If the weather wasn't going to cooperate, she may as well go home. She took out her cell phone and dialed in to check her messages. One new message. She pressed a button, and a vaguely familiar voice came on the line.

> *"Hello. This is Delia Wallace. I just want to let you know that I found my cat on the barn roof just like you said. Mr. Casperson had to climb up a ladder and get her down. She's home safe and sound now, and I'm so relieved. I can't thank you enough."*

Mireya smiled and put the phone away as Marta arrived with a steaming hot bowl of soup, a round loaf of bread, a glass of ice, and a bottle of carbonated water.

"I'll be back with your salad in just a minute."

Mireya held up one finger to detain her. "Do you know what the weather is supposed to be like tomorrow?"

"The last thing I heard was that the rain would end during the night. It will be overcast all morning, and more rain is predicted for the afternoon."

"Thanks. The soup looks great."

Marta smiled and left to check on her other customers.

Mireya leaned over the steaming bowl of soup and took a deep breath. Mmmmm. The loaf of bread had a small depression cut out of the top. The standard procedure was to ladle some of the soup out of the bowl and into the depression in the bread. As you ate the soup, you also ate the soup-saturated bread that formed the bowl. You repeated the procedure until the soup was gone and the loaf of bread completely hollowed out. It was absolutely delicious. Marta returned with a gorgeous Caesar salad, topped with six huge jumbo shrimp, and a basket with three hot French dinner rolls.

"Oh, my God. That looks so good."

Marta smiled as she put the salad on the table. "Bon appetit." She reached into the pocket of her apron and put a handful of individually wrapped portions of butter on the table. "Whoops. I almost forgot your extra butter."

"Marta, do you think George is still in his store?"

Marta looked at her watch. "Probably. Why?"

"Do you think he'd do a rush job for me?"

"Most likely. Want me to call him?"

"Would you?"

"Sure thing. Slide film? How many rolls?"

Mireya reached into her pocket and put four rolls of film on the table.

"Be back in a minute," Marta said as she left to make the call.

Mireya went to work on the bowl of soup.

A few minutes later Marta returned wearing a jacket. She picked the rolls of film up off the table and put them in her pocket. "He said he would do it for the plovers, but in my opinion that crusty old curmudgeon has a crush on you."

Mireya slapped one palm to the center of her forehead as her chin dropped to her chest. She felt her cheeks flush red.

"He wants me to bring the film over right now, and he'll have it ready for you first thing in the morning."

Mireya pushed her chair back from the table and stood up. “No. Give them to me. I’ll take them. You’re working, and it’s raining.”

“Don’t be silly. The kitchen’s closed, and Ralph can keep an eye on these few tables for five minutes. You sit down and eat your soup while it’s still hot.”

“Are you sure?” Mireya sat down.

“Absolutely.”

“I owe you one.”

“I know. And we’re going to collect it in the form of an autographed copy of the cover that we can frame and hang up in here.”

“Deal.”

Marta put the hood up on her rain jacket and left the restaurant. Mireya watched through the window as she sprinted down the sidewalk.

Chapter 18

Gus Larson delivered Gary's dinner without further comment and then joined a group of what appeared to be his cronies at one of the tables in the front. Gary couldn't quite make out their conversation, but out of the corner of his eye he could see them look his way every so often.

He had obviously struck a nerve with his questions and was now the object of some suspicion. He finished his dinner, which was surprisingly good, left some cash with the check on the counter, and walked over to the table where Gus was visiting with his friends. Conversation immediately ceased, and Gus stood up a little straighter, looking tense.

"The chicken was great, but now you got me thinking about fishing," Gary said to Gus and gave him the biggest smile he could manage. The men in the group exchanged a few nervous glances but said nothing. "You guys look like serious fishermen. If I finish up early and have a little extra time, where would I go to do some trout or bass fishing around here?"

Gus's shoulders slumped visibly as he released some of his tension. He turned to one of the men at the table. "Where've you been lucky lately, Andy?"

"I like Indian Lake over near Brimson, northwest of Highland."

“Thanks,” Gary replied. “One thing about Massachusetts is that there are too many people and not enough lakes. I got spoiled living in Wisconsin when I went to college.”

Gary thought he heard an audible group sigh as the men relaxed, smiled, and nodded in agreement. He wished them all a good night and left the diner.

Back in his motel room he powered up his laptop and for the first time since he acquired it from the company was grateful for its wireless Internet capabilities. While he was waiting for it to log on, he decided to call home and say goodnight to Sandra.

The phone rang twice. “Hi, Dad!” a young voice exclaimed, followed by an irrepressibly cute giggle. The sound of her voice never failed to lift his spirits.

“Oh, my God, you’re psycho!” Gary exclaimed with exaggerated surprise.

“That’s PSYCHIC, Gary, and we have caller ID, so my phone says G-A-R-Y right on it. You can’t fool ME anymore.” She was alluding to the days when he would call the house pretending to be Santa Claus, or the Easter Bunny, or the Tooth Fairy. He got away with it, too, until he was foiled by technology.

“Well, I’m going to reprogram that phone to say D-A-D. What do you say to that?”

“OK, Dad. Mrs. Matthews says you’re just a little insecure.”

“Really?” Gary took the cell phone away from his ear and gave it a look of total incredulity.

"Yup. And she said I should always call you Dad, because you're comfortable in that role."

"Well thank you…or her…I guess."

"What did you do today, Dad?"

"I fell in a lake. What did you do?"

Peals of laughter were her only reply.

"Seriously! I really did. I was taking pictures of the biggest beaver lodge I ever saw in my life, and I lost my balance and fell off a log right into the lake."

"How deep was the water?"

"Deep enough to get my pants really wet."

"What's a beaver lodge?"'

"It's a house that the beavers build to live in, only it wasn't just one lodge it was a whole bunch of lodges right next to one another, kinda like the townhouses in our neighborhood."

"Did you see the beavers?"

"No, the lodges were all empty. It was like a beaver ghost town."

"Where did they go?"

"I don't know, honey. I'm going to try to figure that out tomorrow."

"You better wear your bathing suit." More giggles.

"Very funny. I'm not going to fall in again."

"Sure, Dad."

"I'll call you tomorrow night, OK? Now give the phone to Mrs. Matthews, OK?"

"OK. Goodnight, Dad."

"Goodnight, sweetheart. I love you."

"I love you too, Dad."

After checking in with Mrs. Matthews, Gary closed the cell phone and sat down with his laptop. He typed in Pine Point Power Company and clicked on the search button.

Chapter 19

Mireya awoke to the “tap, tap, tap” of a tree branch against her window. She looked at her watch. Eight thirty. She must have been pretty tired to sleep this late on a field trip, especially when she got to bed at an hour that she considered early.

The room was uncharacteristically dark for this time of day. She rolled over and looked out the window. The sky was completely overcast, downright ominous. So much for the WBZ weather center. No doubt they would have a full explanation for this weather reversal involving troughs and stalled fronts. What a job. You get paid a fortune to state your opinion, and nobody ever expects you to be correct. As she thought about it, Mireya decided it must actually be hard to do your best day after day when everyone’s expectations are so low.

She got up and walked to the window. The branches of the trees in back of the inn were dipping and waving wildly in the wind. She looked at her watch again. If she hurried, she could get a quick bite to eat and be at George’s when he opened his shop. She looked out the window again. Why bother? She would be taking no photographs today.

Just as she started to turn away, something caught her eye. She pressed her face and both her palms against the glass and searched the trees. What had she seen? She was staring at a maple tree as if it were one of those optical illusion pictures with a hidden image imbedded in it. Like the pictures, an image materialized from the camouflage and she realized that she was looking at a turkey buzzard perched in the tree, and he was staring in her direction. In fact, he was staring AT her. For a moment she met his gaze and was immediately filled with a dark foreboding. As she jumped back from the window, the buzzard flew out of the tree and disappeared. She put one hand on her chest and exhaled sharply. This was not going to be a good day. She should pick up her pictures and go home.

By the time she dressed and packed up her things, the dark premonition began to subside along with her feelings of urgency. She avoided the window.

After checking out of the inn she decided that she would never make it home without at least a cup of coffee. When she found an empty parking spot directly across from the Lighthouse restaurant she took it as a sign and went in. There was a TV on in the bar area and as she drank her coffee and ate her bagel, she watched the very same weatherman predict light rain and gusty winds for the afternoon. Go figure.

She got another cup of coffee to go and walked the two blocks to George's Photo Stop. An old-fashioned bell attached to the door announced her entrance into the tiny shop. George was obviously in the darkroom, so she went over to the other side of the shop to check out his wall-sized bulletin board. The board was an ever-changing collage of prints, most of which he took himself, but he would occasionally pay a customer the supreme compliment of asking for a copy of one of his or her pictures to add to the display. Mireya's work had been on display more than a few times.

George had a passion for photographing insects, and a picture of a spider's web lightly coated with snowflakes absolutely captivated her. It was the angle at which the sunlight hit the web that gave it such an ethereal effect. She was so absorbed in her analysis that she didn't realize George had entered the room until he dropped an envelope and four boxes of slides on the counter. She straightened up and turned around.

George looked more like a retired sea captain than a photographer, and he always seemed to be blushing whenever Mireya was around. She thought about Marta's comment the night before and decided that he probably just had a naturally ruddy complexion.

"Aah…" she pointed back at the wall. "Love the web."

George smiled and nodded. He opened the envelope and took out some prints. "I took the liberty of printing your cover photo." He slid the prints toward her.

Mireya was stunned. It was the last shot of the day. Light perfect, background perfect, focus perfect, mother plover poised over the nest…What she had not seen through the viewfinder of the camera, but which was perfectly visible on the enlargement, was a tiny hole in one of the eggs and a tiny beak poking through it. What luck! How could she ever have thought this would be a bad day?

"That's it," she said. "I'm done."

George smiled and nodded again. "Yeah. That's what I thought."

Mireya handed him a credit card and glanced at the invoice on the counter. "Wait, George. You forgot to charge for the prints."

"No charge."

"Don't be silly, George, there's six of them here."

"I was hoping I could have one for the wall."

"Of course. Sure." She slid one off the stack toward him and put the rest back in the envelope.

He put the credit card slip on the counter for her to sign, and then slid the picture back to her with a felt-tipped pen. "I thought maybe you wouldn't mind putting your John Hancock on this, too." This time he was really blushing, and so was she. He had never asked her to sign a photograph before. She put her signature in the lower right hand corner, thanked him again, and left the shop.

She felt a few isolated drops of rain as she returned to her car. Let it rain, she thought. Let it rain for a month. As she put Wellfleet behind her, she also left behind the dark premonition she had experienced earlier.

Chapter 20

Gary drove through the center of Beaver Bay looking for someplace to eat breakfast. After another night at Cobwebs Я Us, he hoped he would have time to find another hotel as well. On the north side of town he found an International House of Pancakes. Perfect. He ordered a huge plate of eggs, pancakes, and sausage, and was on his third cup of coffee when he decided on a course of action. He would call the landowner and ask him about the lake point blank. His reaction to the question might tell him more than the answer he gave.

He looked at his watch. It was 9:05. He took out his cell phone and dialed his office.

"Hawthorne & Associates. Gary Coakley's office."

"Joan!"

"Good morning, Gary. How's it going out there?"

"It's interesting. Can you look up a phone number for me?"

"Of course. What do you need?"

"Paquette Investments."

"Hold on." There was a pause as she scrolled through her electronic Rolodex. "I've got it. (212) 555-3404."

"Great."

"Is everything OK?"

"Yeah. I'll probably talk to you after I check out the aerial photos at the Regional Planning Commission offices. I might need you to do a few things for me."

"Like what?"

"We'll talk later. I have to make this call. Meanwhile, check your e-mail so you'll be up to speed when I call back."

"OK, later."

"Thanks, Joan. Bye."

He smiled. Joan sensed there was a mission imminent, and she was never happier than when given a mission. She was sharp and dedicated, and he wouldn't trade her for all the hot Natalie types in Boston.

He poured himself another cup of coffee from the bottomless pot and dialed the number for Paquette Investments.

"Paquette Investments. How may I direct your call?"

"Good morning. My name is Gary Coakley. I'm the engineer in charge of the environmental site assessment requested for Mr. Paquette's Minnesota property. May I speak to Mr. Paquette please?"

"Mr. Paquette is not in the office at the moment, but if you can hold I will try to forward your call."

"Thank you."

He listened to about forty-five seconds of Frank Sinatra singing "Strangers in the Night."

"This is Nelson Paquette."

"Good morning. My name is Gary Coakley. I'm in charge of the environmental site assessment on your Minnesota property."

"How's it going? Is there something I can help you with?"

"I have a few questions concerning the lake on the property. The locals refer to it as Pine Lake."

"What about it?"

"Some of the local people were talking about how great the fishing used to be in that lake. They say there aren't any fish anymore and alluded to the old Pine Point Power Company as the cause. Is there any chance the power plant dumped any of its coal ash on that piece of land in the past?"

"Absolutely not. But what would that have to do with the fishing?"

"Coal ash is highly contaminated with many toxic substances, such as arsenic, strontium, cadmium, selenium, and mercury to name a few. Any site where dumping occurred could have very contaminated soil and groundwater."

"That's very interesting. But I'll tell you why there aren't any fish. My father was an avid fisherman and used to stock the lake every year. He gave blanket permission for the locals to fish in the lake because he only made it up there a few times each year and it seemed like a waste. As the years went by and he got older he almost never had time to go up there so he discontinued stocking it. It didn't take long for the locals to fish it out. They were supposed to throw back everything under ten inches, but nobody ever did. That's why there's no fish."

Gary paused to assimilate the story. "Well, that would certainly explain it. Thank you for clearing that up for me."

"My father always said that the simplest explanation is usually the correct one. No illegal dumping, just too many fishermen."

"It probably wasn't illegal back in those days, and I subscribe to the simplest explanation philosophy as well. Thank you for your time."

"No problem. If you have any more questions feel free to call again."

"Thank you. Good bye." Gary closed his cell phone and stared into his coffee cup.

Chapter 21

Nelson Paquette stormed into his offices and blew by his receptionist's desk without so much as glancing at her. She stood up in a feeble attempt to hand him some phone messages.

"Coffee!" he barked over his shoulder. She dropped the messages and scurried to the coffee maker.

Once inside his office he hurled his coat onto a chair, sat behind his desk, and swiveled his chair toward the window. He didn't bother to look around when his receptionist delivered his coffee and his messages. This was not the way he wanted to start his day, with a call from a nosey engineer while he was still in his pajamas.

He turned back to his desk, picked up the phone, and pushed a button.

"Norman? Bring whatever we've got on Gary Coakley and get in here!" He slammed the receiver down and swiveled back to the window. Looking out over lower Manhattan usually validated him in some way, especially during these post 9/11 days, even if it only made him feel like a survivor.

He felt no such comfort today.

A moment later Norman entered his office carrying a file.

Paquette turned to face his assistant. "What do we know about this guy? Refresh my memory."

"Gary Coakley, 43 years old. Born and raised in West Hartford, Connecticut…Eagle Scout…All-State athlete in baseball…B.S. Civil Engineering from Northeastern University…M.S. Geotechnical and Environmental Engineering from the University of Wisconsin, Madison…crew team captain at Northeastern…Oh! Hiked the Brooks Range one summer."

"Where's that?" Paquette asked.

"Alaska. Let's see…Married to Karen Anne O'Day in '86…daughter Sandra Jean born in '94…Wife killed in a car accident in '97…currently single, living with his daughter in Brookline…current employment is Hawthorne & Associates…That's about it."

"Great! A geotechnical Boy Scout."

"Is there a problem?"

"Yes. I'd say there's a problem. He just called to ask me if Pine Point Power ever dumped ash on my land."

"How in the hell did he figure that out from the visual on-site?"

"Oh, I think one of the locals mentioned the current lack of fishing opportunities, and he figured it out."

"What did you tell him?"

"I flatly denied it, of course. Told him my father stopped stocking the lake. He seemed to buy it, but these God damned geotechnical dweebs just don't seem to be able to leave an 'i' undotted."

"What are you going to do?"

"Are you absolutely sure we can't buy this guy?"

"No way in hell!"

"I want you in touch with all the locals. If he so much as asks one question, he has to be removed from the case. Is our man at Hawthorne ready to step in?"

"He is. How are we going to get Coakley off the case?"

"Call your guys in Massachusetts. Tell them to be ready. If we have to, we're going to distract Mr. Coakley."

Chapter 22

Al stepped out of his kitchen door and stood in the breezeway. He was still dressed in his sweatpants and pajama top. If he wanted to he could darn well stay that way all day. He was starting to adjust to the no rules aspect of life as a retired widower. Still, he looked around to see if any of his neighbors were in evidence. He stepped into the backyard and squinted up at the sky. Another lousy day. No matter. He and Connor would rather watch another Red Sox game and maybe some of the NBA playoffs than mow the lawn any day. *Where did that dog disappear to?*

"CONNOR!" Al looked around the back yard.

"CONNOR! HERE BOY!" He walked back into the breezeway and toward the front of the house.

At that moment, the mailman pulled up to Al's mailbox, stuffed some mail in it, and sped off to the next mailbox, which was all of two hundred feet down the street.

Al looked at his watch.

"Eighteen minutes late," he muttered. "How can you be eighteen minutes late when you get to drive a Jeep around your route? It's not like you can get stuck in traffic in these neighborhoods." He began walking down the driveway shaking his head when he realized he was still carrying his coffee mug. Connor would have this all over him in a heartbeat. He dumped the leftover coffee on the lawn and set the mug down on the step by the kitchen door. On his way back down the driveway he called his dog.

"CONNOR! COME ON, CONNOR!"

There was still no sign of him.

Al retrieved his mail from the box and looked up and down the street.

"CONNOR? HERE BOY!" It wasn't like Connor to miss mail call. Al hoped he hadn't wheedled his way into somebody's kitchen. Al's phone number was on Connor's collar so if that were the case he would just have to wait for the person to phone him.

Where the heck did he go?

"CONNOR!" Al decided to walk down to the end of the block just in case Connor was somewhere in the neighborhood. Maybe he was just out of earshot.

"CONNOR!" He tried to peer into the back yards of the houses he passed.

"CONNOR!"

"C-O-O-N-N-O-O-R-R!!!"...

Chapter 23

Gary was traveling south on Route 61, on his way to the office of the Lake County Regional Planning Commission. When the Mobil station came into view, he slowed the car. Maybe it wouldn't hurt to have a friendly conversation with another one of the county elders. He decided to pull in, check out the doughnut supply, and top off his tank.

He parked in front of the gas pumps and got out of the car. The proprietor emerged from the garage and waved at him, with what looked like the same greasy rag in his hand.

"What can I do you for today?" the old man asked. The crevice that appeared on the lower half of his face might have been mistaken for a smile if he'd had any teeth.

"I need to top off my tank and thought I might as well grab some doughnuts at the same time."

"Sold the last one about a half hour ago, but I can help you out with the gas."

"Darn!" Gary snapped his fingers and feigned deep disappointment.

"So where are you off to today?"

"Research."

The old man gave him a questioning look.

"Over at the county offices. Maps, photos, and so on. Not nearly as much fun as hiking up to the lake yesterday. That's a very pretty spot."

The old man nodded.

"Hey, maybe you could tell me where the nearest one-hour photo place is. Yesterday I took some pictures of the biggest beaver colony I ever saw, and I want to make sure they came out OK before I go home. My little girl loves that kind of thing."

"If you're heading south, there's a CVS in Two Harbors that could probably do it."

"Thanks. That huge colony is completely empty. What do you suppose happened to all those beavers?"

"Don't know." The old man looked reflective. "Ain't been any beavers up there for twenty years or more. I'm surprised there's anything left."

"Gus Larson said there aren't any fish left in the lake. Maybe the beavers ate them all and moved on."

The old man smiled again. "I ain't no expert, but I think beavers are vegetarians."

"Oh, right," Gary replied. "Trees…or something."

"They eat the bark."

"Bark," Gary repeated, nodding. "So you have no idea what happened to them?"

"Well, I ain't seen a lot of people walkin around in fur coats."

"Right. Trapping beavers is illegal, isn't it?"

"Nope. You can get a license. There's a season for it just like hunting. Ain't nobody ever set traps on Paquette's land, though. His wife was one of them animal rights people. Hated leg-hold traps. Always tryin to get them outlawed." He hung the nozzle back on the pump and replaced the gas cap on Gary's car.

"I guess it will remain a mystery," Gary said as he handed his credit card to the old man.

"Suppose so," he replied and took the credit card inside to the register.

Gary couldn't tell if this guy really didn't have a clue or was just playing it close to the vest. Either way, his suspicions were mounting by the moment.

From the gas station he went straight to the county offices. They were all contained on the second floor of a modest wood frame structure, a space that seemed much too small to contain all the departments listed on the door. There appeared to be only one clerk and one telephone with four different lines. Gary walked up to the counter and laid his map down on it.

"Can I help you?" the mousy, middle-aged woman asked.

Gary turned the map around and pointed to it. "I'd like to see the aerial photographs of this parcel from 1955 to 1975."

She studied the map for a few seconds. "Certainly. It will just take a few minutes."

"Thanks," Gary replied and watched as she disappeared into a back room. He looked around the office. There was a horseshoe-shaped counter, behind which were a few business machines, including a fax, a printer that must have been connected to a computer in another room, a copy machine, and lots of file cabinets. The walls were institutional yellow. This could be the clerk's office in any town or county building in rural America.

The clerk returned carrying a large file that she dropped on the counter and opened. She flipped quickly through the photographs in the file, looked a little confused, then flipped through them again more slowly.

"Those years seem to be missing," she said. "I have 1955," she handed him a photograph, "and the next one is 1980."

"Any idea what could have happened to them?"

"Not really. Maybe they got misfiled. I could look around and see if I can find them for you."

"OK, thanks," he said and handed her his card. "If you find them, would you please call me on my cell phone?"

"Sure, no problem," the clerk replied.

The clerk watched Gary closely as he turned to leave. As soon as the door closed behind him, she picked up the phone.

Gary sat in his car for a few minutes, contemplating this latest lack of information. The little suspicions that had been nagging him morphed into a full-blown bad feeling. He took out his cell phone, dialed his office, and was relieved to hear Joan's voice.

"Joan."

"Gary."

"I'm glad to get a hold of you."

"Where else would I be?"

"Nowhere. I mean, I'm glad you didn't take an early lunch or something."

"You mean like, when the cat's away…"

"No. Quit, will you? I need some help out here."

"Shoot."

"Did you read the documents I e-mailed you?"

"The 50-megawatt, coal-fired regional power plant?"

"Right."

"They're printed out and sitting right in front of me."

"Great. I need you to find the names and current addresses of as many of the former managers of that plant as you can. Then I need you to set up interviews with any that are still in this area. I suspect that at some point the power company made a contract with Paquette to dump its ash on the parcel that I'm inspecting out here, but I don't want you to mention that when you set up the interviews. It probably wasn't illegal then, but if the soil and groundwater are as contaminated as I suspect, it will have a very big financial impact on any future use."

"OK, I'm on it. Anything else?"

"Look into the flight alternatives for me. I may have to stay out here longer than I planned."

"You got it."

"You're the best, Joan."

"Yeah, well, talk is cheap."

"Will you PLEASE quit?"

"My job?"

"Badgering me for a raise."

"You're my boss. I can't badger anyone else."

"The company reviews salaries in September. I can't do anything until then, and you know that."

"You know what they say about the squeaky wheel."

"Yeah, when no grease is available, the squeaky wheel gets replaced."

"I guess that's my cue to get back to work."

"Buh-bye, Joan."

"Wait! I forgot something."

"What's that?"

"It's Jim. He's constantly in here asking about you. At least three times yesterday and again first thing this morning. He won't say what it's about."

Gary paused a moment to consider the possibilities, then smiled. "It's Wednesday, and he's already thinking about the weekend. I guarantee he's trying to fix me up again. Damn guy just won't quit."

"So you don't want to talk to him."

"Absolutely not. If I do manage to make it home for part of the weekend, I am dedicating all my attention to a beautiful young lady named Sandra."

"I hear you. Later."

Chapter 24

Norman put down the receiver and folded his hands. This was the call he'd been dreading since his meeting with the boss earlier this morning. He knew Paquette would want this information immediately. Norman just wished he could wear a sign that said, "DON'T KILL THE MESSENGER!"

Norman left his office and strode across the small lobby in the direction of Paquette's office. As he approached the door, Marcie, their receptionist, stood up behind her desk and flagged him down.

She was not, by most men's standards, an attractive woman, although she did have two remarkable attributes, or three if you counted them individually, and she took care to make the most of them. She always wore dark red lipstick to highlight her pillowy lips, and tight fitting, low-cut sweaters to accentuate an eye-popping, gravity-defying, colossal pair of breasts. The fact that she could stand erect without toppling onto her face defied the basic laws of physics.

When she came for her interview he had been in Paquette's office. They peeked out the door to see what she looked like, and Norman blurted out "Holy cow!" Paquette had laughed until he cried.

Though woefully underqualified, she still got the job. The endearing thing about her was that she had no idea she was incompetent, and came to work each day brimming over with enthusiasm and good intentions.

"Mr. Sears," she said, holding her index finger to her lips as if telling him a secret. In hushed tones but with an accent that landed her smack in the middle of Brooklyn, she said, "I don't think you should be goin in there right now."

"Why?" Norman replied.

"He's in a really bad mood today, and right now he's on the phone with Cindi. He doesn't want to be disturbed." She pronounced the last word "distoibed."

Norman smiled. His first instinct as a cutthroat elitist Manhattanite was to cut her down with some insidious verbiage that would have her scratching her head and consulting a dictionary, but as usual, he couldn't bring himself to follow through. Being mean to Marcie would be sort of like kicking a puppy. Way too mean for most of the human race.

"It's important business, Marcie," Norman said in the same conspiratorial pseudo-whisper that she used. "But thanks for the warning."

"OK, you're welcome," she mouthed and quietly sat down in her chair.

Norman entered the office without knocking and crossed the room to stand in front of the desk. Paquette looked annoyed, but found a way to end his phone conversation. He sat back in his chair and looked at Norman.

"What?"

Norman garnered his courage. "The clerk from the Lake County Offices called. Coakley found out about the missing aerials."

"And?"

"He called his secretary and asked her to find out if any of the Pine Point Power management team is still in the area. He wants to do some interviews."

"SONOFABITCH!" Paquette stood up so fast his chair flew back and slammed into the window.

"That's it! We have to get him out of there. Leave it to us to get Dudley Fucking Due Diligence for an engineer." Paquette began to pace back and forth behind his desk.

He stopped and looked at Norman.

"These 'operatives' of yours…" He used the first two fingers of each hand to make quotation marks in the air when he said "operatives." "They aren't twisted, or sociopathic, or anything?"

"They're gay." Norman began to shift his weight from one foot to the other.

"Gay?"

"Yeah, well, one is a real tough guy type and the other one is…not so tough."

"Perfect." Paquette shook his head and let out a huge sigh. "Tell them to pick up the kid ASAP and take her to the house in Truro. You…" He pointed his finger at Norman, who was still shifting his weight back and forth like a mongoose facing down a cobra. "Get your ass down there and make sure nobody fucks up or gets carried away. Tell those two faggots if they harm one hair on that kid's head my next order of business will be to hire two homophobic psychopaths to rip their lungs out. Do you think that's clear cut enough for them?"

Norman nodded and remained silent. A feeling of dread began to creep over him the way poison ivy crawls up a tree.

Paquette continued, "They get half when they deliver the girl safely to Truro and the other half when the deal is in place and we let her go."

"Anything else?" Norman asked, not really wanting to hear the answer.

"Isn't that enough?" Paquette opened his locked desk drawer, took out a thick envelope, and handed it to Norman. "This is the first half. They don't know our names so they can't slip up in front of the kid. Just make sure you don't. Now hurry up and get down there."

Norman turned to leave, then changed his mind and turned back to face Paquette again.

Paquette, now seated at his desk, looked up at Norman and raised his eyebrows. "WHAT?"

"I was just thinking that this whole kid-snatching idea might be a little extreme."

Paquette was out of his chair and around his desk in one intensely aggressive move that had Norman taking a few faltering steps backward.

"EXTREME? I'LL TELL YOU WHAT'S EXTREME! PISSING AWAY A **TWENTY MILLION-DOLLAR** LAND DEAL OVER

AN ENGINEERING REPORT. THAT'S EXTREME! NOW STOP THINKING AND GET YOUR ASS DOWN TO TRURO!"

Though he made a good attempt at remaining outwardly cool, Norman withered emotionally and mentally in the face of this attack. He turned slowly and walked toward the door.

"Norman."

Norman stopped and looked back at his boss.

"Look, Norman. We have insiders at both Hawthorne and Sund Oil. We railroad this deal through, take the money, and run."

"Easy for you to say. You're the one with the beach house in Belize."

"Your cut will be large enough to give you the freedom to go anywhere you choose."

Norman nodded, though he remained unconvinced.

Chapter 25

Al pushed his Hungry Man microwave dinner across the table, barely touched. Connor had never missed lunch before. Actually, it was dinner; Al had gotten into the habit of eating his biggest meal at noon. Although, in truth, his evening meal was pretty large also.

After his wife died, he swore he would never eat another Lean Cuisine meal again as long as he lived. It seems that these days eating healthy means going hungry 24/7. Those healthy meals were so "lite" they couldn't fill a hole in his back tooth. He just didn't care anymore about the state of his cholesterol, his blood pressure, the extra twenty-five pounds he put on, or the fact that he could no longer pass a cardio-pulmonary stress test. He did take the pills his doctor prescribed, but he blew off the heart-healthy diet and the exercise regime. The only sport in which he participated as a non-spectator was fishing. He decided to live his life on his own terms, and if it cut him out of a few years, what would be the difference?

What he did care about most in his day-to-day life was Connor. After his wife, Connor was the best, most true-blue companion he had ever had. *So where had his best friend disappeared to?*

He couldn't stand sitting around doing nothing. Maybe Connor followed one of the kids on a bike and got too far away to find his way back. Over the years, Dorchester had become part of the suburban sprawl surrounding Boston, a never-ending series of residential subdivisions punctuated by the occasional shopping plaza. He got up from the table, grabbed his jacket, and headed for the garage. He backed the '96 Crown Victoria sedan slowly down the driveway and rolled down both the driver's and passenger's side front windows.

He adjusted his wiper speed to the lowest setting to accommodate the mother-in-law rain that had begun again, and drove slowly down the street, calling his dog after every house he passed.

Chapter 26

Mireya returned to her house in Cambridge in a much better mood than when she left. She burst through the kitchen door, dropping all her gear on the floor.

"GINA! ARE YOU HERE?" She kicked off her shoes and made a beeline for the refrigerator, where she grabbed a bottle of her favorite Nantucket Nectars Ice Tea. She took a long drink as she walked to the hall.

"GINA!" she yelled up the stairs. She listened for a few seconds, and when Gina didn't answer, she continued walking to her office. There was a note on her desk. It said, "Gone to the market." –Gina. She could never figure out whether Gina knew somehow that she was coming home early or whether she always left a note just in case.

She never felt that she had a meaningful or lasting bond of any kind with her own mother, but Mireya imagined that her connection with Gina was much stronger, more spiritual, than a normal mother-daughter relationship would be. It was Gina who kept her in touch with her roots, kept her grounded.

She looked across the room and noticed the light blinking on the Lost Friends message machine. She dragged her chair over and sat down next to it with a notebook and pen in hand. There was one new message. She took a long drink from her bottle of ice tea and pushed the button.

After the customary few seconds of blank tape, a woman's voice announced,

> *"My name is Karen Iverson and I'm calling from Newark, New Jersey."*

Mireya wondered why callers almost always included their location; as if it would make a difference whether they were calling from Kabul, or the house next door. She supposed it must seem significant to them.

> *"I'm calling about my cat, Rosco. He's been missing for about three days, and I have absolutely run out of ideas of where to look. My number is (201) 555-5489."*

Mireya sighed. "Another wayward kitty. OK." She dialed the number.

"Hello."

"This is Mireya from Lost Friends returning Karen Iverson's call."

"Oh, thank God! This is Karen."

"Why don't you tell me about Rosco?"

"He's six years old. He's a very large orange-and-white tabby. He's basically an indoor cat. He's neutered and never wanders. I know all about you because you found my brother's dog last fall. I have my Visa number ready for you if you're ready for it."

"OK. Go ahead." Mireya wrote down the number. "How long has Rosco been missing?"

"It's been three whole days now."

"I'd better get going on this right away, then. I'll get back to you soon."

"Thank you so much."

Mireya hung up the phone and ran the credit card information through the machine. She sat back in her chair, exhaled deeply, and closed her eyes.

She whispered, "Rosco…"

An image immediately began to take shape in her mind, but she was confused because she was unable to see any details. She was confident of her connection with the cat, yet she saw nothing. She remained patient, watchful, concentrating on Rosco. As the moments passed, a claustrophobic, trapped feeling slowly overtook her. As she stared at the dark image in her mind she realized that she was literally in the dark. She was in a small dark space, lying wedged between two unidentifiable objects. She let her consciousness spiral down, to the cat; the cat trapped in a small, dark, uncomfortable space. Suddenly she felt as though she was suffocating, and very, very thirsty. She grabbed her throat, her breath was becoming raspy…

Mireya's eyes snapped open and she gasped for air. She immediately took a drink from her bottle of ice tea.

"Holy shit. Poor thing," she said, still holding her throat. She scribbled down everything she could remember about Rosco's location, picked up the phone, and dialed Karen's number.

"Hello." Karen answered the phone on the first ring.

"It's Mireya. Your cat is stuck in a small dark space. I'm thinking it's a closet because there seems to be a lot of stuff on the floor. Maybe a cabinet. Anyway, you better act fast because he's badly dehydrated, barely conscious, and he's not going to last long."

"We've looked in all the closets in the house. If he were somewhere in the house we would have heard him. He's very vocal."

"Attic? Basement? Garage?"

"I'm going to check all those places again."

"Drawers. I think you should check all drawers large enough to hold a cat. Be sure to call me when you find him. Good luck."

"Will do. Thank you so much."

Mireya relaxed back into her chair and reflected on the dire nature of the cat's situation. She searched her memory for any missed clues, anything at all. From her extensive experience in situations like this, she was sure that they would find him, as long as he had not left the property.

She got up and went to the window. A light, misty rain was falling. She came home from the Cape a day early with a photograph that she was sure was destined for the cover of a national magazine, and she probably just saved the life of a lost, trapped cat. Why, then, was she once again experiencing this sense of foreboding, this feeling of impending evil? She should be having a good day. No, she should be having a great day.

She pressed her forehead against the cool glass of the window and stared at the raindrops that were clinging to the outside. Occasionally, one of the tiny drops would fall on top of another, increasing its mass sufficiently for gravity to pull it downward. It would soon collide with another tiny drop, making it bigger still, and increasing the downward momentum in a kind of snowball effect, until the drop became so large it simply rolled to the bottom of the window and disintegrated against the sill.

Life could be like that, she thought. A series of chance encounters could generate momentum in a certain direction, could influence one to choose a certain path that once begun, made changing course as difficult as opposing the force of gravity. The more time you spent focused in a particular direction, the more momentum was generated, the greater were the forces of inertia that swept you down the path, and the less likely you would be to see the sill blocking the terminus.

She looked past the raindrops. On the other side of her yard a large bird flew down and landed on the fence. As she stood transfixed, the buzzard slowly turned and stared back at her.

Chapter 27

Rick Turner eased the old van to the curb and turned the key off. The engine sputtered to a halt. He leaned back in his seat and held his hand out to his partner. Paul reluctantly passed him the bottle of Jack Daniels.

"Take it easy on the booze, Rick. We can't afford to blow this gig."

"Yeah, well, why don't you blow *this* gig," he said, pointing to his crotch."

"For God's sake, Rick, I'm serious!"

Rick took a big swallow from the bottle and smiled. "So am I."

Paul couldn't keep from laughing, and some of the tension that had built up during the drive to Brookline dissipated.

"Anyway," Rick said, "I don't know why we have to waste time hanging around here. We should go right to the playground."

"Look, genius. We can't hang around the playground any longer than we have to. Somebody might remember this lovely rust bucket. It doesn't exactly blend in with middle class, suburban America, and neither do you."

"Don't dis my wheels," Rick said followed by a loud belch, "and I ain't dressin up in preppie clothes for nobody."

"I'm just saying, it would have been easier if we had rented a…hey, here comes a bus."

They watched as one by one the buses rolled up to the front of the elementary school across the street. A light, misty rain began to fall; Rick rolled his window down halfway so that he could have a clear view of the front entrance. A loud bell rang, and almost immediately children began pouring out of large sets of doors at both ends of the building. Some began to board the buses, others collected around long racks of bicycles, and many stood at the curb waiting to be picked up by one of the dozens of soccer-mom vehicles lined up all the way to the corner.

"Have you ever seen so many SUVs and minivans in one place in your life?" Paul asked.

"Not even in P-town at the height of family vacation season." Rick replied. "Now what do you suppose these people really need with four-wheel drive vehicles? Is there even a dirt road anywhere in this county? Do you suppose they tool around the backyard just for fun? Kinda tough on the petunias."

"It's the latest fashion. Family urban assault vehicles," Paul replied. "Do you see what I mean about your wheels not blending in?"

"Well, you are my fashion queen, but the day I blend in with this group I will buy a gun and shoot myself."

"You already own a gun."

"Oh. Right. Well, I'll buy a bigger one. Just to be sure."

The buses began to roll out of the schoolyard. "Give me the bottle," Paul said as he reached over and tapped Rick on the arm. "Maybe we should call this off. It's raining harder."

"Can't. It has to be today."

"What if she doesn't walk the puppy?"

"Why the hell wouldn't she? She has every other day right after school."

"H-e-l-l-o-o-o," Paul said, making a gesture toward the windshield. "It's raining."

"What? Dogs don't piss on rainy days? We're sticking to the plan. The rain is good. There'll be less people around."

Rick passed the bottle back to Paul and started the engine. He pulled the switch for the windshield wipers and nothing happened. He turned the switch on and off several times. Still nothing.

"Don't do this to me, you old whore!" Rick cursed through clenched teeth. He slammed the heel of his hand into the dashboard next to the wiper switch. After a few seconds, the wipers dutifully began to make their swath back and forth across the windshield.

"Works every time," Rick said and looked over at Paul, who was slumped in his seat, one hand covering his forehead and eyes as if he were in pain.

"What the hell's your problem?"

"Nothing, nothing at all," Paul raised both hands. "Just drive."

"Fine." Rick pulled the old van away from the curb and accelerated down the street.

Chapter 28

Helen Matthews peered out the sidelight of the front door. It was raining, and she hadn't dressed Sandra in her raincoat and hat this morning. The day started out so beautifully she didn't think about it, and besides, the weatherman had said the rain would be southeast of Boston, on the Cape.

She was always on edge when Sandra's father was out of town, but she couldn't pinpoint the reason. He was as easy to work for as anyone she had met in her life, appreciative and undemanding. She was required to be in the house from seven o'clock until nine o'clock in the morning, and from three o'clock until six o'clock in the afternoon. Basically, as long as she put Sandra on the bus each morning and met her when she got off in the afternoon, her hours were completely flexible. Gary got her a pager in case he or anyone from Sandra's school needed to get in touch with her when she wasn't at the house.

She saw the bus turn the corner onto their street. She stepped out onto the front landing and opened her umbrella. When the bus came to a stop in front of the house she was waiting at the curb, ready to tuck Sandra under her arm and her umbrella as soon as she stepped off the bus. They hurried back up the steps and into the house. Scooby was barricaded in the kitchen, and immediately began to bark when he heard Sandra's voice.

"Scooby-Don't! Did you miss me?" Sandra climbed over the barrier and picked up the puppy. "Are you ready for your walk?"

"Oh, Sandra, honey. I don't think you should go walking in the rain."

"It's not raining very hard, and I promised Dad. Like he always says," she lowered her voice as much as she could and pointed to the center of her chest. "'My word is my bond.'"

Mrs. Matthews laughed, "Well I still don't think he would expect you to go out in the rain."

"Don't worry. I'll wear my boots, and I can try out my new Snoopy umbrella!"

"OK, but you go once around the playground and then you come straight home. No playing around in the puddles, boots or no boots." Mrs. Matthews helped her on with her slicker, hat, and boots, and handed her the Snoopy umbrella as she went out the door.

"Just once around and right back here, Sandra," Mrs. Matthews called.

Sandra turned around and walked backward, waving with the hand that held the leash. "Don't worry, I'll be right back." She turned around, skipped a few steps, then jumped in the air and landed on both feet squarely in the middle of a puddle, making a huge splash that startled the puppy.

Mrs. Matthews shook her head. She could hear the sound of Sandra giggling as she and Scooby disappeared through the gate to the playground.

Chapter 29

Rick slowed the van as he went by Gary's street. He rolled the window down a little farther and scanned the neighborhood for activity. Everything was quiet. Maybe the rain was keeping everyone indoors as he had hoped, everyone except one, that is.

"All's quiet," Rick said to Paul, who had just taken a good belt from Rick's bottle of Jack Daniels. "Hey! Easy does it, loverboy. Jack is *not* your friend, remember?" Rick grabbed for the bottle, which Paul kept just out of his reach. "Come on, give it up."

Paul screwed the cap back on the bottle and stowed it under the seat.

"Fine. It's time to take care of business, anyway. Everything looks quiet in the hood, and I'm sure the bus hasn't been here yet so I'll take the long way around to the other entrance."

"Why the long way around?"

"I figure all the non-SUV-owning soccer moms are watching out their windows for the buses. We can't have them noticing my beautiful set of wheels now, can we?"

"*Very* good thinking. Sometimes you surprise me, Rick."

"Why, because I'm not as dumb as I look?"

Paul looked over at Rick and smiled sweetly. "No, baby, you really *are* as dumb as you look. It's just that sometimes…"

Rick cuffed the back of Paul's head, and they both burst into laughter.

This is more like it, Paul thought. He had never been involved in anything criminal before and had to defer to Rick's experience. Although he would never say it out loud, this was the first moment he thought they might actually get away with this.

Rick pulled the van over just before the entrance, parking behind a tall hedge that would hide it from anyone who happened to be on the playground. "I'm going to go have a cigarette over by that tree. You get in the driver's seat. When I signal, start the engine. When I go through the entrance, you drive up to the gates so I can jump in the side door after I grab her. Got it?"

"We've been over this a hundred times. Of course I *got* it." Paul was becoming more and more irritated, unaccustomed as he was to taking instructions from Rick.

"Don't get touchy on me; I'm just makin sure."

"Believe me," Paul hissed, "When I get *touchy*, you'll know it."

"Well," Rick got out of the van and shut the door. "I guess I have that to look forward to."

He walked backwards away from the van, keeping his eyes on Paul.

Paul avoided making eye contact as he climbed over the console and into the driver's seat. Finally, he smiled.

"Caught you!" Rick shouted, pointing at Paul.

Paul cracked up, pounding the steering wheel with one hand, and prominently displaying his middle finger with the other. He watched

Rick walk over to a large maple tree, lean against it, and light a cigarette. This was another part of the plan that made him nervous. Rick was standing in plain view. To say he stood out like a sore thumb would be an understatement.

He was a big burly guy, taller than six feet. He was dressed in leather boots with thick heels, faded jeans, a leather vest over a Harley-Davidson T-shirt, and a worn-out baseball cap sporting the Daytona 500 logo. A thick, untrimmed beard completed the picture of a guy who was totally out of his element in this neighborhood.

Rick was still smiling. From this vantage point, he could see more than half the playground, and so far it was completely deserted. The rain would work to their advantage as long as the kid still walked the puppy.

He was halfway through his second cigarette when he saw her, a tiny brightly clad figure carrying an umbrella and leading a puppy. He got Paul's attention, pointed to his eyes, and then in the direction of the playground. Paul started the engine and let it idle.

There was an asphalt path or sidewalk around the entire outside edge of the playground. He imagined that on a sunny day there would be kids on skateboards and bikes, in-line skaters, and mothers pushing strollers everywhere. For now, there was just the one child and her puppy. She was basically following the sidewalk, making small detours to splash around in the puddles that were forming everywhere. He would let her go all the way past the gates, after which the path was close to the hedge, offering him the best cover.

She was closer now. He could see that she was dressed in a bright yellow rain outfit and carried an umbrella with some kind of cartoon figures on it. He could hear her laughing and talking to the puppy, and singing some kid song. He relaxed against the tree with his arms folded and watched her approach. If there was ever a time in his life when he was that carefree, he couldn't remember it.

He felt a hint of remorse at the idea of curtailing her happy-go-lucky stroll in such a scary way. The rules of engagement were that she was not to be harmed in any way, she would not be held for ransom, and she would be returned to her home after an unspecified period of time. Beyond that he knew nothing, but the whole deal was a no-brainer for him. They would be paid twenty thousand dollars to pick up the kid, keep her safe for a period of time, and then let her go. To him, it didn't even seem like a crime.

He continued to lean against the tree while she skipped past the gate. When she disappeared on the other side, he walked quietly through the gate and onto the path. She was still alone on the playground. He accelerated quickly and grabbed her from behind, placing one hand over her mouth.

She immediately dropped the leash and the umbrella and began to kick both her legs. He turned and ran toward the gate. He was about ten feet away when his feet got tangled in something and he lost his balance. He twisted his body in the air so that he would land on the grass and not on the asphalt. He took the weight on his elbows so as not to crush the child and slid under the hedge, momentarily losing his grip on her.

She scrambled free and crawled out from under the hedge.

He jumped to his feet and immediately fell down again.

"Shit!" The puppy was jumping on him, and its leash was tangled around his legs.

Sandra grabbed the puppy, yanked the leash free, and ran. Rick caught up to her in three or four strides and grabbed her again. This time he kicked at the puppy to chase it away and sprinted out the gate and into the waiting van.

The van sped away from the curb as the side door slammed shut.

Scooby-Doo saw the thing that took his GIRL away, but being a hound, he didn't process visual information very well. He put his nose to the ground and followed the footsteps of the MAN all the way to the curb. The trail of information stopped there. He looked down the street and sniffed the air. Nothing.

He put his nose down again and followed the footsteps back through the gate and under the hedge. He came to the place where they fell and his tail began to wag. SHE had been here, on the ground. He investigated the entire area, and then followed the steps of the MAN back to the umbrella. His tail wagged out of control. This was HERS, but SHE was not here. He would wait. SHE would come.

A gust of wind rolled the umbrella about halfway across the playground where it wedged against the jungle gym. The puppy followed and sat down next to it. Shivering in the rain and wind, he began to cry. It started as a high-pitched bark and ended as a howl, rising and falling like a canine dirge, a vocal expression of all the loneliness in his little heart.

Chapter 30

Helen Matthews put down her cup of tea and looked at the clock again. Sandra should have been back fifteen or twenty minutes ago. She went to the front door, opened it, and looked down the street. No sign of her. It was raining harder now and she couldn't imagine that Sandra would be playing on the swings or the jungle gym. She closed the door and shook her head.

"Children," she muttered and went to the closet to get her coat and an umbrella. "I'll probably find her splashing about in a big puddle catching her death."

She checked her coat pocket for her keys, stepped outside, and locked the door behind her. As she opened the umbrella a gust of wind caught it and nearly pulled her down the front steps.

"Oh, good Lord!" she exclaimed and aimed the umbrella against the wind. "What could I be thinking letting a child outside in this?" She hurried down the steps and walked briskly toward the playground.

As she passed through the gates she got the impression that the playground was completely empty. Naturally. All *responsible* mothers and caregivers kept their children inside on days like this. She turned right and started down the sidewalk that paralleled the edge of the playground. "What would Sandra be doing out in this with her puppy?

Could she have gone to a friend's house and forgotten to call?" Mrs. Matthews asked herself as she surveyed the area. But something else felt wrong. She scanned that entire end of the playground again. *No monitors! Where are the monitors?*

She went past the seesaws and was walking by the big swings when she heard a noise. It sounded like a cry of some kind. She did a slow 360-degree turn, but saw and heard nothing. She had continued down the path no more than thirty yards when she heard it again. This time she recognized it as a howling dog, and turned in the direction of the sound. She walked toward the center of the playground, and what she saw stopped her in her tracks. Sandra's puppy was sitting by the jungle gym next to Sandra's new umbrella.

Why would Sandra tie her puppy to the jungle gym and leave him there? And why would she leave her umbrella behind when it was raining so hard?

"SCOOBY-DOO!" Helen called. The puppy stopped howling and pricked his ears. "I'M COMING, SCOOBY!" She walked a little faster.

Scooby immediately began to run toward Helen, dragging his leash behind him. He wasn't tied! How could Sandra have left the playground without him following? She picked up the leash and scanned the playground. She could see both entrances. It was completely deserted.

As she picked up the little umbrella and closed it, the realization of what must have happened hit her like a sledgehammer. Her heart began to thud in her chest, each beat sending waves of fear radiating through her body.

"OH, NO! GOD, NO! PLEASE, GOD, NO!" She began to cry. "SANDRA! S-A-N-D-R-A!" She ran for the gate, and she had nearly made it when she felt a crushing pain in her chest. By the time she reached the street she could hardly breathe. She leaned against a lamppost and fumbled through her pockets for her pills. Her hands were shaking so badly she spilled several on the ground before getting one in her mouth.

She paused for only a few seconds longer before stumbling her way down the street. She leaned heavily against the front door and cursed her aging hands as she struggled to get the key in the lock. When the door finally opened, she literally fell into the front hall and scrambled toward the kitchen without bothering to close the door.

She was on her hands and knees when she entered the kitchen and pulled herself up on the counter just enough to grab the cordless phone. She collapsed back onto the floor, propped herself up against the cabinet, and dialed 911.

"Brookline Police Department. What is the nature of your emergency?"

Helen was slumped against the cabinets, legs splayed out on the floor, her torso moving in small shallow jerks as she tried to catch her breath. "I…help…"

"Ma'am. Can you tell me if you need an ambulance?"

"Somebody took…child…"

"It's OK, ma'am. I've already dispatched an officer and an ambulance to your address. Can you tell me your name?"

"Sandra…please…"

"Your name is Sandra? Someone will be right there to help…"

"NO! Missing…have to…find…"

"Sandra is missing? Can you tell me your name?"

Helen watched the hand that held the phone drop to the floor as if in slow motion, as if it belonged to someone else. Her fingers opened, and the phone slid several inches across the tile. The puppy trotted into the kitchen, sniffed the phone, and began pushing it across the kitchen floor with his nose.

Helen had moved past her fear and her pain. Now, in a dreamlike state, she would have smiled if she had been able when she realized that the last thing she would see on earth was the puppy's wagging tail.

Chapter 31

The back of the van was full of junk. Rick sat in a mangled beanbag chair with Sandra in his lap. Between the chair and the side door there was just enough room for him to stretch out his legs.

Paul sped down the street, anxious to get away from the neighborhood. He didn't so much as pause at the stop sign at the end of the block and practically took the corner on two wheels.

"For Chrissake, Paul! Slow down! You wanna get pulled over?"

"I can't help it. I drive fast when I'm nervous."

"Well, stop it! We can't afford to attract any attention."

"Sorry. And ixnay on the amesnay."

Rick looked at Paul and rolled his eyes. He loosened his grip on the child and took his hand off her mouth. She was crying, catching her breath between sobs. She pressed her left hand against her head, just above her temple. He eased her off his lap and onto the beanbag.

Rick knelt on the floor next to Sandra in a clumsy attempt to comfort her. He asked in a soft voice, "Does your head hurt?"

"I WANT MY PUPPY!" she screamed.

"*Why* would her head hurt?" Paul asked.

"I tripped over the puppy and fell with her. She hit her head."

Paul inhaled sharply through clenched teeth and shot Rick an admonishing look. "That's it. I'm pulling over. You drive and I'll look after the little one."

"Fine by me," Rick replied. "Who do you think you are anyway, Mother Fuckin Theresa?"

"And furthermore, I don't think it's appropriate to use language like that in front of an eight-year-old girl. It's a very impressionable age." Paul got out of the van and walked around to the side door. Rick slid it open and held his fist in Paul's face, his middle finger prominently displayed.

"Why don't you make an impression on this?" he said.

Paul pushed him aside and climbed into the van. "I don't have time for your crude remarks."

"Well, e-x-c-u-u-u-s-e me," Rick replied as he climbed into the driver's seat. "Why don't you hook up with Dr. Fuckin Spock," he muttered under his breath.

Rick pulled the van back out into traffic; Paul turned his attention to Sandra.

"Show me where you hit your head, Sandra."

She stopped crying long enough to point to the spot on her head. Paul examined it carefully. There was a red mark but not much swelling.

"I think you'll survive. Does it still hurt?"

She shook her head.

"Then why are you crying?"

"I want my pup…pup…puppy!" She started sobbing again.

"You'll get him back real soon. When you go home he'll be waiting for you."

"He's all alone and what if he can't find his way home?" Tears were streaming down her cheeks. Paul reached into the front and grabbed a box of tissues. He tried to dry her eyes but she would have none of it.

"Was your puppy wearing a collar?"

Sandra nodded.

"Good! The first person who finds him will read what's on his collar and bring him right home."

"They will?"

"Sure they will. It's the law. Right?" He reached up and tapped Rick on the shoulder.

"That's right. It's the oldest law in the books. Everybody knows about it," Rick replied.

Paul put the box of tissues in Sandra's lap and climbed back in the front.

Sandra continued to cry softly.

"How are we going to cheer her up?" Paul whispered.

"How the fuck would I know?" Rick replied.

"Will you *please* watch your language? She's a very young girl. We have to set an example."

Rick looked at Paul in disbelief. "*We?* You mean, you and me?" He pointed back and forth between Paul and himself. "*We* have to set an example? Who do you think we are? Ozzie and Fuckin Harriet?"

"Shhhhhh!"

"*Fine.* Just leave me alone and let me drive."

"OK. But we didn't have time to shop on such short notice. We don't have anything to feed her. Let's stop and get some cold drinks and munchies. Something she'd like."

Rick let out a huge sigh and nodded. "Whatever. But let's just put a few towns between us and that playground first."

Chapter 32

Scooby-Doo nosed the phone around the kitchen floor. Some noise was coming from it, but he didn't hear his name. Sometimes he heard his name. Sometimes his GIRL put it near him, and he heard his name.

He trotted over to Mrs. Matthews. She was quiet. He sniffed the hand that dropped the phone, then sniffed her face and wagged his tail. She didn't move. He gave her a few puppy licks on her face and wagged his tail harder. She still remained quiet.

He sat on the kitchen floor and turned his head in the direction of an unusual noise. It got louder and louder until it seemed to be coming into the house. Unable to contain his curiosity, he trotted out of the kitchen, through the hall, and stopped at the wide-open front door.

Chapter 33

Officer Mike Braden didn't have to check the number on the mailbox to know which house called in the emergency. As he turned the corner with lights flashing and sirens wailing, he noticed the front door standing wide open on the third house to his right.

As he pulled up to the curb, he could see the ambulance round the corner right behind him. He jumped out of the cruiser, and as he ran up the walk a puppy bounced down the steps wagging his tail and dragging a leash.

He scooped the puppy up and approached the front door. He knocked loudly and called into the house, "POLICE OFFICER!…MA'AM?" The EMTs were running up the walk behind him. He entered the house and walked down the hall to the kitchen where he found Mrs. Matthews on the kitchen floor.

"IN HERE!" he yelled unnecessarily. The EMTs were right behind him.

The medics immediately went to work on Mrs. Matthews. Mike began a room-by-room search of the house to look for other occupants. He had just finished when a voice came over his radio.

"Five."

"Five," he replied.

"Do you have an ID on the caller yet?"

“Yeah. I found her wallet. Matthews, Helen. Date of birth: eleven, oh-five, thirty-five. Address: two-nine-two Arbor Drive in Brookline.”

“Anyone else in the house?”

“Negative. Just a puppy.”

“The phone number is a listing for Gary Coakley. See if you can find out who else lives there. There might be someone named Sandra.”

“Ten-four.”

It didn’t take much detective work to figure out who occupied this townhouse. There were family pictures on every wall in every room of the house. He assumed the man was Gary Coakley. In some photographs he posed with a woman and a little girl. Wife and daughter, no doubt. In the most recent pictures, the wife was missing.

In the kitchen, traditional schoolroom artwork covered the refrigerator, attached to the door with a collection of magnets that looked like Snoopy. Most of the drawings were colorful crayon portraits of the puppy. The artist wrote the name Scooby prominently on many of them and the initials S.C. in the bottom corner of all of them; he jotted that down in his notebook. The most recent addition to the display, judging by the date on it, was a math test. Underneath a large gold star and “100!” in red felt-tipped pen, the name Sandra Coakley identified the student.

The EMTs carried Mrs. Matthews out of the kitchen on a stretcher. When the commotion died down, Mike heard the telltale beep-beep-beep of a phone off the hook. The cordless handset was on the floor underneath the overhang of the cabinet. He placed it back on the base unit and opened the address book on the counter beside it. Taped inside the front cover he found one of Gary Coakley's business cards. He wrote down the office and cell phone numbers, and then took one more look around the house. He picked up the puppy and the crate that he found in the front hall and returned to his patrol car.

Chapter 34

Paul tapped Rick on the shoulder several times with his left hand and pointed to something down the street with his right. "It's a 7-Eleven. See it? In that little strip mall. Let's stop there."

Rick slowly turned to look at Paul. "You are s-o-o-o hyper. Chill."

"Just pull in there. Don't be giving me a hard time."

"OK, but I'm not parking out front. I'll pull around the back and you can go in. I have to take a leak."

Paul shot him a look of total disgust. "Fine. Just don't let anything happen to her."

"Give me a break. And get me some more beer."

Rick let Paul out in the parking lot, then pulled the van up to a large dumpster around the side of the building. He got out and walked behind the corner of the dumpster, where he was out of the public view but could still keep an eye on Sandra.

He turned away from the van, unzipped his fly, and relieved himself. He noticed an old golden retriever sniffing around the other side, scarfing up some French fries that were scattered on the ground. When Rick zipped up and stepped back, the dog immediately approached him, sniffed the dumpster, and lifted his leg on the same spot.

"Well aren't *you* a cool dude. Come on, boy."

Rick walked back to the van and slid open the side door. "Come on, buddy! Get in! Let's cruise!"

Connor obediently jumped into the back of the van and went directly to Sandra, who was huddled in the beanbag chair crying softly. Tail wagging, Connor began to lick the tears off her face. Sandra brightened immediately and threw her arms around the big golden dog. Connor sat down and leaned into her embrace, happy (as any golden would be) for any form of physical contact.

About ten minutes later, Paul came jogging around the corner of the building toward the van. Rick marveled at how a grown man could struggle under the weight of two little shopping bags. Paul opened the passenger side door of the van and thrust the bags onto the floor.

"You gotta go back," Rick said.

"What?" asked Paul still trying to catch his breath.

"You gotta go back in and buy some dog bones."

"Why?"

"For him." Rick aimed his thumb toward the back.

Paul peered around the passenger seat, lowered his sunglasses, stared at the pair on the beanbag chair, then turned his disbelieving eyes back on Rick.

"Are you stealing this dog?"

"No way. Just borrowing him for awhile."

"This is really low."

"What? Lower than snatching someone's little girl? Are you afraid of having pet thief on your rap sheet? Get real, and go get some bones. He's hungry, and she really likes him."

Using his middle finger, Paul slowly pushed his sunglasses back up onto the bridge of his nose, slammed the door, and jogged back to the store. He returned a few minutes later with a box of Milk Bones for large dogs.

"Can we get out of here now, or have you picked up a stray cat?"

"Think whatever you like, but she ain't crying any more." Rick pulled the van back out into traffic and headed in the direction of the Cape. "I hope you bought enough for a long ride. We're going to hit the bridge right at rush hour."

Chapter 35

Gary sat at the counter in the Brown Bear diner, working his way through a monstrous cheeseburger and an equally impressive basket of curly fries. He was mentally sifting through all the disturbing details he'd uncovered in the last twenty-four hours: the beavers, the fish, the Brown Trout/Brown Bear, the missing aerials, and the general unwillingness of the locals to talk to him.

Individually, they weren't much cause for concern, but this was definitely a situation where the whole was much greater than the sum of the parts. He was getting a glimpse of the big picture, and it was ugly. He only hoped that Joan would dig up a former power plant employee who could confirm or deny the dumping.

"Is that your phone?" Gus asked as he walked by with a pot of coffee.

Gary snapped to attention, grabbed his backpack, and dug through it for his phone. Maybe it was Joan with some good news, or the county clerk with the missing photos. He answered the call just before the answering service kicked in.

"Hello, Gary Coakley."

"Mr. Coakley, my name is John Murphy. I'm a detective with the Brookline Police Department."

A few seconds of confused silence passed before Gary answered, “What can I do for you, Detective Murphy?”

“It’s John. Please.”

“OK, John. It’s Gary. Again, how can I help you?”

“Do you leave your daughter in the care of Helen Matthews?”

“Yes. She’s my housekeeper and babysitter. Why?”

“We answered an emergency call at your house today. Helen Matthews had a heart attack.”

“Oh, my God! Is she all right? Where is she?”

“I’m sorry. She passed away. They weren’t able to resuscitate her.”

“Oh, no! How is Sandra taking it? Can I talk to her?”

“That’s the problem. We can’t find her.”

“What? What do you mean?” Gary checked his watch. “She should have been home from school two hours ago. It’s almost time for her dinner.”

“Actually it’s been longer. The elementary schools had an early release today. Some kind of teachers’ meeting. When the officer and EMTs arrived at the scene, the front door was open and except for the puppy, Helen was alone in the house.”

“Did you check the neighbors? Maybe she went to play with a friend after school.”

“We have every available officer going door to door around the neighborhood. We think Helen may have been walking the puppy. She was wearing a raincoat, and the puppy was dragging a leash. We found two umbrellas on the front walk. One adult-size and one child's umbrella with pictures of Snoopy on it."

"That's Sandra's."

"That's what we thought. Can you give me the names of Sandra's closest friends? It might help to shorten our search. I'd also like the name of her teacher so we can get a list of her classmates. By the way, where are you?"

"I'm about an hour north of Duluth, Minnesota."

"Whoa. It'll take you a while to get home. I'll give you a number where you can reach me with your ETA after you make your flight arrangements."

Gary gave John the names of every friend of Sandra's he could think of, ended the call, and immediately dialed his office. He cut Joan off in the middle of her greeting.

"It's Gary."

"What's wrong?"

"My housekeeper, Helen, had a heart attack and died this afternoon. Sandra's missing."

"What do you mean…missing? Missing how?"

"I mean she wasn't in the house, and the police can't find her!"

"How can I help? Tell me what to do."

"Get me back to Boston ASAP. It will take me a little over an hour to get to the airport. Get me on any plane and call me as soon as you have the flight information. Then call this number…(617)555-0212 and ask for detective John Murphy. Give him the same information. He said he could call airport security and expedite my check-in and boarding."

"I'm on it. When it's arranged, I'm going to your house. If they find Sandra, she'll be more at ease with somebody she knows."

"Thanks, Joan."

"OK. Get to the airport. If you think of ANYTHING else, call me on my cell phone. Anything at all."

"OK. Later."

Gary shoved the cell phone in his pocket, tossed a twenty-dollar bill on the counter, and ran out of the diner.

Chapter 36

Rick piloted the old van smoothly through the moderate traffic on Neponset Avenue to the interchange for Route 3. Once on the highway, both he and Paul relaxed. It was a straight shot to the Sagamore Bridge, which spanned the Cape Cod Canal and connected mainland Massachusetts to the Cape.

Paul took a cold Budweiser out of one of the bags and handed it to Rick.

"Are you hungry, Sandra?" Paul turned to look at the pair occupying the beanbag chair. Without loosening her grip on the dog or making eye contact with him, she shook her head.

"Thirsty? I have some Juicy Juice." Paul held up a bottle containing a purple liquid.

Sandra shook her head again.

"Well, your dog is hungry. He was eating trash off the ground when we stopped. You better feed him some of these Milk Bones." Paul held out the box for her.

For the first time Sandra's eyes met his.

"His name is Connor," she announced indignantly, as if daring them not to refer to him correctly.

"You named him already?"

"I didn't name him. THAT'S his name."

"How do you know that?"

"It's written on his collar, and you two are breaking the law!"

Paul and Rick exchanged a curious glance. "What do you mean?" Paul asked.

"When you find a lost dog with a collar you're supposed to take it right home. It's the oldest law in the books. You even said so."

"Oh, right." Paul stifled a laugh. "We *are* going to take him home, the same time we take you home. We don't have time to do it right now.

"I really like the name Connor, don't you? I think it fits him."

Sandra nodded.

Paul opened the box and took out two bones. "Here. Give him these. I know he's hungry, and we need to take good care of him while we have him."

"Pets are a big responsibility," Sandra said as she accepted the bones.

"You're absolutely right. You know, if everyone felt that way there wouldn't be so many abandoned pets filling the pounds. I mean, do you know how many innocent animals are killed each year because people don't take responsibility?

"You know, if more people were like you…"

"Hey!" Rick slapped Paul on the shoulder with the back of his hand. "Why don't you spare us the animal welfare lecture, huh?"

"Come on! You give money to the no-kill animal shelters every year, too. This is something I'm very passionate about, so what's wrong with sharing my views and feelings on the subject?"

"Number one, I give that money to shut you up, and number two..." Rick lowered his voice to a whisper. "I don't think you should be gettin too familiar with her."

"Why not?" Paul whispered back. "Don't you remember the guy said that once we have her our number one priority is to keep her happy and safe. I'm just trying to establish a rapport."

Rick looked at Paul and shook his head in disbelief. "The more details she knows about us, the more she can tell the cops when we let her go."

"Oh. I never thought of it that way." Paul turned to look at Sandra again.

She still had one of the bones in her hand. Connor was sitting at attention, totally focused on Sandra and the treat, a few stringy droplets of drool hanging from the corners of his mouth.

Sandra held out her hand and Connor immediately responded by giving her his paw. She broke the bone in half, gave him a piece, and smiled a little as he crunched it up enthusiastically. Next, she showed him the palm of her hand and then lowered her arm so that her palm was parallel to the floor. He immediately lay down, his tail thumping against the floor of the van as he anticipated his reward.

Paul sat back in his seat, reached out, and touched Rick on the arm. When Rick turned to look at him he said, "The dog was a brilliant idea."

Rick smiled and sat up a little taller, pleased with the compliment.

Chapter 37

Gary collapsed into his seat in first class only moments before the attendants sealed the doors and prepared the plane for take-off.

Compliments of detective John Murphy, a security officer had met him at the ticket counter, expedited his check-in, then escorted him through the X-ray machines and metal detectors and delivered him to the gate where the plane had already finished boarding.

Gary chalked up a few points to Detective Murphy in the credibility column. It was a start. If his daughter were waiting for him when he got off the plane he would genuflect in front of the guy, and be forever indebted. Until then, the jury was still out.

His anxiety over Sandra's disappearance had made him incapable of grieving for Mrs. Matthews. As he stared at his reflection in the plane window, he thought of her for the first time. She had been such a comfort, such a solid influence in both their lives; he couldn't imagine how they would replace her. Her diligence, that peerless work ethic so rarely found these days, her kindness, and her impeccable morality were exactly the qualities he wanted Sandra to emulate.

As he thought about Helen, his mind bounced back to Sandra. The police found two umbrellas on the front step, Helen was wearing a raincoat and the puppy was dragging a leash.

His interpretation of this evidence was that Helen and Sandra were walking the puppy together and ended their walk at the house of one of Sandra's many friends so that she and Sandra could play together for the afternoon. Then Helen returned home alone with the puppy and had a heart attack, probably as she approached the house.

So why had she kept Sandra's umbrella? The friend's mother probably promised to keep the girls inside and to drive Sandra home at dinnertime. That would explain everything, and furthermore, the friend would have to be within walking distance of his house so the police would most likely have found her by now. Right.

He checked his watch. They'd been in the air for about an hour and a half. That would put them about halfway to Boston. He grabbed the Airfone and called John Murphy's cell phone.

"Murphy."

"John. It's Gary Coakley."

"You're here already?"

"No. Calling from the plane. Any news?"

"Nothing. None of Sandra's friends have seen her since she got off the school bus. The bus driver remembers that it was raining and Mrs. Matthews met Sandra at the curb with an umbrella. They exchanged hellos."

"Have you checked *all* her friends?"

"All but three who aren't home yet. We're thinking that maybe she went shopping or to a movie and out to dinner with one of those families. Something along those lines. We have officers watching all three houses, as well as one keeping your secretary company at your house."

"You might try Chuck E. Cheese's. Birthday parties at that place have been the cool thing to do in her group lately. I don't remember her mentioning anything about it but that doesn't mean..."

"We checked the two closest ones already, and when we interviewed the mothers none of them was aware of any parties or outings planned for today."

There was a long silence. Gary was at a loss for something else to suggest. "So what now?"

"We also have to consider the possibility that she may have seen your housekeeper die and been traumatized by it. Children do unpredictable things when they're extremely frightened. She may be hiding somewhere. Sometimes they think they're to blame in some way."

"I can't stand the thought of my daughter wandering around alone and frightened." Gary made no attempt to hide the anxiety and frustration in his voice.

"We took a recent school picture of her from your house. It's going to be on the late news tonight and in the paper tomorrow morning. Just as a precaution.

"Your secretary has already been on your computer and made up a missing child flyer that she plans to get into circulation tomorrow. We'll find her.

"Oh! And I was supposed to tell you that Joan drove your car to your house. I'm sending a car to pick you up at Logan and bring you directly to the police station."

Gary took all this information in and once again, as had happened so often in recent days, warning flags were popping up behind his thoughts.

"John. What aren't you telling me?"

"Nothing, really. Look. We're coming up to a shift change and I have to assign some officers to relieve the ones I have out on your case. We'll go over everything when you get here."

"OK. I'll see you later."

"Right, Gary. Hang in there."

Gary replaced the phone and repeated the words, "Nothing, really..."

Chapter 38

After a long stretch of rush hour stop-and-go at the Sagamore Bridge and slow-moving commuter traffic through all the bayside towns on the lower arm of the Cape—Sandwich, Barnstable, Yarmouth, Dennis, Brewster, Orleans—they were finally rolling along smoothly on the lesser traveled roads of the outer Cape.

Rick and Paul had relaxed into their usual repartee of benign bickering; Sandra was sharing a box of Teddy Grahams with Connor.

They weren't too far from their final destination when they heard a muffled bang and the van began to vibrate noticeably.

"Shit!" Rick pounded the steering wheel with the heel of his hand.

"What is it?" Paul looked back toward the source of the sound and the vibration.

"We got a flat."

"Do we have a spare?"

"Marginal, but it will get us where we're goin."

"We have to get off the main road first. You can't change it here. Too many cars. What if somebody stops to help? Like a cop for instance."

"No shit, Sherlock. You mean I can't call the auto club?"

"Cut the sarcasm and get off this road!"

"Just chill before you have a stroke, or give me one."

Rick turned down a side road and went far enough to be out of sight of the main drag. Fortunately, there were no houses on this stretch of road. He parked the van, got out, stretched, and sauntered around the front of the van and up to a short stretch of beach fencing along the side of the road. He carefully set his beer can on the ground, unzipped his fly, and relieved himself on the fence. After a loud, ceremonial belch, he zipped up again and retrieved his beer can.

The passenger side door of the van flew open and Paul jumped out, followed by Connor. Connor immediately trotted over to the fence and lifted his leg on the same spot Rick had used.

"I swear you are the coolest dog, Connor," Rick said without disguising the admiration in his voice.

"What do you think you're doing?" Paul said in a whisper that was as loud as a shout.

"Can't a guy stretch his legs for a minute? Not to mention his dog."

"We have to get to Truro! And it's *not* your dog."

"Well excuuuuse me, but I believe we *are* in Truro, and you know what they say. Possession is nine-tenths of the law."

"I don't care *what* they say. *We* have to get going."

Moving with exaggerated lethargy, Rick walked to the back of the van, opened the doors, and pulled out a jack, a tire iron, and a spare tire. He dragged the equipment around to the passenger side wheel and knelt down to position the jack.

Paul ran to the back and slammed the doors shut, clearly exasperated.

A large gull swept low over the beach fencing, past the two men and across the road. Connor sprang into action, pursuing the gull out into the street with as much speed as he could summon.

The sound of screeching tires filled the air followed by a sickening impact and the excruciating sound of a fatally injured dog in agony.

Chapter 39

Gary walked through the doors of the Brookline Police and Fire Municipal Safety Complex for the first, and he hoped last, time. Funny how you could live in a town for a number of years and not ever have an occasion to see the inside of its police department. In fact, the only time he had ever been in any police building was when he took his Boy Scout troop to one for a guided tour.

It was larger than he expected, but then Brookline was deceptive. It was primarily residential, but had a population of more than 60,000, necessitating a sizeable police force.

The officer who picked him up at the airport guided him through a warren of corridors to a door with a sign that identified the occupant as Detective J. Murphy. Gary thanked her and stepped inside.

The office was small, but its cramped feeling was the direct result of the mountains of clutter that covered every surface. The wall to his left supported a bank of file cabinets over which hung two large bulletin boards. Layers of papers pinned on top of more layers of papers secured by hundreds of colored pushpins covered every inch of the boards.

The top of each file cabinet was home to a large stack of papers and/or files. Some of the file drawers, full to bursting, were pulled open, with stacks of files resting on top of them so that it was impossible to open the drawer above.

On the wall to his right another bank of file cabinets was in pretty much the same condition as the cabinets on the left, except that a dry erase board hung above them. It was disconcerting to see the name Coakley written in red marker on the case list.

There was just enough room for a desk and two padded metal chairs in the center of the office. The two windows behind the desk provided a view of the parking lot. The desk itself was a miracle of disorganization. The computer keyboard sat on top of a stack of files so high Gary pictured the detective standing up to type. Even the CPU held a stack of papers that seemed to defy gravity.

As the two men shook hands, they made eye contact, sizing each other up, each wondering whether this meeting would be cooperative or adversarial.

Gary couldn't help but notice that the detective looked completely at home in the middle of this chaos. He was slight in stature, but with an intensity about him that was somehow reassuring.

"Thanks for your help in expediting my return, John."

"No problem. I wish I had better news for you."

"What *is* the news?"

"There isn't any. The last three houses we were watching were dead ends. We haven't got a single lead. However, the *Boston Globe* is going to run a picture of your daughter and a missing person's story on the front page tomorrow."

"John, what is it that you know that you haven't told me?"

The detective moved a stack of papers and uncovered a small tape recorder.

"When I listened to the 911 recording, another possibility occurred to me. It sounds to me like your housekeeper was calling to report a missing child, not to ask for medical assistance."

"What?" Gary leapt out of the chair. He stood against the edge of the desk, towering over the diminutive detective.

"Let me play it for you." He pushed the button for playback.

Operator: Brookline Police Department. What is the nature of your emergency?

Mrs. Matthews: I...help...

Operator: Ma'am. Can you tell me if you need an ambulance?

Mrs. Matthews: Somebody took...child...

Operator: It's OK, ma'am. I've already dispatched an officer and an ambulance to your address. Can you tell me your name?

Mrs. Matthews: Sandra...please...

Operator: Your name is Sandra? Someone will be right there to help...

Mrs. Matthews: NO! Missing...have to find...

Operator: Sandra is missing? Can you tell me your name?

"That's all there is. What do you make of it?"

Gary was so shaken he was unable to answer. He sat heavily back onto the chair, gripping his knees with both hands, and still they shook. John picked up the phone and punched a number.

"Suzy. It's Murphy. Could you bring a couple cups of coffee in here? Thanks."

Gary found his voice. "Why would anyone want to take my daughter? I'm not a wealthy man."

"That's what we're trying to figure out. Let me ask you a few questions." He pushed the record button on the tape recorder.

"Has anyone made any threats against you, anonymous or otherwise, even in jest?"

"No."

"Are there any family members, perhaps from your wife's side, who wanted custody of the child? Has anyone complained about not seeing her enough?"

"No."

"So your relationship with your wife's family is good? Friendly?"

"Yes."

"Have you noticed anyone unusual hanging around your neighborhood lately? Anyone you didn't recognize or any strange vehicles parked on your street at any time?"

"No."

"Well, think about it. Sometimes in these situations, if you keep thinking back over the last few days, you might come up with something you normally would have just dismissed.

"Would Sandra have walked the puppy on the playground alone?"

"Probably."

"You mean it's your policy to allow her to go to the playground all by herself?"

"Yes. What are you saying?"

"I'm saying she's only eight years old."

"*Look.* I could have gotten a lot more house for my money. But I wanted to live in *that* neighborhood. The schools are great and my child can walk to that big beautiful playground on a sidewalk, without even crossing a street! There's even a group of non-working mothers who take turns spending after school hours on the playground as monitors. Haven't you talked to the ones who were there today?" Gary felt caged in the small office. He sat with his hands and jaws clenched.

"It was raining this afternoon and we don't think anyone was there.

"We have no idea if she walked the puppy alone or if Mrs. Matthews was with her. Maybe she was gone too long and Mrs. Matthews went after her. Maybe they went together and she ran off to get help when Mrs. Matthews fell ill. We just don't know. We have to consider every possible scenario until we can find somebody who actually saw her."

Gary buried his face in his hands.

"Look, Gary. I'm not trying to make this out as your fault or anyone's fault. These are just questions I have to ask. I understand how you feel."

"How could you *possibly* understand how I feel?"

John turned and matched the intensity of emotion in Gary's eyes and voice.

"*I'm* a father too. *I* have two little girls, ages six and nine. *I'm* living my worst nightmare, every father's worst nightmare. *Right* now, *through* you!"

Gary looked away and leaned back in his chair. "So what do we do now?"

"Based on the evidence that Helen Matthews left us," John tapped the tape recorder, "We have to consider this case a possible abduction. We're going to interview every woman who monitored the playground in the last two weeks to find out if anyone suspicious has been hanging around or anything unusual has happened. I have a technician setting up recording and tracing devices on your phone at home."

"What can I do?"

"You can wrack your brain for anything, even the smallest thing that could shed some light on this…and wait."

Gary jumped up and leaned over the desk, shouting. "WAIT! YOU WANT ME TO GO HOME, SIT AROUND, AND WAIT?" His anger and frustration were reflected in every syllable.

"Gary. This story is going to be all over the eleven o'clock news and all over the papers tomorrow morning. If she's just missing we'll find her. If she was taken and there is some kind of profit motive, we should hear from them soon."

"And if not?"

"If it was a random pick-up, by someone who just wants the child…"

"What! What are you saying? The next step is to get her picture on a carton of milk?"

"I'm saying it's too soon to know. Hundreds of children disappear every year for any number of reasons. Without any evidence to go on, we can't even make an educated guess. For now, we just have to do our homework and wait."

"Jesus Christ." Gary was on the verge of tears as he collapsed back onto the chair.

"You need to go home now, and stay by the phone."

Gary sat, staring down at the floor. After a long silence he rose to his feet and offered the detective his hand. "Sorry. I..."

"No apologies. Finding your daughter is my job. *I* apologize for not doing it quicker. But make no mistake. I will not stop until I *do* find her. You have my word."

Gary nodded and left the office. His frame bent under the weight of his desperation, taking inches away from his true height. Fear and emotional exhaustion aged his face.

The detective sat down and rested his elbows on the edge of his desk. Nearly hidden behind his impossible mountain of paperwork, he could no longer keep the positive spin on his emotions he had displayed for Gary's benefit.

Suzy arrived balancing two cups of coffee in Styrofoam cups, one on top of the other. John waved her in and took both cups. He turned and set them on the windowsill, knowing he would drink them both before they even started to cool down. Weary, worried, and with a deepening sadness, he opened the slender file labeled Sandra Coakley.

Chapter 40

Al Sullivan sat motionless at his kitchen table, staring into his morning coffee mug like a gypsy reading tea leaves. He hadn't been to church in years, but he would have welcomed some kind of divine intervention now. He'd already called all the animal control officers in the immediate and not-so-immediate vicinity with no result.

And, he had to call the police department to find out who to call because dogcatcher wasn't listed under town services in the phone book. He thought that this was yet another example of turkeys taking over everyday life. Why can't they just call a spade a spade? A dogcatcher is a dogcatcher. A garbage man picks up the garbage and puts it in a truck. He is not a sanitation worker. He ain't sanitizing anything. The same guy had been cutting what was left of his hair for decades, but suddenly he wasn't a barber anymore; the sign on the door identified him as a hair stylist. What a load of crap.

The phone rang, diverting his attention from his coffee. His only phone was mounted on the kitchen wall. He put a twenty-five-foot cord on it so he could walk around the room. He got up from the table and grabbed the receiver.

"Hello."

"Hi, Gramps."

"Hey, little girl. What's new?"

"What's wrong?"

"With me? Not a thing."

"I *doubt* that. You haven't sounded this down since Gram died."

"It's nothing for you to worry about."

"Tell me, Gramps. I bet I can help."

"I *doubt* that," he said mimicking her tone.

"Well, you'll never know unless you tell me."

"OK. You win. Connor is missing."

"Missing?"

"Yeah. He disappeared yesterday and was gone all night."

"Did you call animal control?"

Al smiled. Today's youngsters probably wouldn't know what a dogcatcher was. "I did. All of them up to two towns away."

"That's terrible. I just love Connor. You must be so lonely."

"Well, nothing to be done but wait at this point. Except maybe take out an ad in the paper and offer a reward."

"Not true."

"Not?"

"I told you I could help."

"OK. I'm listening."

"See, my roommate has this cousin, and…"

"Hold it! Is this going to be a really long one, because I only have a half cup of coffee here."

"Come on, Gramps! Give me a break!"

"Sorry. Go ahead."

"So this cousin's mother lost her little dog. It was this Peek-a-poo…"

"Sounds like a new fangled way to check diapers or something."

"Gramps!"

"Sorry. Go on."

"Well for your information a Peek-a-poo is a Pekinese crossed with a poodle."

"Why the hell would anyone do that? They want the worst of both worlds?"

"Come on, Gramps."

"Sorry, but that kind of stupidity always gets a reaction out of me."

"I know. Anyway, the dog was lost for three days, and you know she lives in Portsmouth, Rhode Island, which is near Newport."

"Thanks for the geography lesson."

"Shhhh! So somehow she got the number of this pet-finding service. It's a woman who can find any pet. She does it by mental telepathy."

"Oh for Chrissake, Patricia! Who do you think you're talking to?"

"Stop. Seriously, Gramps. You gotta hear this."

"Is there any way to make you stop?"

"No. So she talked to the woman on the phone, and told her the dog's name, I can't remember the name though, and what the dog looked like, and the lady found the dog. Guess how?"

"Just get it over with and tell me."

"OK. She communicated with the dog, and the dog told her she was on a boat. Of course you know how many boats there are in Newport, so the dog showed her a picture of the flag the boat was flying."

"What do you mean a picture?"

"Well I guess the dog was looking at the flag and the lady got a picture of it in her mind."

"What a load of crap."

"Seriously, Gramps. The lady drew a picture of the flag and faxed it to the owner. They took it around to the marinas and they found the dog. The fax was a perfect replica of the flag on the boat. Explain that."

"I wouldn't waste my time."

"You know what the best part is?"

"There's more?"

"Absolutely. It only costs fifty bucks to sign up. If she doesn't find the pet, that's it. If the pet is found you have to pay fifty more."

"Fifty dollars down the toilet."

"I think Connor is worth it, and anyway her success rate is like ninety percent. Hey, Donna just came in. I'll get a phone number from her and call you back. Bye."

Al took the receiver away from his ear and looked at it in disbelief. Mental telepathy. Unbelievable. Maybe he could make up some missing dog posters, put them around town, and offer a reward. Yeah, that's the thing to do. Mental telepathy. What kind of turkey does she take her old granddad for?

He hung up the receiver, and shuffled off to his bedroom to find a good snapshot of Connor.

Chapter 41

Al hung up the phone and sat down at the kitchen table. He had pushed the photograph album, poster paper, and markers aside. In front of him was a notepad with a phone number on it and his Visa Card. His granddaughter had browbeaten him into calling the Portsmouth woman who had found her dog on the boat. Kid should go to law school. He had to admit that the lady hadn't sounded like a crackpot. She had been just as skeptical as he was…and just as desperate. He drummed his fingers on the tabletop for a few minutes while he stared at the phone number. He got up and started pacing the kitchen floor.

"I must be nuts to be even considering this. Great. It was bad enough I talked to Connor all day. Now I'm talking to the four walls. Jesus H. Christ! The things I would stoop to for that dog.

"This is a new low in my life as an intelligent life form. It's like the invasion of the bodysnatchers, except instead of aliens it's turkeys taking over. Well, who's gonna know? Nobody's here but me. *I'm* gonna know, that's who! I guess I'm gonna have to watch my back come Thanksgiving time."

He picked up the notepad, walked over to the phone, and dialed the number.

Chapter 42

Mireya leaned back in her chair, her steaming hot mug of coffee cradled in both hands. She shelved the condor manuscript for the time being and decided to press on with the piping plovers until she finished it. Between the remaining research and the writing she should be done with it in a week, two weeks tops.

She had been to a specialty photo store in Boston that morning and had prints made from her twelve favorite slides. They were spread out all over her desk. She was having a difficult time selecting the ones she would send with the manuscript. Aside from the one she imagined as a cover photo, she liked most of the others equally. The "smart crow" shot would be one to use, and she had a picture of a boot print in the sand, directly over a plover's nest complete with three squashed eggs. Beyond that she was stumped.

As she sat contemplating the others, the Lost Friends phone rang. She swiveled her chair to face the machine and waited for the message.

After her outgoing message and an unusually long period of silence, a man began to speak.

"Hello...This is Al Sullivan. You've never met me but I live in Dorchester...Mass. and I've lost my golden retriever, Connor. I just talked to a lady who lost a dog that you found on a boat in Newport and she thought you could help me.

My dog disappeared yesterday. He's never been away from this house overnight since he was a puppy. I've looked everywhere. I've called all the dog...ah...animal control people in the area and nobody's found him. My number is (617)-555-4521.

Please call me if you think you can find him."

Mireya jotted down the number, picked up the phone, and dialed.

"Hello."

"This is Mireya from Lost Friends returning your call."

"Wow. That was fast."

"I happened to be sitting next to the phone when your call came in."

"Why didn't you just pick up?"

"I never pick up. As you can imagine I get a lot of crank calls. Most of them are discouraged when they hear the machine and hang up."

"Yeah, I can see that might happen. I sorta feel like I'm on a crank call right now."

"Why don't you tell me about Connor."

"He's a really big…I mean *really* big, weighed a hundred and two pounds at his last vet appointment…golden retriever. He's gettin a little gray around his face, but he's real handsome. Everyone thinks so. And smart, too."

Mireya couldn't help smiling. She loved people who loved their pets. "How old is Connor?"

"He was nine years old last month. They say that's old for a golden, but Connor is in perfect health and he's very active, just like his old man."

Mireya smiled again. "Did you understand my payment terms? I need a fifty-dollar deposit now and fifty dollars when you find Connor, alive or deceased. I take Visa or MasterCard. Is that acceptable?"

"No problem. You can find animals even if they're dead?"

"Absolutely. In spite of what current Christian religious teachings would have us believe, animals do have spirits, and they don't die when the animal dies. But let's not get ahead of ourselves here. Give me your card number and I'll get to work finding Connor."

After hanging up the phone, Mireya entered the number into the machine and relaxed into her chair, eyes closed. It took a minute to chase all the plovers and buzzards from the forefront of her consciousness, but as soon as she made room for him she whispered "Connor…"

Immediately a crushing pain filled her chest. She clutched her sides with both arms as a defense against the pain. She had the sensation of lying on a hard surface, and when her vision cleared she could see pavement right in front of her eyes. The pain was unbearable.

She opened her eyes and sat up, breaking her connection with Connor. She was on the verge of hyperventilating.

"Oh, no!" She burst into tears. She covered her face with both hands, leaning against them, her elbows on her knees. After a few minutes, she composed herself and picked up the phone.

"Hello." She heard Al's hopeful voice on the line.

"Mr. Sullivan. It's Mireya. I'm sorry to have to tell you that Connor is deceased. I'm very sure that a car hit him."

"When?"

"I'm not exactly sure, but it was during the day.

"Where?"

"I can't say for sure, but in twenty-four hours a dog can't go very far unless he's been stolen. Call the police in your town and surrounding towns. Usually a dog that is hit is reported to the police department, and they contact the DPW to pick the dog up and dispose of it. If the dog is wearing a collar the police contact the owner."

"Nobody contacted me, and Connor is wearing a collar with his name and phone number on it."

"Police departments get very busy and they don't give these kinds of things priority. You need to contact them."

"You're sure?" Al's voice was beginning to break up.

"Very sure. Please call me when you find him."

"OK."

As Mireya hung up the phone and wiped her eyes, she heard Gina coming into the house.

"REY?"

"IN HERE!"

Mireya turned in the direction of the door as Gina poked her head into the office.

"You've been on the Friends phone. Rey, did you find another deceased one? You look terrible."

"Gee, thanks, and yes, I did. I never get used to it."

"Thank God for that. "How did your trip to the Cape go? Good news?"

Mireya reached over to her desk and handed Gina one of the eight by ten-inch prints George made.

"Wow! Looks like cover material to me." She quickly scanned the rest of the pictures on the desk.

"I can't believe how those eggs blend into the sand. No wonder people step on them.

"Have you eaten?"

"No. I've been working all day. I want to finish this up because I also have the condor article to do."

"You've still got to eat. I'll make you something."

"No, Gina. I'm going out for a run. I've been dressed for it since noon, but these sidetracked me." She pointed to the pictures.

"Well work up an appetite while you're out there because I'm making you some eggs when you return. And no more coffee! You'll be up half the night." She picked up Mireya's mug and headed for the kitchen.

Mireya stepped out of the house and closed the door. She stretched a few times, jogged down the front walk, turned toward the river, and started to run. She planned to run fast and far. She would run until she left the memory of Connor behind.

Chapter 43

Gary had just returned from his morning walk with the puppy. As he stepped into the front hall and unhooked Scooby's leash, the emptiness of the building that had once felt like a home overpowered him.

The two people who had defined the character of this house, who filled his heart with joy and gave meaning to his life, were not here. One would never return, and the other, well, it was too painful to contemplate.

He walked to the kitchen and poured himself a cup of coffee. From the kitchen window he saw the school bus roll up to his front walk and slow almost to a stop before continuing down the street. Force of habit, he assumed.

He walked to the small den that he used as an office. The police had used his desk to set up their tracing and recording equipment. He was going to offer the police officer who was monitoring communications a cup of coffee.

As he entered the room, the phone rang. The officer sat up at the desk, put on his headset, and pointed to the phone he wanted Gary to answer. Gary put down his coffee and grabbed the receiver.

"Hello."

"Gary? It's Mom. Any word yet?"

The officer took off his headset and sat back.

"Mom! I told you not to call this number. The police are monitoring it in case anyone calls about Sandra."

"Well, *I'm* calling about Sandra."

"No, Mom, that's not what I mean. I mean if anyone calls to give us information about Sandra."

"I'm sorry. I'm just so worried. She's my only grandchild."

"I know, Mom. Just call me on my cell phone. Not this phone. Is Dad there? Let me talk to Dad."

"Hello, Son."

"Dad. I need a favor."

"Anything."

"I want you to call everyone in the family you can think of. Give them my cell phone number. Tell them not to call the house number under any circumstances. If they do, they're interfering with the police investigation. Better yet, tell them not to call me at all. If I have any news, I'll call you and you can spread the word to everyone else. OK?"

"Will do. Any news at all?"

"Nothing yet."

"OK. Goodbye, Son. We're all praying for her."

"I know. Thanks, Dad."

"Gary! Wait. I thought you were going to hang up. Your mother wants me to ask…*again*…if you want us to come up and stay with you."

"No. I really mean it. I appreciate Mom's good intentions, but the police are here around the clock and it would just be too much. I'm fine. I couldn't take anyone hovering over me, if you know what I mean."

"Of course I do, but I was required to ask, if you know what *I* mean."

"Oh, believe me. I understand."

"OK then. I'll get off the line. Call if you get any news at all."

"I will. I promise. Bye, Dad."

"Sorry," he said to the officer as he hung up the phone.

"No problem." The officer gave Gary an understanding smile.

Gary went into the living room, turned on the TV, and sat down to finish his coffee. The Today Show took a break for local news, and there on the screen was his daughter's picture. His copy of the *Boston Globe* was on the coffee table; the same picture was staring back at him from the front page. He picked it up and flipped it over.

He had felt helpless when his wife died, but there was a finality to that situation. Arrangements had to be made, and then life went on. Like it or not.

This was entirely different. He couldn't act because he didn't know what had happened, what was happening now, or what would happen. He was freefalling in a void of zero information.

The waiting was torture. He was an engineer through and through. He never thought of himself as blessed with even the smallest shred of imagination. Yet waiting, powerless in this information vacuum, led his mind down path after path, through countless scenarios, each one more horrible than the next.

He suddenly realized he was staring into the bottom of his empty coffee cup. As he got up to go for a refill, the doorbell rang. He opened the door, expecting yet another neighbor with a bundt cake. His kitchen counter was already covered with so many desserts he came to the conclusion that these women must bake in their sleep.

Instead of a neighbor, he was face to face with John Murphy.

"John!" Gary thrust out his right hand without realizing that he still held his empty coffee mug.

"Oh! Sorry." He tried a rapid transfer to his left hand, fumbled the mug, and dropped it on the floor.

"Shit!" He cursed under his breath. "Give me a second, John." He grabbed a dustpan and brush out of the hall closet and began to sweep up pieces of the mug.

"Gary. Take a breath."

"I know. This waiting is making me crazy. Come on in. I'll get us a cup of coffee."

John followed Gary to the kitchen. "Better make yours decaf."

Gary retrieved two mugs from the cabinet and filled them.

"You want something to eat? We got bundt cake, coffee cake, pound cake, lemon poppy seed…whatever, cinnamon things…I have no idea what those two are…"

"No, thanks. The coffee will be fine. I just ate breakfast. What about you?"

"Enough, already. I just got off the phone with my mother. You don't want any of this stuff? What kind of cop are you?"

"The usual kind. I don't see any doughnuts."

"No. No doughnuts. Just the homemade…stuff. So what are you planning to do today?"

"We started questioning the playground monitors at about seven-thirty this morning."

"So early? That's great!"

"Women with school-age children are up early, and everyone is eager to cooperate."

"Anything new?"

"Actually, one of them remembered seeing a guy that looked out of place a couple weeks ago. She said he was dressed like a…" He took a small notebook out of his pocket and put on his reading glasses. "motorcycle guy. Those were the words she used. He was a big guy wearing a leather vest and jeans. He had tattoos on his arms, a reddish brown beard, and he was wearing boots. She said he walked around the playground once and then left. He may have driven off in an old van. She wasn't sure. She didn't actually see what vehicle he got into, but she saw a beat up old van go by right after he left."

"That isn't much."

"No, but it's something."

"Any calls from the TV or newspaper stories yet?"

"Not yet."

"This waiting is killing me. I want to do something."

"It's early yet. It hasn't been twenty-four hours. Did you get any sleep?"

"You're joking, right?"

"Yeah. I suppose I am."

Chapter 44

Nelson Paquette sat at his desk as he did every morning. He drank the coffee his secretary made and delivered to him just like every other morning. His computer was on, like it always was. The same stack of files had been on the corner of his desk for weeks. His appointment book lay open before him, and under Thursday, May 23rd, the page was blank.

In reality, Nelson Paquette was a man with nothing to do. Paquette Investments no longer had any investments or any clients. His only real employee was his secretary, who was too dumb to know the difference. Little did she know that she was hired because of her lack of qualifications. He occasionally shuffled files around, wrote fictitious lunch meetings and appointments in his book, and surfed the Internet in the guise of doing research.

He liked making money, but he never enjoyed working. All he wanted to do was make a killing on his father's real estate and retire.

His secretary's voice came over the intercom in the hushed tones of a professional golf commentator. It could have been sexy if it weren't for the horrible accent.

"Mr. Paquette. Norman is on line one."

He picked up the receiver and pressed a button.

"Good morning, Norman. How's your visitor?"

"As good as can be expected, given the circumstances."

"What do you mean? Did something happen to her?"

"Not really. She was walking her puppy when they picked her up. Of course, they left the puppy behind and she was upset. Then she formed an attachment to an old dog they found. *But* when they stopped to fix a flat tire, the dog got hit by a car and was killed. So, as you can imagine, she's pretty upset. She cried half the night."

"Jesus Christ. Is nothing we do uncomplicated? What about the driver that killed the dog? Did he see the girl?"

"They said they handled it."

"What did they do with the dog?"

"They left it there. They didn't want to upset the girl by putting its body in the van."

"Can the dog be identified?"

"No. They took its collar off."

"Jesus Christ!"

"I think everything is OK. I just wish the kid wasn't so unhappy."

"I'm sure you'll think of something. Just make sure she eats and drinks and doesn't stay out in the sun too long or anything."

"Right. I'll call you later."

He hung up the phone, worried. What had seemed before like a bold move, a daring ruse, began to smack of desperation. He was sure that to Norman it had always appeared so.

During the dot-com days he had made his mark by acting aggressively and with confidence. It seemed unwise to change his style now. And if things went really wrong, they could just release the girl and they'd be in the clear. Wouldn't they?

There he was, second-guessing himself again. He never used to do that. He picked up his empty coffee cup and hurled it at his office door. A moment later, the door opened slowly and Marcie peeked in at him.

"Is everything OK, Mr. Paquette?"

"No. Everything is not OK. I need another cup of coffee."

Chapter 45

After a fitful night Mireya awoke unrested. Images of Connor haunted her dreams. Even Gina's prayers left her spirit unsoothed.

She hoped Connor's owner found him so that he could be properly laid to rest. In her opinion, there was nothing more undignified than the body of a cherished pet dumped in a landfill, without recognition of its lifetime of loyalty and devotion to its family. No tears of love and sorrow or words of thanks and praise to ease the passage of its spirit into the next life. No memory of a last comfort or kindness, no final hug to overshadow the fear or final pain of relinquishing the only life it's known into the unknown.

Mireya knew she would get no work done in this frame of mind, so she dressed in her running clothes. A morning run followed by a hot shower usually energized her. She ran down the stairs and paused at the front door.

"GINA! I'M GOING ON A RUN."

"NO BREAKFAST?"

"WHEN I GET BACK, OK?"

"OK."

Mireya did the three-cemetery loop in record time, but skipped her usual meditation by the Charles. She would only sit and dredge up thoughts of Connor, so she opted to go straight home.

She went in the kitchen door and straight to the refrigerator for a bottle of water.

"Are you ready for breakfast, Rey?"

"I want to take a shower first."

"You might want to check your machine. You have a message. I didn't hear what the guy said, but he sounded agitated."

"OK. Thanks."

Mireya guzzled half the bottle of water as she walked to her office. She sat down next to the machine and pushed the button for playback. She recognized Al's voice immediately.

> *"This is Al Sullivan. I've called every police department in a three-town radius of Dorchester and nobody has found a golden retriever. I think you must be wrong about Connor. If he was hit on the road, somebody should know about it. Please call."*

Mireya immediately dialed Al's number.

Al picked up on the first ring. "Hello."

"Hello. It's Mireya. I'm definitely not wrong about Connor, but let me try to get some more details about the location."

"Why the hell didn't you do that in the first place?"

"Usually people find their pets in their own town, so it's not necessary."

"Why the hell don't you do it anyway, just in case?"

"First of all, let me say that I am a lover of all animals. The reason I know that Connor is dead is that I felt what he felt when he died. I saw what he saw through his eyes. As you can imagine, it was very upsetting, not to mention painful."

There was a short pause, and when Al spoke, skepticism had replaced the anger in his voice. "Right. If he's dead for sure then I don't know why either of us should bother. He ain't coming back."

"You have to find him because you need closure."

"Closure. I hate all them new-age yuppie words: closure, significant other, post-traumatic stress, inner child, flight attendant, and especially animal control person. What the hell's wrong with dogcatchers, stewardesses, boyfriends and girlfriends, and garbage men for chrissake!"

"I'm sorry, I…"

"And I really hate all them initials. You got your ATM, your SUV, PC, PMS, VHS, DVD, EMTs, and HMOs. And half the time a TV ain't even a TV. It's a monitor. I mean you can't even be retarded anymore! You have to be mentally challenged! I'd like to challenge the morons who made up all this stuff."

"OK. I see that I didn't explain myself very clearly. Don't you think Connor deserves to be laid to rest in a way that honors his life?"

There was another long silence. Al couldn't hide the emotion in his voice. "Yes, I do. But why do you care? Oh, right. You get another fifty bucks if I find him."

"I won't take the money."

"Then why…"

"Look. I was only in touch with Connor for a moment, but I could tell that he had a magnificent spirit. It would kill me to think that he ended up in a dumpster."

After a long pause Al replied, "Me, too. Please find him."

Mireya relaxed back into her favorite chair and concentrated on the rhythm of her breathing. She had to relax. Anxiety and anticipation would work against her. Animal communication is all about listening. The images had to flow from Connor to her, not the other way around. It took much longer than usual, but when she finally achieved inner calm she whispered, "Connor…"

Again, she immediately felt the crushing pain in her chest, and felt the hard surface of the road beneath her. As the image in her mind slowly cleared, she could see the pavement, and feet, a woman's feet clad in New Balance running shoes with short tennis socks.

Beyond the woman there was some fencing, and a small sign with the letters CCNS. The sneakers moved away and she could see that the woman was wearing tan shorts and a navy blue shirt with a picture of a whale on it. There were some words, but she couldn't read them.

Suddenly, the woman fell to the pavement. For a moment Mireya was staring into her eyes, then her pupils dilated and she was gone.

Mireya's eyes snapped open. She was still hugging her ribs. She relaxed her arms, grabbed her pen, and frantically scribbled everything she had seen into her notebook. She stood up and began to pace back and forth across her office, staring at the notes she just made.

"Oh, my God…What happened to her? Where are they? The fence…It looks just like beach fencing. Maybe they're near a beach…the sign…CCNS…CCNS…Oh, my God! Cape Cod National Seashore. They're on the Cape!"

Mireya ran to the phone and dialed Al's number.

"Hello."

"It's Mireya. I've located Connor on part of Cape Cod. He's in one of the areas designated as the Cape Cod National Seashore, so you should start with the town of Chatham and work your way north. The towns that contain part of the National Seashore are Chatham, Orleans, Eastham, Wellfleet, Truro, and Provincetown. It should be one of those."

"Are you sure?"

"Pretty sure."

"How the hell would he get all the way to the Cape?"

"Maybe somebody picked him up. Did he like to ride in the car?"

"Oh, yeah. Loved it."

"Maybe someone took him for a joy ride."

"Possible. Do you know anything else about the location?"

"Just that it wasn't a main highway. It was a small side road."

"OK. I better go make the calls."

"Let me know what you find?"

"Sure thing."

Mireya hung up the phone and resumed her pacing. Then it hit her!

"This happened yesterday."

She ran to the kitchen. "Gina! Is today's paper here?"

Gina pointed to the other side of the room. "On the chair."

Mireya grabbed the paper and examined the front page. There was a picture of a beautiful little girl who disappeared from a neighborhood in Brookline. She flipped through the front section and then the local news. There was nothing about a murdered or missing woman.

"Maybe it's too soon. Maybe she lives alone and nobody has noticed she's missing."

"What are you talking about?" Gina asked.

Mireya sat in the chair and covered her face with her hands. She rocked back and forth a few times, then carefully placed both hands on her knees and looked up. Fear showed plainly on her face.

"What's wrong, Rey?" Gina put her arm around Mireya's shoulders. "What's got you so scared?"

Mireya looked into Gina's eyes, searching for strength.

"I think I just witnessed a murder."

Chapter 46

Gina sat down across from Mireya and took hold of her hands. "How did you witness a murder?" she asked in a quiet, but commanding voice.

"The dog," Mireya replied without taking her eyes from Gina's. "The deceased dog from yesterday. It was the last thing he saw before he died."

"You're sure?"

Mireya nodded.

"What are you going to do?"

"I don't know."

"You could try the police."

"No way, not again. You know what happened the last time."

"Do you know where it happened?"

"Not really. Somewhere on the outer Cape. Probably yesterday afternoon, but there wasn't anything in the paper this morning so I guess they haven't found the body."

"You didn't see anything else? Tell me everything you remember."

"She was wearing running shoes, tan shorts, and a navy blue shirt with a picture of a whale on it and some writing too, but I couldn't make out what it said." Mireya's voice was shaking. Gina squeezed her hands.

"What did the whale look like? Was it a photograph? Or maybe a drawing?"

"It was a drawing. Like an outline of a whale's shape. In fact, it looked vaguely familiar."

"Like maybe a logo you've seen before."

"Maybe."

"That isn't much to go on. Why do you think it was a murder? What did you see to make you think that?"

"At first she was standing nearby, probably looking down at the dog. I could only see her feet. Then she moved a few steps away."

"Did you get a look at her face?"

"Not at first. When she moved away I got a look at what she was wearing, then she turned, as if she were looking at something or someone else. I could see part of the back of her head, and her right ear. She had short blonde hair. Bleached, I think.

"Suddenly she fell to the pavement. I don't think she tripped or lost her balance because she would have tried to catch herself, break her fall. She didn't. She hit the pavement like a ton of bricks. She made eye contact for a few seconds, and then she was gone. Her pupils dilated and I just knew she was dead."

"Maybe the owner of the dog was so distraught, he lashed out at her. Killed her by accident."

"I don't think so. The owner of the dog lives in Dorchester, and when he called me the dog had been missing for a day. Whoever had the dog on the Cape stole him."

"OK. It would make sense that if she were murdered, the killer would hide the body. That's why there was no mention of it in the paper. She could be listed as a missing person for a long time."

"I know. I need to find her. Somehow."

The phone in her office began to ring. Both women ran to the office where they stood poised over the Lost Friends machine. As soon as Mireya heard Al's voice, she grabbed the phone.

"It's Mireya."

"Oh. You picked up. I think I found him."

"Where?"

"He's in Truro, near the Wellfleet line, on a small street called Collins Road. The dog they found wasn't wearing a collar, so I'm driving to the Cape this afternoon to identify him. They were just about to dispose of him when I called."

"I'm so sorry about Connor. I can tell that he was a great dog."

"Yes, he was, thanks. I'll call you tomorrow."

"Have a safe trip."

Mireya hung up the phone and dug out her street atlas of the Cape. "Truro, near the Wellfleet line. Collins Road is off Route 6…I know that area. It connects to Pamet Road and Ballston Beach.

"Gina, I just can't get over the feeling that I've seen a shirt like that somewhere." Mireya took a Cape Cod travel guide down off her bookshelf. "Maybe if I look through the list of tourist attractions, restaurants, and hotels in each of the towns near there, something will trigger my memory."

"You go to the Cape so often, I'm sure it will come to you."

"Unfortunately, I always go to the same places, my favorites, and pretty much ignore the tourist stuff."

"And a whale would be a pretty common image to be associated with anything on Cape Cod."

"True. Still, there was something about it..." Mireya followed Gina to the kitchen.

"I'm going to make you breakfast while you study the book."

Gina poured two cups of coffee, then took hers over to the stove where she began preparing some eggs.

Mireya went through the listings and descriptions of every restaurant, boutique, hotel, motel, and tourist trap in Truro, then moved one town north to Provincetown, the biggest tourist destination on the Cape. By the time she finished eating her breakfast, she had exhausted all the listings for Provincetown and turned to the chapter on Wellfleet, the town south of Truro.

Gina had just poured her a third cup of coffee when she shouted, "I've got it. It's Moby Dick's! It's on Route 6 on the north side of Wellfleet. I can't believe I didn't think of it! It's probably no more than five minutes from the scene of the murder. The waitresses wear shirts like the one I saw on the dead woman, and they sell them in the restaurant."

"So she could have been a waitress there."

"Maybe." Mireya was back to studying the map. "What if I searched the conservation land to the east of Collins road here?" She tapped the map with her finger. "If this crime was committed on impulse, maybe they dumped her body here. I mean, they probably wouldn't have a preconceived plan for it."

"Are you completely sure about this, Rey?"

"Absolutely. Hey! I have an idea how to confirm it."

She grabbed her cell phone off the table and dialed the number listed for Moby Dick's in the guidebook. A young voice answered.

"Moby Dick's."

"May I speak with the manager, please?"

"Sure. Just a moment. Is there a problem?"

"No. Not at all."

"OK. Please hold."

Mireya listened to the sounds of a busy restaurant in the background. A few minutes later, a woman picked up the phone.

"This is Mary, I'm the shift supervisor."

"Mary, this is detective Rey, of the Provincetown Police Department."

Gina rolled her eyes in disbelief.

"Is anything wrong?"

"No, I'm just following up on a missing persons report. Can you tell me if any of your waitresses failed to show up for work yesterday?"

"Yeah. Dawn Royce. We were left really shorthanded."

"Have you been in contact with her since then?"

"No. We've called her several times but we just get the machine. Is she in trouble?"

"No. These are just preliminary questions. Someone will be out there to talk to you if it goes further than this. Thank you for your time." Mireya hung up the phone.

"Her name is Dawn Royce. She didn't show up for work yesterday, and they can't reach her by phone. If it's not her, it's a very big coincidence."

"I'm sure it's not a coincidence, Rey, but it doesn't get you any closer to finding her."

"I know."

"How much do you think the dog saw?"

"I don't know, but I think I'm about to find out."

"I'll stay with you, Rey. I have no plans for this afternoon."

"Thanks."

Mireya went to her office and sat in her favorite chair. She smiled weakly at Gina, and closed her eyes. After a few minutes she whispered, "Connor…"

The too familiar crushing pain returned to her chest. She immediately doubled over and hugged her knees. An image assembled in her mind and played like a movie scene in slow motion:

She's lying on the pavement looking at the running shoes. They move away from her. She forces her eyes to look up. The woman wearing the Moby Dick's shirt is crying, agitated. She's looking down at the dog. Suddenly she turns in the opposite direction, lifting her arm as if to point at something. She's looking at something like a window. It's hazy. There's something ***in*** *the window. A girl. The girl is pounding on the window and screaming. An object is hurtling through the air. It's metal and looks heavy. The woman turns too late and it strikes her squarely in the temple. She falls to the pavement. She makes eye contact with Mireya briefly, then her pupils dilate and she's gone.*

When Mireya opened her eyes she was lying on the floor in the fetal position, crying. Gina rushed in and helped her into her chair. While she frantically wrote everything that happened in her notebook, Gina went to the kitchen and returned with a cup of herb tea and a steaming hot damp towel for Mireya's face. Mireya immediately unfolded the towel, leaned back in her chair as far as she dared, and covered her face with the towel. Breathing in the steam soothed her aching lungs and had a relaxing effect on her mind.

"Are you ready to talk about it?" Gina asked.

"I saw the woman. She was pointing to a window. There was a little girl in the window. She was beating her hands against it and screaming. Somebody threw a heavy metal object at the woman's head. It hit her here." Mireya pointed to her temple. "She fell to the pavement and died."

"Where was the girl?"

"She was behind a window of some kind."

"Like a window in a house."

"Not really. It was a smaller window. Kind of square. It was very hazy."

"Do you think the girl was in danger?"

"I don't know. She was screaming and crying. Not a good sign."

"Do you remember what she looked like? Would you recognize her again?"

"She had shoulder length dark hair. She was very pretty, even when she was crying. I had a feeling that she didn't belong there. And again, there was something familiar…"

Mireya sipped her tea. She was exhausted.

Gina left the room and returned a minute later with the morning newspaper. She handed it to Mireya. Mireya set her teacup down and unfolded the paper. She was looking at the front page of the *Boston Globe*.

"Oh, my God…"

Chapter 47

Al Sullivan arrived at the Truro Department of Public Works less than two hours after talking to Mireya. He parked in front of a small building attached to a large three-bay garage.

He sat in his car not knowing what to do. He absolutely did not want this dog to be Connor, but he desperately needed to find his dog. If it's him, I need to know, he thought, and sitting here is not going to change the truth.

Mustering his courage and his strength, he reached for the handle and opened the car door. Slowly he got out and even more slowly he closed the door. For the first time in his life he felt like an old man. For the second time in his life, he felt as though he would soon be faced with something he couldn't handle.

He heard heavy equipment operating on the other side of the garage. He walked in the direction of the noise and found a young man moving a pile of gravel with a huge front-end loader. To his dismay, the young man saw him right away and stopped the machine.

Al waved.

As he approached the machine, the young man jumped down out of the cab.

Al extended his hand. "Al Sullivan. I called about the golden retriever you found. The one that was hit."

The young man shook his hand. "Oh. Sorry." Al was surprised by the look of genuine sadness on his face. "He's over here." He pointed to the back of the building and Al followed him over to a blue tarp that was weighted down with a brick on each corner.

"I'll leave you alone," the young man said. "But come get me if you need any help moving him. He's a big dog."

"Thanks." Al appreciated the reference to Connor in the present tense. He hesitated for a moment, then removed two of the bricks and pulled the tarp back. He stood for a few minutes, trying to see Connor in the dog that lay before him. It was definitely Connor, but the love and joy that sprang from his heart and shone through his eyes every waking moment of his life were gone. His eyes were dark and sunken. His lustrous golden coat was dull and matted. His tongue looked thick and purple, his mouth open in a final grimace frozen by death. But it was Connor.

Shocked by the appearance of his dog, he returned to the car and retrieved a blanket from the trunk. He laid the blanket out on the ground next to Connor, then dragged him to the center of it and carefully wrapped him up. It took him three tries to lift Connor off the ground. He could feel the eyes of the young man on him, wanting to help but maintaining a respectful distance. When he got to his car he looked at his open trunk, unable to put Connor inside. Instead, he laid Connor on the hood, opened the back door, and then slid Connor onto the back seat.

Closure. If this was closure, he didn't want any more of it. Closure sucks. He slammed the door, slammed the trunk, and slid behind the wheel, numb.

The outpouring of grief that would surely come was preceded by a fit of rage. How could anyone let this happen to such a beautiful, innocent creature? If he ever found the asshole that stole his best friend and robbed them of their future, he would rip him a new one. Al decided that the best way to get home without an emotional breakdown was to spend the time imagining new and gruesome ways to put this guy in a hurt locker.

He started the car and drove slowly out of the parking lot. It would be a long drive home. A very long drive.

Chapter 48

Gina sat at the kitchen table, head bowed, eyes closed, hands folded in front of her. When Mireya walked through the kitchen door, fresh from the whirlpool tub wearing a bathrobe and with a towel wrapped around her head, she saw much more than an old woman dozing at the kitchen table.

She saw a timeless face, the wisdom of its years etched proudly in the furrows on its brow and the lines in its cheeks. This was the face of a woman who was at peace with her world, who found a place for every living thing in its natural order. A lifetime of love and laughter left its telltale marks around her eyes and mouth. A lifetime of meditation and spirituality cloaked her countenance in serenity.

Gina opened her eyes as Mireya took a seat across from her and folded her arms on the table.

"Am I in your prayers, Gina?"

"Always."

"Have you been praying for guidance? What am I going to do?"

"You know the answer to that. You've witnessed a murder. You have information as to the whereabouts of a kidnapped child. You have to tell someone. The child is at risk."

"Who? The police? They'll never believe me. They'll laugh me out of the station."

"I think you should talk to the girl's father. I just watched the news, and they said there still aren't any suspects in the case, and nobody has contacted the father with any kind of ransom demand.

"He won't believe me. They're all the same. Even the people I help don't really believe in me, they're just desperate."

"They have a puppy. You will know things that nobody outside their home could know. You can convince the little girl's father that you're legitimate. You know you can do it. You must believe that you can."

"You know how I hate to talk about it."

"I know, but you have a gift. The price of that gift is an obligation to do the right thing. You have a responsibility to the girl that you cannot ignore. Her father will be desperate for information. You'll have to try to make him believe you."

"I'll have to get him alone. I can't talk to him with the police around."

"In the newspaper it said that she might have been taken from the playground where they walk the puppy. I bet you can find him there. Maybe you can find some clues there, too."

"I'm sure the police have been over that playground with a fine-tooth comb."

"Yes, but they don't have your special insight."

Mireya sighed loudly and laid her head on top of her folded arms. "OK. I'll try. I hope you're right."

Gina got up, walked behind Mireya's chair, and planted a kiss on top of her toweled head. "You have the truth in your heart. Do the best you can. Nobody can ask more."

Chapter 49

Mireya had no trouble locating Gary's house. She drove slowly by, then parked at the end of the road near the entrance to the playground. She got out of her car and looked back down the street. If this wasn't the picture of the American suburban family neighborhood she didn't know what was.

She felt alone and out of place. A little voice in her head told her that she would find no friends here. She should leave. She wanted to leave. But she knew that she had to stay. Her responsibility to Sandra Coakley forced her to stay. Somehow, knowing the child's name made her obligation to help more real.

She turned and walked onto the playground. It was large and well manicured. To her left was a basketball court and beyond that two tennis courts. The center of the playground was a recreation center for young children. There were seesaws, small swings, big swings, a huge sandbox, and one of the most ornate jungle gyms she had ever seen. It had dozens of slides, ladders, tunnels, raised platforms, and bridges; it reminded her of the Habitrail habitats they sold for hamsters.

As a teenager on in-line skates whizzed by her, she realized she was standing on a wide sidewalk that followed the outer edge of the entire playground. Here and there shade trees protected wooden benches, providing a comfortable vantage point for watchful parents.

And there certainly seemed to be a lot of watchful parents on the playground today.

She decided to follow the sidewalk and make a slow tour of the place. There were two large entrances, one on either end. Halfway down the long sides were two smaller pedestrian gates. A hedge around the entire circumference was meant to shield the playground from the streets. On both ends the hedge was quite tall, but on the long sides she could look right over it.

As she walked around, she noticed many places where children took shortcuts through the hedge, opening spaces big enough for an average-size adult to squeeze through. Basically, Sandra could have been snatched from just about anywhere. You didn't have to be Sherlock Holmes to figure that out.

When she completed her circle, she headed for the big swings and took a seat on one. From there she could view the entire playground. She would wait for as long as she had to. She could use the time to collect her thoughts and garner her courage.

As she sat swinging gently in the fading sun of late afternoon, she was careful not to slip into her personal Twilight Zone. She could not afford to have him walk the puppy right by her while she was oblivious to everything outside her own head. Watching people on the playground—coming and going, walking, jogging, skating, and pushing strollers—was like watching fish in a tank. It was relaxing if you didn't try to read too much into it.

The shadows were growing longer, and more people were leaving than arriving. She supposed the family supper hour was drawing near.

Her legs were getting numb from sitting on the swing. She stood up and stretched, thinking she would go for another short walk when she spotted him. It had to be him. He was a tall man with sandy colored hair and broad shoulders—and he was walking a beagle puppy. As she got closer, she could see he was wearing faded jeans and a dark blue, short-sleeved shirt.

She was on the path now, and as she got closer his sadness was evident in the way he carried himself. His head was down, his shoulders slumped forward as if they bore the weight of the world. Without looking up he automatically moved to his right to allow her room to pass. She stepped to her left and blocked him.

He looked up with startled green eyes. Green. They were the ancient barren green of glacial ice and water. Sea foam green, like a vast sad sea, endlessly empty on the surface and out of touch with the explosion of life below.

"Sorry," he said and moved left. Mireya moved right to counter.

"Are you Mr. Coakley?"

He held out his hand to stop her. "Please. No press. I need a little peace."

"I'm not the press. I'm Mireya Richardson, and I'm an animal communicator." She held out her right hand.

As he took her hand in a firm grasp, he looked into her eyes. They were dark, fathomless, mesmerizing. For a moment he felt as though he were being drawn into their depths, like he was being pulled outside of himself, floating downward…

He stepped back abruptly and looked away, mildly alarmed and confused. "Ah…sorry. What's an animal communicator?"

"Someone who can communicate with animals in a telepathic way."

"You're an animal psychic?"

"No. I'm not a psychic. I can't predict the future. I can only communicate with them concerning present and past events."

"Right. Very interesting. Nice meeting you." He stepped around her and walked away.

She turned and watched him continue on his way with the puppy trotting along beside him. She knew it wouldn't work. He was obviously a really nice guy, politely excusing himself when he had really wanted to laugh in her face. She longed to go home, but the image of his daughter screaming and beating her hands against the window rooted her to the spot.

"YOU'LL WANT TO LISTEN TO WHAT I HAVE TO SAY BECAUSE I HAVE INFORMATION ABOUT YOUR DAUGHTER!"

He spun around and marched back to her, anger replacing the sadness on his face. "Listen! You cannot begin to imagine the hell I've been through these last twenty-four hours. The last thing I need is some whacko weaving telepathic psycho-babble about my daughter!"

"I'm NOT a whacko, and if you'll let me, I can prove it."

"How?

"Give me permission to communicate with your puppy."

"Sure. Why not. Knock yourself out." Gary stood with his arms defensively folded across his chest. When he looked down at the normally boisterous puppy, he was amazed to see that Scooby was sitting perfectly still, his attention riveted on Mireya.

Mireya looked down at the puppy. "What's his name?"

"Why don't you ask him?"

Mireya lifted her head and shot him a hostile look through narrowed eyes.

Jesus! He took a step back. Where did that look come from? His wife used to give him that look when she was supremely annoyed. It was a kind of castrating glare that never failed to freeze him in his tracks. Was this some kind of genetic thing that all women got? And the way they made their eyes smaller when they did it. It was like they were focusing the beam of a laser or something. He didn't know this woman from a hole in the wall, and he was scared.

"Well?"

"Oh. Scooby. My daughter named him Scooby-Doo, but the last day I saw her she told me she was changing it to Scooby-Don't because that's what we were always saying to him."

Mireya smiled and lowered her eyes to look at the puppy again.

"He says that you were very angry with him this morning."

"Really?"

"Yes. Apparently he had a little accident in your bedroom closet."

Gary looked startled and took another step back.

"Am I correct?"

He nodded.

"And I guess you'll be needing a new pair of wingtips."

"Why? There's nothing wrong with the ones I have."

"Really?"

"Really."

"Better check on that before the next time you're required to dress up in formal attire."

"I have to go." Gary cut across the park at a brisk walk, making a straight line for the entrance, and home.

She watched him go, the puppy running along beside him. When they disappeared through the gates, she returned to her seat on the swing. He'd be back.

Chapter 50

Gary practically ran back to his house. Who was this woman? How could she know what was going on in his house? She couldn't. She was just another whacko who made a lucky guess about the closet. He found the whole encounter deeply disturbing. Anyway, he was about to prove her wrong. He entered the front door and immediately went upstairs, with the puppy still on the leash.

Once inside the bedroom he dropped the leash and entered the small walk-in closet. He wore the wingtips so infrequently, business casual being the dress code of his office, they were in the back partially hidden behind his laundry basket. He reached in and grabbed one. It looked in perfect condition. He had to search around for the other one. When he located it, he was shocked to see that the toe had been chewed completely open. He stared at the shoe in disbelief.

"Scooby. How the hell can this be?"

He dropped the shoe and grabbed the puppy's leash again. "What else could she know?"

He picked the puppy up and ran back down the stairs, right into the path of the police officer on duty manning the communications station.

"Going out again?" the officer asked.

"We didn't finish our walk. I've really been drinking too much coffee."

The officer smiled and waved him out the door.

Gary forced himself to walk until he was out of sight of his house. He broke into a run and prayed that she was still hanging around.

When he passed through the entrance he slowed down and began to scan the playground. How could a complete stranger know things about his closet that even *he* didn't know? He couldn't explain it, but he was going to make sure that she did.

He spotted her sitting on a swing and headed in that direction. She stood when she saw him approach. She was a little taller than average with a slim but athletic build. He thought she had two remarkable features. Her dark, thick, straight hair hung down to her shoulders and shone like highly polished, antique mahogany. Her eyes were riveting, mysterious, dark and dangerous. He wouldn't make the mistake of staring too deeply into those again. Overall she had a vaguely exotic look that he found intriguing.

By the time he reached her she had taken a seat on one of the swings. He sat on the swing next to her. For a few minutes neither of them spoke.

Gary was the first to break the silence.

"There's no way you could have known about that shoe. Hell, *I* didn't even know and it's *my* shoe in *my* closet.

"I mean, do you actually expect me to believe that this puppy told you about it? That's not possible."

Mireya just looked at him and remained silent.

"So maybe you got lucky. Puppies have accidents and chew up shoes. Happens all the time.

"Aren't you going to say anything?"

"You seem to be doing just fine all by yourself."

"OK. Fine. I gotta get back." He got up to leave.

"He also told me you spent the night in her room last night. He usually sleeps in a crate by the front door, but you let him stay upstairs last night. That's why he had the accident. He said you laid on her bed, and you were holding something new. Or, I assumed it was new because it still had the tags on it."

"How can you know these things?" He thought about the new stuffed Snoopy dog he bought Sandra at the airport.

"I appreciate that things not widely understood can be a little hard to accept."

"That's an understatement!"

"Look. I didn't want to come here. I'm not at all comfortable talking about this, but I have a responsibility to Sandra. I believe she's in trouble."

"OK. Just tell me what you know, and I'll decide what to do with it. Tell me how you came by information about my daughter."

Mireya stretched, then sat back down on the swing and took a deep breath, like she was preparing for another argument.

He soon found out why.

"One of the things I do is find lost pets for people. I'm able to find them because…"

"Wait. You don't have to be with the animal to communicate with it?"

"No. It can be anywhere. Distance is meaningless."

"Jesus! OK. Forget it. Go on."

"I can find them because I can see what they see, and I try to deduce their location from what I see around them."

She looked over at Gary.

He nodded.

"A man from Dorchester called me this morning because his golden retriever went missing yesterday.

"Anyway, when I contacted the dog, Connor, I discovered that he had been hit by a car."

"Where *is* this dog?"

"You mean, right now?"

"Yes, now."

"Well his owner went to Truro to identify him and by now he's probably back home, laying him to rest, saying a prayer, whatever. I'm not exactly sure."

"Are you saying the dog died?"

"I know, it's so sad. I have a really hard time when they die, especially in such a painful way. I just hate suffering. And the owners suffer too. It's so hard to give them news like that."

"I'm a little confused. How can you know that the dog died?"

"I asked him to show me where he was because his person, Al…"

"Excuse me. His person?"

"Yeah. They don't really understand the concept of ownership very well. So I told him Al wanted to find him. All he could do was show me what he saw during the last moments of his life."

"Are you telling me that you can communicate with an animal that's dead?"

She nodded.

Gary stood up and walked a few steps away. "This is just too much to swallow."

"Here we go again," she said under her breath.

"What?"

"OK. Did you ever have a pet that died?"

"What's that got…"

"Did you?"

"Yes, a cat."

"What was the cat's name?"

"Now look…"

"The name!"

"Mae West."

"Thank you." Mireya closed her eyes, gave herself a push on the swing, and after a moment whispered, "Mae West." She was quiet, swinging gently back and forth. After a minute she opened her eyes and looked at Gary.

"She was a long-haired cat. I think she was your wife's. You didn't like her much. She used to sleep on the closet shelf on top of your sweaters. It made you angry, because she got her hair all over them. She also liked to sleep under the hood of your car in the warm engine compartment. That's how she died."

Gary was staring at her with his mouth wide open. It took him a minute to recover his voice. When he did, he asked, "Would you please tell me exactly what you know about my daughter?"

"There was a woman standing in the road near the dog. She was very upset. She may have been the driver of the car that hit him. She was pointing to a small window. I could see Sandra's face in the window. She was screaming and beating her hands against it. I recognized her face from the newspaper. Somebody threw a heavy metal object at the woman and hit her in the head. She fell to the pavement right in front of the dog and died. We found the dog in the town of Truro, near the Wellfleet line. That's on Cape Cod."

"So you're saying the people who have my daughter are potential murderers?"

"I guess so. Yeah, maybe."

"Anything else at all? Where was this window? What kind of window was it?"

"I don't know. The image was hazy. Was she walking the puppy when she was taken?"

"We aren't sure. We think so."

"May I?" Mireya pointed to Scooby.

"Of course."

Mireya stared at the puppy for a few minutes, then she looked at Gary.

"He dropped something!"

"Who?"

"The man who took Sandra!"

"Where?"

"Over there, I think." She pointed to the far entrance, jumped off the swing, and ran toward that end of the playground with Gary and Scooby close behind. When she reached the sidewalk she slowed to a walk.

"He fell down somewhere near the entrance and dropped something."

"He fell?"

"Yeah. Scooby tripped him."

Gary looked at the puppy. "You did that, buddy? Nice try." He gave the puppy a pat.

"Why don't you just ask Scooby what he looked like?"

"I did, but he's like eight inches tall! All he noticed was the guy's feet. He was wearing thick-heeled black boots. Even if Scooby were full grown, he probably wouldn't be able to give us a good description. Hounds operate about ninety percent on smell."

They were walking along the hedge when Gary suddenly realized the puppy was straining at the end of the leash and wagging his tail. He reached under the hedge with the puppy and pried a small object out of the dirt. The rain had covered it with a thin layer of mud.

"Did you find something?"

Gary backed away from the hedge and stood up. "It's pretty soggy from the rain, but it's a book of matches."

"Where from?"

Gary held the matchbook at arm's length. "The Atlantic House, Provincetown, Mass."

"The A-House. That's interesting."

"Do you know the place?"

"Sure. It's very well known, although for obvious reasons I've never been inside. It's a men's bar. A gay bar."

"So now you're saying that my daughter has been kidnapped by a murderer who is gay?"

"Possibly, but I wouldn't worry about the gay part."

"Excuse me?"

"The gay…thing. Isn't that better than if he were the other way?"

"I see your point. I feel s-o-o-o much better."

Mireya shrugged.

"We need more information. We'll never find this guy without a description, or a car, or something."

"I've had a very long day. I'm going home. Why don't you give that matchbook to the police? There still might be a fingerprint on the inside."

"I'll do that. How can I get in touch with you?"

Mireya pulled a business card out of her pocket and handed it to him. "I put my cell number on the back. You can call me anytime."

Mireya began to walk away and then turned around, walking backward so that she could see Gary.

"Hey! About Mae West…"

Gary looked up. "What about her?"

"You aren't a cat person, are you?"

"No."

"Well, Mae said to tell you 'No hard feelings.' She says that she's still just a big hairy broad."

Once again, Gary looked stunned. "That's what I used to call her."

Mireya smiled and waved, then turned around and jogged back to her car.

Chapter 51

Mireya had exceeded the burden of proof. He was a believer, but still unable to process the overload of new ideas that only an hour ago he would have considered preposterous. Ridiculous. Absurd. Outrageous. All of the above.

Her last insight into the realm of his animal relationships had rocked him. That cat died almost ten years ago yet she had every detail about what happened exactly right.

Animal spirits. He wasn't even sure he believed in human spirits! But how else could he explain it? He had always believed that people lived on after death, because eventually their bodies were reabsorbed into the natural world and became part of other living things. He now had to reorganize his thoughts. If Mae's spirit could be hanging around, then why wouldn't Karen's be here, too?

A flood of emotions he thought he had locked away permanently came rushing back. He sat down on one of the wooden benches and buried his face in his hands. The unshed tears of the last twenty-four hours, and the last three years, finally found their release.

"Oh God, Karen. I've lost our little girl! I'm so sorry!" Guilt welled up in him, extinguishing the hopes and dreams that illuminated his life. He was overwhelmed with grief for his lost family. He realized that he felt the loss of his wife more acutely now than ever because of Sandra. Whenever he looked at his little girl he could see his wife, in her eyes, her hair, her smile. Now he'd lost that link, potentially forever.

The child of his heart was in the hands of a murderer. His only hope was to trust in the unexplainable and uncanny abilities of a woman whose eyes were fascinating and frightening, and drew him to them like a child to a haunted house.

He had no idea how long he languished in his private well of grief before the antics of his impatient puppy brought him back to the present. Dusk was fast approaching, the playground was nearly empty, and he was very sure Scooby was thinking about dinner.

As soon as he cleared his head, he dug out his cell phone and called up John Murphy's number from its memory.

"Murphy."

"John, it's Gary. I need to see you."

"I'm in my car, on my way back to the station. Why don't I drop by your house? I could be there in about ten minutes."

"Great. I'll see you then."

Gary had just enough time to get home and get the puppy fed before the detective knocked on the door.

"John. Thanks for coming." He let the detective into the house and from the look on his face, Gary surmised that the police were still empty-handed, or perhaps clueless was a more accurate word.

"I found something unusual on the playground."

"Really? What is it?"

Gary took the matchbook out of his shirt pocket, being careful to handle it by the edges. He handed it to John.

"I thought there might still be a viable fingerprint on the inside."

"Maybe, but I doubt if it was there when she was taken or we would have found it."

"I don't think so. I had to crawl under a hedge to get it, and it was covered with mud. The puppy actually sniffed it out. I'd really like you to check it for prints. See where it's from? A little unusual for a family playground, don't you think?"

"The Atlantic House. Provincetown. So? A lot of families vacation on the Cape."

"I guarantee you they don't visit this place. It's P-town's most famous gay bar. Men only."

"You're thinking about the biker-type that one of the mothers saw?"

Gary nodded.

"It's worth a try." He took an evidence bag out of his pocket and carefully dropped the matchbook into it, then knelt down in front of the puppy.

"Good work, young man. I'm going to give you a special citation if this is a clue."

He stood up and turned back to Gary. "I'm on my way home. I'll drop this off at the lab and put a rush on it. I just authorized an officer to monitor your phone for another twenty-four hours. Keep your fingers crossed."

"Thanks, John. See you tomorrow."

The detective nodded and left.

Gary took out Mireya's card and turned it over in his hand a few times. He felt the tiniest flicker of hope rekindle in his heart.

Chapter 52

Mireya parked in her garage and began the long trek up the walk to her house. Her limbs became lead weights as what was left of her energy quietly drained out of them. Contacting Connor had been extremely hard on her, but not nearly as hard as the contact she made with Gary Coakley. Communication with animals was usually easy. Communication with humans was a nightmare.

She had lived with this "gift," as Gina called it, for most of her life. As a child, it seemed like a natural part of life; she supposed that everyone possessed the same rapport with the animal world that she did. Gina had always known about it. However, her parents didn't find out until the day her cat, Sneakers, died violently in the jaws of a neighbor's dog. Although she was nowhere near the cat at the time, she experienced its pain and terror seemingly firsthand.

Gina had tried to explain her ability to Mireya's father, but his reaction was to permanently ban all animals from their household and to completely discourage any and all discourse on the subject of animal communication. Her mother just let the whole topic float by unnoticed.

Life went on smoothly until Mireya reached the seventh grade and graduated to a different private school where she immediately made two new friends. By Christmas they were inseparable…and Mireya made one of the biggest mistakes of her life. She confided in them. Naturally, they didn't believe her and required proof. She proved herself in much the way she did with Gary, by telling them things she could not possibly have known. She was unprepared for their reaction.

They believed she had been spying on them through their pets and no longer trusted her. At school she was labeled as a freak and treated as an outcast. In truth, it had never occurred to her to extract private personal information from a pet. She would have felt like a peeping Tom.

Her father made her stick it out at that school for two years in spite of her unhappiness. She survived by isolating herself, refusing to be involved in any extracurricular activities. She attended classes and went home. If she had free time during the day, she spent it in the library, studying. `

The payoff was that she graduated from the eighth grade first in her class and was accepted into the most competitive private high school in Boston, leaving her former friends behind. There she fine-tuned her techniques for self-isolation. She was required to participate in an extracurricular activity and a sport, so she joined the photography club and learned to row singles from her father. The school didn't have a team, but she got credit for participating in competitions through her father's club.

She learned to be pleasant if not friendly around people. She never asked for, or volunteered, any nonessential information. She even devised a way to appear to make eye contact without really doing it.

For the most part, she kept her eyes downcast. She was labeled shy and demure.

When her father died, she sold the Marblehead estate where she grew up and the house on Beacon Hill that her father had bought so that Mireya wouldn't have such a long commute to high school. In spite of his insensitivity and lack of ability to deal with, or even acknowledge, her special needs, he never thought of sending her to boarding school and spent all of his free time doing almost anything she wanted.

As her thoughts drifted back to the present, she stopped halfway up the walk to admire her little house. Well, it wasn't exactly little. It was a fully restored, antique colonial house in the historic district of Cambridge, just a short walk to Longfellow Park and the Charles River. Compared to the eighteen-room mansion in Marblehead and even the brownstone on Beacon Hill, her house was modest. She didn't need a staff, just Gina, who didn't even live with her, and a gardener who came once a week to tend the yard.

Still, she couldn't have afforded it without her trust fund. Her father had been the rebel of his Brahman clan, running off after law school to do *pro bono* work on an Indian reservation, and marrying a Native American woman without the blessing of his family. His parents disinherited him, but his grandfather left him a small trust fund, which he used to start his law firm. He nurtured that fund over the years and left it and his real estate holdings to Mireya.

She could afford to live comfortably in her house near the Charles for the rest of her life, but did so with the knowledge that no member of her father's family would ever acknowledge her existence. So be it. Gina was her family. She didn't need or want anyone else.

In fact, her life was perfect. She loved every single thing about her life as an eco-activist, especially championing the cause of endangered species. She loved her home in Cambridge, and she loved that every so often she got to reunite somebody with a treasured pet.

As she entered the house she called out, "GINA?"

"IN HERE!" Gina was in the parlor, reading a book.

"How did it go? Were you able to find him?" she asked when Mireya entered the room.

Mireya nodded.

"And? You told him?"

Mireya nodded again.

"Did he believe you?"

"I convinced him."

"I knew you could. What now?"

"We found a very good clue, a book of matches the kidnapper dropped when he took the girl. I'm hoping there's a fingerprint inside. Gary's going to give it to the police."

"Will he say how he found it?"

"I don't know. I hope not."

"What's next?"

"Just wait, I guess."

"You have a couple messages." Gina inclined her head in the direction of Mireya's office.

Mireya nodded and trudged into her office. Please, God, no more animals in trouble tonight. She was just too tired.

She pushed the playback button on her machine and flopped into her chair to listen.

> *"Hello. This is Karen Iverson. We found Rosco in the trunk of an old car that my husband is restoring. I don't know how he got in there, but the reason we didn't hear him is that my teenage son works out in the garage and always has his music blasting. We took Rosco to the vet and they had to keep him overnight to give him fluids, but he's home now and he's fine.*
>
> *We are so thankful for your help."*

The next message was from Al Sullivan.

> *"Yeah. This is Al Sullivan. I just wanted you to know that I went to Truro and I found him. It was Connor. I brought him home. I...just want to say that I appreciate whatever it was you went through to find him for me. You were right. It means a lot. I would have never known what happened to him. Thanks."*

Mireya dragged herself back out into the living room and collapsed on the couch. Gina closed her book and took off her reading glasses. "You look exhausted."

Mireya nodded.

"You did a good thing. I'm proud of you."

Mireya answered with a shrug.

"You will believe it, too. Tomorrow, when you are rested, you will believe it in your heart."

This elicited a smile.

"You should eat something. I made some split pea soup."

Mireya stretched. The weight of her own arms was almost too much for her. "I'm too tired to eat. I'm going to sleep, probably for a week."

It was Gina's turn to smile. "It's in the fridge if you change your mind. I think I'll go home now unless you'd like me to stay over."

"No. I'm fine. I'll see you in the morning."

Gina walked over to Mireya, recited her nightly prayer so softly that if Mireya hadn't heard it a million times, she wouldn't have recognized it. Gina kissed the top of Mireya's head and quietly left the room.

Chapter 53

Gary grasped the edge of the sink with both hands and leaned against his arms. He stared at his incomplete reflection in the steamy mirror and wondered if he was looking at the face of a fool. He had been unable to come to grips with the new reality revealed to him the night before.

Had she been for real?

Or was he hallucinating under the stress of his daughter's disappearance?

He just didn't know.

Her eyes haunted him, as did the possibility that their unusual sight could lead him to Sandra. He knew he would call her. He also knew that he would tell no one about her, especially the police.

When he entered his kitchen, he noticed a cup of Dunkin' Donuts coffee on the counter. He picked it up and went to the den where he found the *cop du jour* sitting in his chair, a Dunkin' Donuts bag and the morning paper on the desk. The officer was reading the sports page.

"Is this coffee for me?" Gary asked.

"Yeah. I don't know how you take it so I got it black. I brought your paper in. I hope you don't mind."

"Of course not, and black is perfect. I'm going to walk the puppy."

The officer nodded and went back to the paper.

Gary got Scooby out of his crate and took him out the front door. He sat on the front steps with his coffee and watched as the puppy took care of business and sniffed his way around the tiny front yard. Every so often Scooby would find a spot that smelled especially intriguing and would practically glue his nose to it as his tail wagged furiously.

What would it be like to get so much information from your nose? Gary supposed that it would be as foreign to him as getting information telepathically from an animal. Many animals and insects communicate through scent, dolphins and whales communicate with a kind of sonar, bats use an echolocation system to communicate and navigate the night skies. Why was he having such a hard time with this telepathy concept?

He never realized, until now, how narrow-minded he had become. The mind of a child can embrace, imagine, or enhance an infinite array of possibilities. At what age did he become a dullard, closed off to the fantastic, the miraculous, the extraordinary phenomena that the universe unfolded every day for him as a child?

He took out his cell phone and Mireya's card. As he stared at the number she wrote on the back, his phone rang.

"Gary, it's John."

"Hey, John, I hope you have good news."

"Not really. We got a poor quality partial of a thumb print off the matchbook."

"Can you use it?"

"It's probably not good enough to get a computer match, but could maybe be used as corroborating evidence if we nail the guy on something else."

"I was hoping…"

"I know, but don't give up yet. We're still interviewing people in the neighborhood. I've got a message from a parent whose teenage boy was playing basketball the day the biker was seen walking around the playground. She says he remembers the guy so I'll be talking to him and a few of his friends after school today. Hopefully I'll get a more complete description."

"Let me know what happens."

"Count on it."

Gary closed his phone feeling as though he couldn't count on anything coming from the police investigation. They just didn't have anything to go on. He opened his phone again and dialed Mireya's number.

When she answered, he thought for a moment that he had the wrong number. Her voice sounded tentative, almost diminutive on the other end of the line. Missing was the confidence with which she had argued her case the night before.

"Hello?" she said again.

"Sorry. Hi. Is this Mireya?"

"Yes."

"This is Gary…from last night. Did I wake you?"

"No."

"I'm sorry. I just…You sound different on the phone."

There was a long silence.

"Is it OK that I'm calling you?"

Another silence.

"Because you gave me your card and said to call anytime."

"Right. It's fine."

"I thought you might like to know about the matchbook."

Another silence.

"I gave it to the police, but all they could find was a poor quality partial of a thumbprint. They aren't likely to find a match."

"Oh. Sorry."

Now it was his turn to be silent while he summoned up the courage to ask his next question.

"Do you think I could meet with you again?"

"Why?"

"Because you're the only one who has even the slightest clue about what happened to my daughter."

"Did you tell the police about me?"

"No. I couldn't come up with a rational way to explain you to them."

"Good." He could hear the relief in her voice.

"So can I meet with you? Why don't we have breakfast? You pick the restaurant."

"No. Gina…my housekeeper makes my breakfast."

There was another silence.

"You could come here."

"Really? Are you sure you don't want me to take you out to breakfast?"

"No. Thank you. We can meet here."

"That's very kind of you. Where do you live?"

"Eleven Williams Street in Cambridge. It's off Brattle, near Longfellow Park."

Gary wrote the address on the back of her card, beneath her phone number. "What time?"

"An hour?"

Gary looked at his watch. That would be about nine o'clock. "Sounds perfect. I'll see you soon."

He closed his phone. The snap of the cover closing on his StarTac was like a leg hold trap snapping shut on his rational mind, trapping his common sense in its steel jaws. Desperation pulled him down a road he would never walk if he could exercise free will. His love for his child would not allow this path, no matter how far off the beaten track, to remain uninvestigated.

He leashed the puppy. He had just enough time to take him for some serious exercise before leaving for Cambridge.

Chapter 54

Mireya set her phone down on the kitchen table and stared at it with an amalgam of abject horror and disbelief. She could not believe that she had actually invited this man to breakfast at her home. This desperate man who had no trust or belief in her abilities, this man who was grasping at straws much the way terminal cancer patients flock to foreign countries for the latest experimental miracle cure. What do any of them have to lose?

She, on the other hand, had plenty to lose if the police or press got wind of her helping to search for the girl. The least of her losses would be the tranquil harmony of her relatively anonymous existence in this town, and the greatest would be a complete and public loss of credibility followed by total public humiliation. Most of the people who knew her did not know of her animal communication abilities. An exposé could easily ruin her life.

So be it. Gina would give her no peace if she didn't fulfill her obligation to the girl.

Gina picked that moment to walk through the door. She had only to glance at Mireya to know that all was not well. "What's wrong, Rey?"

"He's coming for breakfast."

"He? Who's he?"

“The father of the girl. Gary Coakley.”

“Why?”

“He wants to talk to me. I suppose he wants my help.”

“That’s good, Rey. I knew you could convince him.”

“It’s just an act of desperation on his part.”

“It doesn’t matter. It’s a good thing. You’ll find that child. I know you will. Any luck with the matchbook?”

Mireya shook her head.

“That’s too bad. What time is he coming?”

“Nine o’clock.”

Gina checked her watch. “Well, I’d better get organized.”

“Thanks, Gina.”

“Don’t thank me. Get showered and dressed. He’ll be here in forty minutes.”

Chapter 55

Gary had no trouble finding her house. It wasn't what he expected, but on the other hand he hadn't known what to expect. It was so traditional. He guessed that if he had been expecting anything, it would have been something that was untraditional.

He pulled into the driveway and parked in front of the garage, which was close to the road, leaving just enough room for one car in front of it. It was a small, single car garage made entirely of brick, laid in interesting patterns. The door was made of a dark polished wood. Mahogany? He wasn't sure.

Six brick steps led up to the front walk, which was also made of brick. The house was the only one on the street that was set toward the back of its lot, leaving room for a large front lawn and creating a feeling of privacy in a city neighborhood.

The house itself was an authentic Georgian colonial with a hip roof accented by a row of dentils just below the eves. The entrance jutted forward from the front of the house. The gabled end of its tiny roof faced the street and was adorned with dentils matching the main roof. The front door was wood with twelve panes of glass. The house was classic white with black trim and shutters. Everything down to the brass coach lamp by the front door and the neatly manicured, conservative landscaping screamed historic, authentic, and traditional.

Everything about its owner said the opposite.

Gary didn't hesitate when he reached the front entrance. He had long since convinced himself that Mireya was his only proactive option.

Moments after he rang the bell, an elderly woman welcomed him and invited him in. There was no physical resemblance to Mireya so he assumed she was the housekeeper. She showed him into the kitchen where a table was set for two in a sunny breakfast area. From the table he could look out a large window to a small but colorful garden at the side of the house.

"Can I pour you some coffee, Mr. Coakley?"

"Yes, thank you."

"Mireya will be down in just a moment."

She had no sooner spoken the words when Mireya appeared in the doorway. She had obviously not taken any pains with her appearance. Her hair was pulled back and fastened at the nape of her neck with one of those stretchy cloth things that Sandra used to misplace all over the house. She wore an oversized old T-shirt that had the words Grand Crew over a picture of a wine bottle and two crossed oars. Underneath the picture were the words Harvard Women 1991. Faded jeans, threadbare at the knees, and athletic socks completed her attire. She looked a little surprised to see him and stood frozen in the doorway. Gary was the first to speak.

"Thanks again for inviting me. You have a beautiful home."

Mireya managed a weak smile. "I hope you didn't have any trouble…finding us."

"No, not at all."

Mireya started walking toward the other place at the table but stopped halfway across the room. "Sorry. Gary, this is Gina Rizzo, my housekeeper. Gina, Gary Coakley."

Gina was busy at the stove, but smiled and nodded at Gary.

"Nice to meet you, Gina.

"I was throwing a toy for Scooby on the playground, and he got so tired of chasing it he's sound asleep on the backseat of my car."

"Bring him in!" Mireya and Gina said simultaneously.

"No. He's fine. The windows are halfway down, and it's a chilly morning. He can sleep out there."

"Nonsense," Gina said as she poured coffee for Mireya and set a plate of muffins on the table. "You sit right there, and I'll run out and get him."

Gary began to rise, but Gina put a firm hand on his shoulder and pushed him back in his chair. "I'll be right back."

When Gina left the room, an awkward silence hung over them. Gary picked up the plate of muffins and offered it to Mireya. As she took one, he thought he heard her say "Thanks," but her voice was softer than a whisper and he could have imagined it.

"Did you row on the Harvard team?"

"Four years."

"I rowed for Northeastern. Heavyweight eights."

"Singles."

"No kidding? You're so close to the Charles. Do you ever go out anymore? I assume a Harvard alumna could commandeer a boat somehow."

"I own my own, actually."

"Really? Is it a single?"

She nodded. She actually had two. She and her father used to row pairs, and she kept their boat, although it hadn't been out of the boathouse since he died. She saw no reason to volunteer this piece of information.

Gary decided to change the subject. He was looking around the kitchen. "Mireya is a beautiful name. Unusual."

"It's Spanish. My mother grew up in the Southwest so I guess that's where she heard it."

"You have a lot of Southwestern-style stuff. It makes an interesting contrast with the New England colonial."

"My mother was a Navajo. Full blood. So, I grew up with a lot of this stuff around."

"Is that where you get your ability to communicate?"

"From the Navajo? I can't really say. I've always been able to do it. I took a weekend seminar once with a very gifted communicator who claims that everyone has this ability. That may be true, but clearly some can take it to a higher level than others."

Gina returned with Scooby. When he saw Gary he tried to bolt across the kitchen to him, but the slippery tile floor had him skidding in every direction. He slid to a stop in front of Mireya's chair and looked up at her, tail wagging at warp speed.

Gary was stunned at the transformation that occurred when Mireya looked down at the puppy. A positively radiant smile lit up her face. Her eyes, which had been mostly downcast and appeared somewhat unfocused the few times she did look at him, were now as darkly brilliant as he remembered them.

"Is he telling you anything?"

For an instant, Mireya looked up. The luminosity in her expression, now directed at him, left him breathless.

"He really likes a funny-looking orange toy. He wants you to chase him and try to take it away like Sandra did."

Gary smiled and shook his head. "It's called a Kong. And Sandra, as well as all of her little friends, used to chase him all over the playground for it. If he doesn't give it back to me, I find a place to sit down and wait until he does. I'm too old and too slow to be running after him."

Gina set a bowl of water down near Scooby; he took a big drink and then flopped in the middle of the kitchen floor.

"I seem to want him with me at all times lately. I guess it makes me feel more connected to my daughter." Gary's voice was laden with an apologetic sadness.

"I'm the one person you don't have to explain that to."

Gary got one more glimpse at what he believed was the real Mireya before she raised her shields again. Was it he, or just people in general, that caused her to retreat?

"What's it like?"

"What's what like?"

"Talking to animals."

There was a long silence, and when she finally spoke it was with great reluctance. "It certainly isn't anything like Dr. Dolittle. It's...different for each person I think, but for me...I see images. Pictures. And I get feelings. That's why I can find lost pets. I can see what they see, and I can figure out where they are."

"Unbelievable."

Gina delivered two plates of eggs Benedict to the table and refilled their coffee cups.

"Oh, my God. Except for you," he chided Mireya, "this is the most beautiful thing I've seen in days."

To his surprise, Mireya blushed scarlet.

"I'm sure you haven't been much in the mood to cook lately," Gina said softly.

"I don't cook. I unwrap and eat. My housekeeper was a very good cook, but she died the day Sandra disappeared."

"We read about that in the paper," Gina said. "She died trying to help your daughter. I said a prayer for her."

"Thank you. She was like family. I miss her almost as much as I miss Sandra."

They ate their breakfast in relative silence while Gary tried to determine the best way to bring up the subject he really wanted to discuss. He hadn't been open-minded with her when she sought him out and offered her assistance. Now he was desperate for it.

"So, do you have any more ideas?" he asked.

"Such as?"

"How I can find the guy who took my daughter."

Mireya sighed. "Well, what do we know, exactly…He was wearing black boots with thick heels, and he may or may not hang out at the A-House in Provincetown."

"And," Gary added, "He may have committed a murder."

"Right. What kind of information would we need to move forward?"

"His identity or the identity of the vehicle he was driving."

"Well, I suppose I could try again…"

Gina walked quickly to the table. "No, Rey. I don't think you should go there again." She looked at Gary. "You don't understand what you're asking."

"We're talking about my daughter's life! She's been kidnapped by a murderer! What could be worse than that?"

Mireya looked reflective. "It appears that no ransom demand is forthcoming, so that means that he or they want your daughter. If she is what is valuable to them, then they wouldn't want to harm her, would they?"

"I follow your logic, but what if the guy is a twisted, psycho child pornographer, or…some sleazy white slavery agent, or…"

"Stop! You'll drive yourself nuts letting your imagination run amok like that."

"Mireya. What's the big deal with getting more information from Connor? Look how easily you found out all that stuff from Mae West. What the hell's the difference?"

Mireya sighed and closed her eyes as if to gather her thoughts. "It's so difficult to explain this…"

"I have nothing else to do but listen to anything and everything you have to say. I want to understand. You took me by surprise yesterday, and I apologize for giving you such a hard time."

"OK. If I asked Connor where he liked to sleep, as I did Mae West, he would most likely show me a rug in front of a fireplace, or the family room sofa, or a shady spot in the backyard. No problem.

"When I asked Mae West how she died, she showed me a white car parked in a garage. Then she showed me how she went underneath and climbed up into the engine compartment. I had a sensation of warmth. Next she showed me a series of pictures, starting with you getting into the car. I assumed you were going to work because you were carrying a briefcase. I saw you and your wife standing next to the car with the hood up. Your wife was wearing a red sweatshirt. Her hands covered her face. I assumed she was crying, although there are never sounds associated with anything I see.

"Mae West passed very quickly. Connor didn't. When I asked Connor how he died, I felt a crushing pain in my chest, then I could see the road where he was lying. It was as if I was actually lying on the road, too. I drew the conclusion that a car hit him. The second time I contacted him, I asked him to show me things that were happening while he was dying there on the road. He was weak and in tremendous pain. He was apparently unable to separate his memories from the pain he was experiencing at the time. Some of the images I received were hazy and incomplete. He was in so much pain…"

Mireya covered her face with her hands. "It's hard for me to experience the suffering of a beautiful animal. It's horrible. He was so brave and so kind…"

"What about the 'big hairy broad' comment?" Gary asked. "That couldn't come from a picture. Can't you just get Connor to tell you things?"

"The thing about animal communication is that there's no foreign voice talking in your head like a voice-over in a movie. The most difficult thing is to separate our own dialogue, the dialogue that we all carry on in our own heads, from the dialogue of the animal. Every once in a while, something pops into my head that I recognize as not coming from me. Like the 'big hairy broad' comment. But ninety-five percent of my communication is through images and feelings."

Gary was staring at her, bewildered, amazed, and speechless.

Mireya stood up. "I'm going to try Connor again. We're never going to find Sandra any other way."

Mireya walked to her office with Gina and Gary following. She picked up a notebook and a pen from her desk and sat in her chair. She managed a small smile for Gina, then closed her eyes and tried to free her mind. She whispered, "Connor…tell me about the girl…"

For the first minute or so nothing happened. Slowly, she realized she was staring at a nondescript pile of junk, but she had a definite sensation of movement, like being inside a moving vehicle. She felt somebody's arms around her. She saw one of the arms reach for something. It was a child's arm, and it was wearing an odd bracelet. Medic-Alert. Someone passed the child a box of Teddy Grahams.

Mireya could see the hand of the person passing the box. It looked like a man's hand, but small. A ring that looked like a silver snake coiled around his index finger. The snake had a broad flat head, with red jewels for eyes.

Mireya whispered, "Where are you…" The crushing pain rushed back into her chest, taking her by surprise. She cried out, clutched her chest with both arms, and fell onto the floor.

Shocked, Gary started through the office door toward her, but Gina held him back. "Let her finish," Gina said. Gary backed off, but remained visibly shaken.

Mireya felt herself back on the pavement again. The pain and extreme difficulty in breathing clouded her vision. She saw the running shoes and immediately forced her vision upward, searching for windows. She found them and focused all her concentration in that direction. A girl's face appeared in one of them. She was screaming. Mireya realized the girl was looking right at her and was screaming Connor's name.

Mireya whispered again, "Help me, Connor…"

Mireya tried to pull back from the window so that she could identify its surroundings. She…Connor, was getting weaker. She had to concentrate. A little of the haze lifted, and she realized that the windows were in the rear doors of a battered old green van. There was a big spot of primer just below the window of the left rear door. On the right door she could see the word "oline" spelled out in metal lettering. There was a tire leaning against the back of the van, obscuring the license plate.

The woman ran into her line of sight. The heavy metal rod-shaped object hurtled through the air, striking the woman in the temple. She fell to the pavement, made brief eye contact with Connor, and died. Mireya struggled to get another look at the girl, or at the person who threw the rod, but the light was fading. She could no longer see beyond the dead woman. Her breath…Connor's breath was coming in short, shallow gasps. She was…Connor was fading like the light. Connor. The pain was fading, too. Good. Need to sleep. Don't want to sleep here in the dark, alone. Home. Want to go home…

Gina watched, horrified, as Mireya lay on the floor, her breath coming so shallow and ragged her whole body jerked with each effort. Suddenly, her breathing stopped, and she lay absolutely still.

"NO!" Gina screamed and hurled herself through the door at Mireya, grabbing her by the shoulders and slapping her cheeks. Mireya's eyes opened and she let out a tortured moan as she left the darkness and came back through the agony to the light.

Gary picked her up off the floor, carried her into the parlor, and gently laid her on the couch. Gina placed a pillow under her head.

Mireya's eyes were closed, and she was taking huge gasping breaths, fighting the oxygen deficit she built up during her communication with Connor.

"I'm going to make her a healing tea," Gina said as she headed for the kitchen.

Gary sat on the edge of the sofa, holding one of Mireya's hands in both of his and praying that she had suffered no harm on his account.

Her breathing gradually returned to normal, and just as Gina arrived with a steaming, pungent mug of tea, Mireya opened her eyes.

"Oh, thank God!" Gary cried as he released the tension that threatened to unglue him. "Thank God." He pressed her hand to his cheek and welcomed the waves of relief that washed away his guilt and his fear.

Though her eyes were only half open, he could see that she was erecting no defenses. In their slightly narrowed shape, they reminded him of black cabochons, so black that they reflected no light. He let himself stare back at her, and again he had the feeling that he was losing part of himself; the room was beginning to revolve around him.

She sat up; her eyes now open wide and locked onto Gary's. She squeezed his hand.

"I think we've got him."

Chapter 56

As was his custom every morning, Nelson Paquette was seated in his chair, gazing out over Manhattan through the window in his office. His secretary brought him his messages (most of them totally nonessential) and his coffee (prepared exactly the way he liked it), as she did every morning. But this was no ordinary morning. This morning was a turning point for him. This morning he finally began to regain control of his life. This morning he had an uncontrollable desire to whistle. This morning he had actually been pleasant to his secretary.

He was back on the path to financial security, and nothing and no one could spoil his good mood.

"Mr. Paquette. Norman is on line one."

Paquette turned back to his desk and depressed the talk button on his intercom. "Thank you, Marcie." He never thanked Marcie.

He pressed the button for line one and picked up the receiver. "Norman! How's it going?"

"Better. The guys bought her a puppy, and she's much happier."

"Really? What a great idea. What kind of puppy?"

"How should I know? I'm no dog expert…I guess it could be a golden retriever. It's very blonde and fluffy."

"A golden retriever. That's just splendid. You know, if I were going to get a dog, that's probably what I would choose." Paquette leaned back in his chair and smiled.

"The hell with the dog. Tell me what's going on! When does this end?"

"Will you lighten up? It so happens that *our* engineer arrived in Minnesota yesterday. He will be finished with the site assessment and will give his very positive verbal report this afternoon. He'll hand in the written report on Monday, and the deal will proceed."

"Great. It can't happen fast enough for me."

"Norman. Aren't you enjoying your vacation?"

"Very funny."

"I'll be in the office for a few hours tomorrow morning. You can check in with me then." Paquette hung up the phone.

He reached for the intercom again. "Marcie, would you bring me another cup of coffee when you have a minute? Thanks."

He turned back to his window. The only disappointing part of his plan was that he wouldn't be conquering Manhattan as he had before. No big comeback in this town for him. This time he would take the money and run. He would run right to his house in Belize and live the rest of his life conquering the beach, deep-sea fishing, golfing, and party hopping.

He actually smiled at Marcie when she delivered his coffee, then turned his chair back to the window. He didn't have anything to prove to this town. Let the rest of them run around Manhattan like a bunch of rats in a maze. Let them fight traffic, smog, high blood pressure, and premature heart attacks. He didn't care if the stock market went up, down, or sideways, because the only stock he would be concerned with would be his stock of sunscreen and Marguerita mix.

He would be retired to a life of leisure at the age of forty-two, and he couldn't be happier. He just had to hold it together for this one last deal. So far everything was going according to plan.

Chapter 57

Mireya abruptly turned away from Gary and buried her face in her hands.

"We've got him? Are you serious? What do you have? A face? A name? What…Mireya? Are you all right?"

She slowly lowered her hands and nodded, though Gina was not convinced. She knelt down in front of Mireya and placed the steaming mug in her hands. "Drink this."

Mireya raised the mug to her lips and took a small sip. "Ugh…Too strong, Gina."

"Desperate times require strong medicine. Drink it all."

"You didn't put a lot of Valerian root in here, did you?"

Gina shook her head. "Just a little."

"Good. Stuff makes me sleep like Rip Van Winkle."

"Sleep would be the best thing for you right now."

"Not now, Gina. There's too much to do. What I need is lots of energy and mental clarity."

"I knew you would say that. Drink the tea."

Gary was completely out of patience. "Mireya, would you please tell me…"

Gina raised her hand and cut him off in mid-sentence.

Mireya took another sip of the bitter tea and made a face at Gina. "What this needs is about a gallon of honey."

"Just drink it, Rey, and when you're ready, tell us what you saw."

Mireya took a big swallow of the tea. "Now that's what I call nasty." The face she made reminded Gary of the face the cowboy stars of old western movies made when they downed a shot of rotgut saloon whiskey.

"OK. At first, I felt like I was in a moving vehicle of some kind. I saw a child's arm reaching out in front of me. She was wearing a Medic-Alert bracelet."

"Sandra wears one! She's allergic to penicillin." Gary was on the edge of his seat.

"Somebody passed her a box of Teddy Grahams. I saw a man's hand. It was small, and he had a ring on his index finger. It looked like a coiled silver snake, and the head had red jeweled eyes."

Mireya took another sip of the tea.

"Is that it?" Gary asked.

"No. But if they're feeding her Teddy Grahams, it seems like they're being nice to her, don't you think?"

Gary nodded. "I guess."

"I saw her in the window again. She was screaming, but I could tell that she was looking right at me, and she was screaming Connor's name. She must have known he was hit.

"I could see that the window was in the rear door of an old green van. There was a big spot of primer on the left rear door and the word 'oline' on the right."

"Oline?" Gary asked.

"Right. o-l-i-n-e. Could it be the name of a dealership?"

"Maybe."

Mireya took a notepad off the coffee table and wrote the word down exactly as it looked on the van. She handed it to Gary. He studied it for a moment.

"Econoline! Some of the letters are missing. It's an old Ford van. My roommate had one in college. That's great because it will be easy to spot. Anything else? Did you get a look at the plates?"

"There was a tire leaning up against the back of the van. I couldn't get the plate number, but I'm sure it was from Massachusetts.

"I think they may have been changing a flat. The metal object that killed the woman may have been a tire iron."

"I didn't check the paper this morning," Gary said. "Was there anything about a murdered or missing woman?"

"It wasn't in the *Globe* or on the morning TV news," Gina replied. "I guess they still haven't found the body."

They fell silent for a moment, each feeling guilty about having knowledge of a murder, and no way to explain to the police or the woman's family how they came upon that knowledge. The remains of somebody's daughter, sister, wife, mother, or friend lay hidden somewhere, slaughtered and abandoned.

Mireya was intensely affected because she witnessed this murder. She saw this woman's face. She saw her take her last breath. Gary was terrified that his daughter would meet the same fate. They felt the need to act.

"So now what?" Mireya asked. She was looking at Gina, who took her empty mug and returned to the kitchen.

Gary answered. "I'll tell you what. I'm going to Provincetown, and I'm going to stake out the A-House. When this son of a…shows up in his old van, I'm gonna choke the last breath of air out of him until…"

"*We*."

"*We* what?"

"*We* go to Provincetown."

"No way."

"Way."

"Look, Mireya." He picked up one of her hands and held it in both of his. She turned, but didn't make eye contact. "I can't tell you how much I am in your debt for everything you've done. But…I think you've done enough. I can take it from here."

"Maybe you think you can, but A) you've never even heard of the A-House, B) I have an encyclopedic knowledge of Cape Cod, and C) I've actually seen the van, the ring, and the boots. You haven't."

"How about D) these are kidnappers and murderers, and you shouldn't be anywhere near them."

"Oh, right. And *you* are equipped to handle them because you are…Rambo! Yeah, that's the ticket."

The sarcasm was mounting and her eyes were narrowing. Gary was afraid that the dreaded look would be coming his way soon. "Be serious, Mireya."

"I *am* serious. I mean, you're not going to try to take these guys out, are you? You're going to find them, follow them, locate your daughter, and call the police. Right?"

"Right."

"Well, I'm a professional wildlife photographer. I stalk and photograph very shy, reclusive endangered species. I'm much more highly qualified for this job than you are. What qualifications do *you* have?"

"*I* happen to be an Eagle Scout."

"Great. I'll remember to call you the next time an old lady needs to cross the street, or I need to tie a sheep shank in my mooring line."

"Not all Scouts are into knots."

"Are you?"

"Well, yes, but a lot of other things as well."

"Really?"

"That's right."

"Such as?"

"Photography. It's part of my job. I take pictures, too."

"What kind of camera do you use?"

"Thirty-five millimeter."

"Is it an SLR? Who makes it?"

"Kodak."

"Oh, for crying out loud." Mireya got up and walked to her office. "Not only are you underqualified for this job," she reached deep into her backpack, which was on the floor next to the desk. "but you're not even properly armed."

"Armed?"

"Armed." She pulled out her five hundred millimeter telephoto lens. "I can practically photograph the surface of the moon with this thing."

"And what if I say it's still too dangerous?"

"It's a free country. I can go to the Cape anytime I feel like it. You want to bet who finds Sandra first?"

Gary let out a huge sigh and dropped into Mireya's chair. Before she could say, "Don't!" he leaned back and the chair tipped over. His head hit the floor, his legs flew up in the air, and he flipped out of the chair in a reverse somersault. He landed face down in the middle of her office. He was so embarrassed, even his ears burned red. She stood looking down on him with her hands on her hips as a goose egg rapidly appeared on the back of his head.

Eventually, he rolled over and looked up at her. "OK. You win. We'll go together."

"GINA! WE NEED ANOTHER CUP OF THAT TEA, AND AN ICE PACK."

Chapter 58

Gary sat on the sofa as Gina applied a Ziploc bag full of ice cubes to the back of his head.

"I've told you a hundred times, Rey. You should get that chair fixed."

"I didn't really see the need, Gina, since this is the first time anyone but me has sat in it."

"Yes, and see what happened?"

"It's not my fault he's a klutz."

"I'm not a klutz," Gary interjected.

"Yes, you are."

"You barely know me. How do you know I'm a klutz?"

"I just know."

"Oh, really. What's this supposed to be? Some kind of woman's intuition?"

"Aren't you forgetting that I'm the psychic freak?"

"Actually, I did. I momentarily mistook you for an ordinary, stubborn, opinionated female."

"OK. Fine. I'm going to pack for my trip to the Cape. Take good care of the Boy Scout klutz, Gina."

"It's *our* trip to the Cape, and I'm not a klutz."

"Whatever you say." Mireya left the room.

"I'm really not a klutz," he said to Gina.

"I'm sure you're not, Mr. Coakley."

"Please call me Gary."

"OK. I'm sure you're not, Gary."

"Well actually, I might be a little bit…of a klutz. But not totally."

"I'm sure that's true of all of us."

"You're very kind." He paused to collect his thoughts. "What's with her? Do you mind filling me in?"

"I'm not sure what you mean."

"Yesterday she literally bullied me into believing in her abilities, then this morning, she acted so shy and introverted. Now, she's back to being totally argumentative. She's like a Jekyll-and-Hyde type."

Gina sighed. "Mireya spends all of her time working for environmental issues. She's a self-described eco-activist. Mostly she works to save endangered species by raising public awareness through her photography and magazine articles. She has very little contact with people. You might say she's reclusive. She doesn't have any close friends. In fact, you are the first person invited to this house in the six years she's owned it. She doesn't know how to act.

"You'll only see her outgoing side when she's on a mission, and when she's on a mission she's fearless and relentless. Lucky for you, her current mission is to find your daughter."

"Believe me, I'm grateful. I just thought that maybe it was me. I mean that maybe I had a negative effect on her."

"No. Not at all. She's just who she is."

Mireya ran down the stairs and strode into the room. She was rooting around in the bottom of a large camera bag, looking for unused rolls of film. “I’m definitely going to have to run downtown for some more film.” She suddenly remembered Gary and looked up. “How’s your head?”

Gary took the ice pack from Gina. “It’s just a bump. No big deal.”

“I guess I should fix the chair.”

Scooby came trotting into the parlor.

“Look who’s awake,” Gina said as she scooped him up in her arms. “I’d better take him for a little walk in the backyard,” she added as she left with the puppy.

“Look, Mireya, I had no idea that communicating with Connor would affect you to this extreme. If I had, I would never have asked you to do it.”

“Of course you would have. You’re a desperate parent, and I would have done it anyway because I have an obligation to help your daughter.”

“I don’t think Gina wanted you to.”

“In this case, the more I concentrate on the dog and the longer I stay with him, the more I feel the pain of his injuries. Gina believes that if I were with him at the moment he died, I could die, too.”

“Are you serious? Could that happen?”

“I don’t know. Anyway, Connor died Wednesday. I was just reliving the memory of his death with him. Gina has an Italian name because her husband was Italian, but she’s actually full-blood Hopi.

"My mother hired her to be my nanny and part of the housekeeping staff when I was an infant. She's been with me ever since. I don't know if she believes this because of some Hopi teachings, or if it's just her own personal belief. She's a very spiritual person."

"So when do we leave for the Cape?"

"The sooner, the better. It's Saturday, and beach traffic can have the bridge backed up for miles."

"I'm ready."

"No you aren't. You need to go home and pack a bag. This stakeout could take a few days. We're lucky it's the weekend, though, because people are more likely to be out partying on Friday and Saturday nights."

"Can we bring Scooby?"

"I don't think that's a good idea. I'm sure Gina will look after him while we're gone. What are you going to tell the police?"

"Nothing. They pack up and leave at noon today. I'm sure they never thought a ransom demand was coming. I'm just not wealthy enough for it to be that sort of case. I think they were just going through the motions. Covering all the bases."

"The police will never find her." Mireya's expression and voice seemed far away, as though her mind were in an altogether different location.

Gary looked at her with more confusion than ever. Where was she now? And what was she doing? Daydreaming? Or on a mission?

"It's all just a shot in the dark," he said.

She turned to look at him, her eyes focused back in the present, though not at him. “Not for us.”

Chapter 59

Gary pulled up in front of Mireya's house for the second time in one day. He had left his townhouse the instant the police officers packed up and moved out. They had been apologetic about the lack of progress on the case. He had played the worried, despondent parent, while counting the minutes to their departure.

Mireya was on the front walk. When she recognized his car, she waved him into the driveway. The garage door was open and the garage was empty.

"Pull your car into the garage, and we'll take mine." She gestured toward a shiny new dark green Range Rover parked on the side of the road.

"Why?" he asked through his open car window.

She gave his six-year-old Toyota sedan a disparaging look. "Because mine has off-road capabilities, just in case."

He parked his car in the garage, retrieved his backpack and his duffle bag from the trunk, and carried them over to the Range Rover. He couldn't help but admire the car. He decided eco-activism must pay pretty well.

Mireya pulled the remote control out of her pocket and unlocked her car. When Gary opened the tailgate he realized that she had already finished packing. He took a quick visual inventory. "Were you ever a Girl Scout?"

"No. Why?"

"Because you certainly are prepared. Prepared for any contingency that I can think of."

In addition to what he assumed was her overnight bag, there were wireless communication devices, camping gear, an elaborate first aid kit, an even more elaborate tool box, and lots of photographic equipment. An electric cooler that plugged into a twelve-volt socket built into the cargo area was full of food and drinks.

He pointed to something buried underneath the other equipment. "Is this a…"

"Inflatable life raft."

"And this…"

"Flare gun."

"Unbelievable." He turned and gave Mireya a scrutinizing look. "Do you really think that camouflage pants will help you blend into a crowd of gay men?"

Mireya burst out laughing. "I'm sorry," she said with one hand covering her mouth and one hand up as if to stop him from saying anything else. "This is not a funny situation, but you made me laugh. I can't help it."

"I've been known to have that effect on women. In fact, women I've dated have said those very words to me."

She clapped both hands over her mouth and stifled a snort. It took her a minute to regain control. "It's a mindset really."

Gary looked confused.

"The pants. I'm talking about the pants!"

Gary mouthed the word "Oh," and raised his eyebrows in a look of exaggerated enlightenment.

"You see, I always wear them whenever I'm stalking something. You just never know where you'll wind up."

"So you're superstitious."

"I guess."

"Shall we?" Gary opened the driver's door and gestured her in with a wave of his arm.

He jumped into the passenger seat, and as they drove past the house he saw Gina standing on the front walk. He waved, but her head was bowed, and she seemed to be talking to herself.

"What's she doing?"

"Praying for us."

"That's exactly what we need."

As they drove away, he thought Gina's face looked as though it had been sculpted in stone: timeless, solid, and wise. An uncontrollable surge of hope filled his chest. They were on their way to the Cape, and they were going to find Sandra.

Chapter 60

They made the trip to Provincetown in relative silence. Mireya had withdrawn to her emotionally barricaded self, answering Gary's questions politely, but volunteering nothing. After a while, he stopped trying to make conversation, sensing that she would be more comfortable if he left her to concentrate on her driving and her own thoughts.

When they reached the first of the towns along the outer Cape, he felt his anxiety level begin a slow but steady escalation. They sped along Route 6, also known as the Cranberry Highway, for another half hour when she slowed down abruptly and pointed to a busy restaurant on the west side of the road.

"Moby Dick's," she said.

A moment later she turned right onto a narrow side road, and after driving only a few hundred yards, pulled over and parked. Without saying a word, she got out and walked to the middle of the road. He opened his door and stood up, watching her intently but saying nothing.

"This is where it happened," she said, pointing to the pavement. "Right here."

He walked out to stand beside her. He tried to imagine the green van with the flat tire and the brave old dog that had given them the only clues that could lead to Sandra's recovery.

They stood in silence for several minutes. He considered Mireya a complete and total mystery, unreadable and unreachable. Was she a miracle? An oracle? A heretic? A bipolar schizophrenic? Or was she just an incredibly complex woman with an extraordinary gift? He'd thought of nothing and nobody else since he met her and was still no closer to the truth.

He reached out and touched her shoulder, startling her. "We should go."

"Right," she nodded. "But I feel a little guilty that we aren't looking for the body or something."

"I know. We will. But first we have to find Sandra. She's still alive and needs us more."

"Right." She turned and walked back to the car.

As they approached Provincetown, the Cape looked more and more like one big beach. There was a lot of sand, dunes, few trees, and row upon row of tiny one-room cottages for rent, all with an ocean view. In less than fifteen minutes, they were driving down Commercial Street, the main thoroughfare through downtown Provincetown.

"Jesus Christ. What a scene this is. I could crawl faster than this car is moving."

"And this is still off-season. You should see it in July and August."

Gary stared at the scene in front of him. Commercial Street was barely two cars wide. If a truck stopped to make a delivery in front of a restaurant, it was touch and go as to whether you could squeeze by or have to wait until the delivery was finished. Pedestrians milled around in the street: families, retirees on bus tours, young couples, and gay couples, in all age groups, ethnic groups, sizes, and shapes. Cyclists, joggers, in-line skaters, dog walkers, skateboarders, shoppers, and photographers all added to the chaos.

In particular, Gary noticed several shirtless men in spandex shorts who looked like they spent a lot more time in the gym than biking, sitting on bicycles. "Is it just me, or is it a little cool to be hanging around without a shirt?"

"What do you mean?"

Gary pointed to a couple of them.

"They're gay."

"Gay?"

"Yeah."

"How would you know that?"

"Trust me."

"OK. But what does that have to do with not wearing a shirt?"

"Look at them!"

"I am!"

"Don't you find them attractive?"

"No!"

"Well I do. And I bet that gay men would, too. It's Saturday afternoon. They're probably looking around for dates. Look at that bleached blonde over there in the halter top."

"What about her?"

"Don't you think she's flaunting it a bit?"

"Definitely."

"So what's the difference?"

Gary just shook his head.

"You really are a Boy Scout. You should get out more."

"Look who's talking."

They inched their way down the street, past restaurants, cafés, galleries, gift shops, jewelry stores, T-shirt shops, and a line of would-be artists standing in front of their easels in an open-air painting class on the town common.

After they passed the fire station, Mireya turned right onto a tiny side street. The sign identified it as Masonic Place.

"There's the A-House."

"Where?"

"On the left. The white house with the porch."

"That's it?"

Mireya nodded.

"Where are you going to park?"

"I'm not."

"Why not?"

"There's no on-street parking, and besides, these bars won't be gearing up for some time. It's too early."

"So what are you going to do?"

"I just wanted you to get a look at it. I'm going to go around the block and park at McMillan Wharf where everyone else does. We can check the lot for the van in case they came into town early."

Gary sat back and let out an exasperated sigh.

"Look. Stalking anything takes patience. Knowledge is power. In this case we have it all. We know about them, but they haven't one clue that we're on to them."

"I think you're forgetting how thin our chain of evidence is. But, if this is your idea of a pep talk, I thank you for it."

"You're welcome."

Chapter 61

Mireya parked the Range Rover near the center of the lot. They got out and strolled up and down the rows of cars looking for the old Ford van, but appearing to the world like a young couple enjoying the crisp spring afternoon.

"It's definitely not here," Gary said. "Are there any other parking lots we should check?"

"There's a garage, but nobody ever parks there until this lot is full."

"So now what?"

"Are you hungry?"

"Starving."

"Let's get something to eat, and then we wait. I know the perfect place."

Mireya led him back across Commercial Street to a restaurant called Café Blasé. It had a large outside patio dining area surrounded by a white picket fence and window boxes full of flowers. Large pink and blue umbrellas provided shade for the tables. It was a little early for dinner so they were seated immediately.

Gary held Mireya's chair for her and then sat down. "Don't you think it would be better to get a fast food type dinner and go back to the car or down toward the A-House to eat it?"

"Places like the A-House don't get up to speed for hours, and this is the best people-watching place in P-town. Besides, the crabmeat salad is to die for."

"How are the burgers?"

"I have no idea. I don't eat meat. Just fish. The potato salad is very good if you like onions."

"Gee. Thanks. Potato salad. That'll really stick to my ribs."

"Sorry. I thought all guys like potato salad."

"Sure. Just not as the main course. What time should we get over to the A-House?"

"There's no point in going there. We can't recognize him, only his car. There's no parking at the A-House. This is the main drag, and it's a one-way street. Ninety-nine percent of the cars coming into P-town for the evening will drive right past this table and park at MacMillan Wharf where we parked.

"On-street parking is virtually nonexistent. So, the best way to stake them out is to sit right here and watch for the van. Once the van gets here, then we have an even longer wait until they leave again. Even in the off season, places like the A-House are jumping on a Saturday night."

"So you're saying that I should enjoy the meal because it's going to be a long night."

"Right."

Gary picked up his menu and immediately decided on a cheddar burger, but substituted potato salad for the fries.

Mireya stuck to the crabmeat salad.

They ate their dinners with little conversation, unable to keep their eyes off the steady stream of cars crawling down Commercial Street. They ordered dessert and took as long as possible to eat it. Every time the waiter came to give them their bill, they ordered another round of cappuccinos.

"How many cappuccinos does this make, Mireya?" The waiter had just delivered two fresh cups.

"I'm thinking this would be the fourth."

"That's a lot of espresso. How long do you think we can keep this up?"

"It's a self-perpetuating process. At this point, I'll probably be 'up' for the rest of my life."

"I hear you. Being the professional stalker that you are, I imagine this is an occupational hazard."

"I wish all my stake-outs were as cushy as this one. You can't exactly get a cappuccino delivered to you when you're hanging off a cliff or stuck in the top of a tree or crawling through a swamp."

"Sounds like your job can get a little dangerous."

"Sometimes."

"Seriously, what is the most dangerous thing you have to do in your profession?"

"Probably rock-climbing, although the closest call I ever had was free-diving in the Caribbean."

"That's funny. I was thinking that some of the wild animals themselves might present the danger."

Mireya laughed and shook her head. "No. I've never been in danger from an endangered animal."

"Did you say free-diving?"

She nodded.

"What made you want to try that?"

"At first I just wanted to photograph some Moray eels and a few other types of reef fish, but then I got really good at it, and I was going down all the time. You can get a lot closer to the fish without a scuba tank."

"But don't you have to keep coming up to the surface, oh, I don't know…to *breathe,* for instance?"

"Yes, but I can hold my breath for a really long time."

"How long?"

"I don't know, exactly. Maybe about three minutes."

"Wow. So what happened during the close call?"

"I was wearing a lot of photographic gear; one of the straps got caught on a piece of coral. It was behind my back so I couldn't see it or reach it. I actually thought I was going to drown. I wasted a lot of air panicking, but just as I was about to give up I became calm enough to systematically wiggle out of one piece of gear at a time until I was free."

"You were diving alone?"

"I know. Not very smart. But I was a college kid and I thought I was invincible."

"And now? Have you adopted the buddy system for your adventures?"

"Only for climbing. But I never go anywhere without a really sharp knife." She reached down and unsnapped one of the pockets in her cargo pants and pulled out a compact Leatherman survival tool. "This little thing actually even has a saw built into it. It works, too."

Gary shook his head in disbelief. "Why don't you just get a partner or an assistant?"

"I work alone."

"But it's so dangerous!"

"Listen!" she said and sharpened her focus on him. "Nobody depends on my survival except maybe the endangered species I campaign for. I have the right to make those choices for myself."

"That's really sad."

"Sad? For whom? Not for me."

"Ok. I give up. You're the lone wolf."

"So what's the most dangerous thing a Boy Scout like you has done?"

"Right now I'd have to say it was becoming a parent."

"Well don't worry. This is strictly a recon mission. We find, we follow, we photograph, and we report in."

"Nothing in life is ever that simple."

"Hey, here comes a van."

"It's a Ford, Rey. And it's green."

The van rolled slowly by, just fifteen or twenty feet from their table. There were two men in the front. Mireya stood up to get a good look at the back doors.

"Oline," Gary said.

"That's the one. Take your radio and follow them. I'll get the check and meet you on the street. You need to get a good look at them when they get out of the van."

Gary started to reach for his wallet.

"Never mind that! Go! We'll work that out later."

Gary got up and walked briskly down the street in pursuit of the van. Mireya flagged down the waiter and waved a twenty-dollar bill in his face.

"If you have my check for me in less than two minutes, you get to keep this as a bonus." She looked at her watch. "The clock starts now."

The waiter sprinted off into the restaurant.

Mireya pulled her two-way radio out of her pack, turned it on, clipped it to her shirt pocket, and ran the earphone under her jacket to her ear. She took her camera out and attached a telephoto lens. She put her backpack on and slung the camera over her shoulder just as the waiter returned. She checked her watch.

"Pretty fast." She handed him the twenty, threw four more on the table, and left the café.

Chapter 62

Gary had no trouble walking at a pace that kept him within fifty feet of the van. Just as Mireya predicted, it turned left and headed to the MacMillan Wharf parking lot. The lot was almost full as Saturday night revelers flocked to Provincetown's many clubs and cabarets. Gary hung back and watched as the van cruised up and down looking for an empty spot.

Once the two men parked and left the van, Gary chose a path that would intercept them face-to-face. As he walked toward them, he noticed the boots, beard, and leather vest on the big guy. This could definitely be the one who was seen on the playground. The other one was shorter, slender, and well dressed. Gary wanted to see the snake-shaped ring on his hand, but the man was walking with his hands in his pockets.

Gary was closing the distance. He could see their faces clearly. *Bastards! These are the bastards who took my baby!* Every fiber of his being raged. He wanted to snap the neck of the little one and rip the lungs out of the big one. He had always been a nonviolent person, but he was taller, and just as strong as the biker, and he had the advantage of all the adrenaline that accompanied a father's fury. Mireya made a mistake sending him to do this alone. He was going to blow it.

He had to keep his goal in front of his rage. If he hurt them, they wouldn't lead him to Sandra. He had to find her. He shoved his clenched fists in his pockets. He forced himself to observe their faces, while keeping Sandra's image in his mind. He strode directly at them and, as a concession to his rage, he made no move to the side to let them pass. He forced them to separate and pass on either side. The little one gave him an admiring smile as he passed. Gary nodded at him cordially, while choking back the desire to terminate his life.

He turned and leaned against a car, keys in hand as if he were looking for the right one. When they were a safe distance from him he took out his two-way radio and called Mireya.

Chapter 63

Mireya set off from the café at a brisk walk; by the time she reached the corner of Standish Street she had broken into a run. If the kidnappers were going to the A-House, they would walk down Commercial Street and turn right onto Masonic Place. It was the first building on the left. Her plan was to go down Bradford and approach it from the opposite direction. If she could get there ahead of them, she would find a place to hide and get their picture as they entered the building. *If she could get there ahead of them.*

She had just turned onto Bradford when Gary called her on the radio.

"Mireya."

She slowed to a walk. "I'm here. Did you get a good look at them? Where are they?"

"They just turned onto Commercial. One is a big guy dressed like a biker. He could very well be the one they saw on the playground. The other is short and slim. Very well dressed. Like a preppie. He had his hands in his pockets so I didn't get a look at the ring. Where are you?"

"I'm on Bradford."

"What are you doing on Bradford?"

"I'm going to get there ahead of them and get their picture before they enter the bar."

"Jesus! What if they see you?"

"They won't."

"Ok, but wait for me."

"Forget it. You're too far away. You'll never get here in time."

"I mean it, Mireya."

"So do I. Follow them and let me know when they get to Masonic so I can be ready."

"All right, but *please* be careful."

"Ten-four."

Mireya broke into a run again and sprinted the three blocks to Masonic Place. She slowed down as she turned the corner, hoping to catch her breath before they came into view. As she walked slowly down the street, she looked for a place to hide. After a brief deliberation, she squeezed behind some shrubbery next door to the A-House. With her back against the foundation of the house, and her telephoto lens resting at the level of the trimmed tops of the bushes, she was in a prime location to catch them coming down the street and entering the bar. She was closer than she needed to be and worried that if things were really quiet, they might hear her motor drive as she photographed them.

The Atlantic House was a large white eighteenth century wood-framed building in the Greek revival style, with a long covered porch across the front. An American flag flew from a pole mounted on the porch roof. The porch eaves and railings were festively but tastefully decorated with tiny lights. Old-fashioned pole lamps and wrought iron horse head hitching posts added to the historical feel.

"Mireya." Gary's voice over the radio was so loud and clear, she flinched as though others might hear it.

"I'm here," she whispered.

"They're just about to turn the corner."

"I'm ready."

"What do you want me to do?"

"Nothing. Just hang out on the corner, and I'll meet you after they're inside."

"OK."

She checked the settings on her camera, then zoomed in on the two figures walking down the street. They were already in range. She tried to bring their faces into focus. Damn! They were backlit by the street light, casting their faces in shadow. She would wait until they walked by the pole lamps, which hopefully would provide enough illumination for some good pictures. She held her breath and waited for the right moment. The big guy was walking slightly ahead of the other. As he entered the circle of light, he was looking down at the ground and talking. She depressed the shutter and clicked off several frames, aware that she was getting only a partial profile.

She refocused on the second man. As he walked past the pole light, he grabbed it with his right hand and stopped. He was obviously replying to his partner, but his head was turned and he was looking back down the street. She quickly zoomed in on his hand. He was wearing the ring! She focused and clicked off three or four shots. She backed off on the telephoto just as he turned his head and looked straight into her camera. She captured his face on several frames before he moved past the light and entered the bar with his friend.

She leaned back, exhaled, and wondered how long she had been holding her breath.

"Gary." Mireya whispered into the microphone.

"Here."

"They've gone inside. I'm going to wait until it's clear, then I'll meet you on the corner."

"Ten-four."

She waited for another small group of men to wander down the street and enter the bar, and then she slipped out from behind the bushes, dusted herself off, and walked to the corner.

Gary was waiting. "Rey! Thank God. I'm a nervous wreck."

"When are you going to get it through your head that this is what I do, practically every day of my life? No big deal."

"Really. You sneak around photographing murderers every day?"

"You know what I mean."

"So what happened? Did you get some good shots?"

"I got beautiful face-front shots of the short one. *And* I got a close-up of the ring. The other one was looking down at the ground and I only got a partial profile."

"Damn! That's the one the playground monitors might be able to identify."

"Don't worry. We're going to follow them when they get back to their car. We'll get another opportunity. I'm sure of it.

"Meanwhile, if I hurry down the street, I can get this roll of film developed at the one-hour photo. That will give us something to do while we're waiting for the party boys to emerge."

"Let's go."

"You go back to the car and wait," she said as she handed him the keys. "Just in case they go back to the van early. If you spot them, call me on the radio and I'll run back and intercept you on your way out of town."

"How is it that you have this so figured out?"

"Nevermind. Just go. If I don't hurry I won't be able to get my film in on time." She turned and jogged down the street, leaving Gary to stare after her.

Chapter 64

Gary walked slowly back to the car. He should be skipping and leaping for joy. They had actually succeeded in finding Sandra's abductors, and would soon follow them to her. They had photographs. He had memorized the license plate of their vehicle. These guys were toast just as soon as they gave up Sandra's location. So why was he so worried?

So far this whole endeavor had been a cakewalk, at least for him. Mireya had uncovered the clues and had called all the shots. She seemed to know inherently what would constitute the best and most expedient course of action. So far he was just a bystander. She, on the other hand, could have a promising future as a police detective. Why did he have such an unsettled feeling?

He had still not answered this question when he arrived at the car. He unlocked it, climbed into the passenger seat, and twisted sideways so that he could keep an eye on the van. This wasn't the best spot for surveillance. If it weren't for the roof racks, he wouldn't even be able to see the van, let alone see anyone approach it. He wouldn't know it was leaving until the roof racks disappeared.

He could see Mireya coming toward the car, walking erect, with long determined strides. Her eyes swept the parking lot from one side to the other, missing nothing. Gina had told him that she was on a mission. They both were. He was focused only on the success of this mission, on rescuing his daughter. He hadn't thought about how all of this was going to affect Mireya.

How was he going to explain this to the police without involving her? How could he possibly have found his way to Cape Cod and to these men without evidence beyond what the police had access to? Would the fact that he hadn't shared his information with the police be considered obstruction of justice? And what if he had shared? Would they have taken Mireya seriously? Doubtful. He probably wouldn't have either if he hadn't been desperate.

Mireya opened the driver's side door and got in.

"We have to move the car. We can't really observe the van from here. There's an empty spot near the entrance if we hurry." She started the engine, pulled the car out of its slot and sped down the lane, taking the corner so fast the tires squealed. Gary grabbed the dash for support.

"Jeez, Mireya!"

She floored it and Gary froze when he realized that she was facing down another car head on. He saw the parking spot she was heading for. It was on the end of a lane and just two rows from the entrance. No doubt, the other car was intending to park there as well. Without taking her foot off the gas, she laid on the horn and at the last moment, veered into the spot, slammed on her brakes, and skidded to a halt inches from the car parked in the opposing spot.

The smell of rubber hung in the air, and the occupants of the other car shouted and made obscene gestures before resuming their search.

Who could blame them? He thanked God that they were women and not likely to start a fistfight.

Mireya waited until they were gone before backing out of the spot again. She executed a perfect three-point turn and backed into the spot so the car was facing out. Now they could see the van, though still only the roof, by just looking through the windshield.

She killed the engine and leaned back in her seat.

"There. Now they have to walk right by us to get to their van and drive right by us to leave."

"You're certifiable."

"Hey! There might not have been another available space all night. And now at least you understand why we didn't take your car."

"I really don't think the car has anything to do with it."

"Never mind. We have to decide who's going to take the first watch."

"It doesn't matter. What about the pictures?"

"They close earlier during the off season, and I couldn't talk them into staying late for me." She took the roll out of her pocket and popped it into the glove compartment.

"It's not important. We both know what they look like now."

"Right. So who's taking the first watch?"

"I will," Gary sighed. "With all the espresso I drank I wouldn't be able to sleep even if my daughter's freedom wasn't hanging in the balance."

"OK." She reclined her seat back as far as it would go and put a baseball cap over her face to shield her eyes from the streetlight. "By the way," she lifted the cap off her face as she talked. "You might want to duck when those girls go by."

"Jesus!" They were the occupants of the car they had just cut off. He immediately flattened out his seat. There was a loud click as Mireya depressed the button locking all the doors. After a minute he could hear the group of women talking and laughing as they went by. Thankfully, they ignored Mireya's car.

"Mireya."

"What?" she said from underneath the cap.

"What are we going to tell the police about all this?"

"Let's just find Sandra and worry about that later."

Chapter 65

Gary yawned and stretched. They had decided on three-hour shifts, but he saw no reason to wake Mireya as long as he wasn't sleepy. She must have been very tired; he could tell from her breathing that she fell asleep immediately and remained asleep the entire evening, in spite of the espresso.

It was after midnight, and finally more people were returning to the parking lot than arriving. He observed that there was certainly no shortage of party animals in Provincetown.

Another wave of revelers was returning to the lot. There were two young men walking arm-in-arm, followed by a large group of what looked like teenage girls and boys, although judging from their level of intoxication, some of them must have been of legal age. It was a rowdy bunch, flaunting a wide array of creatively pierced body parts, wearing leather and chains, and displaying outlandishly styled hair in all the colors of the rainbow. The pair appearing most normal in this wave was a Rastafarian-looking fellow with his arm around a voluptuous black woman who wore a long tropical print skirt and a scarf fastened tightly around her head like a chemotherapy patient hiding her hair loss. This town was nothing if not entertaining.

Gary relaxed in his seat and let his mind wander back to the events of the last few days. He would never have believed that his life could take such a bizarre turn. He thought about his last conversation with Sandra, how she'd laughed when he told her about falling in the lake. He would love to hear what her unbiased child's mind would think of Mireya. He smiled at the thought.

The sound of laughter brought him back to the present. A group of four men was almost abreast of their car. Gary reached out and touched Mireya's arm. She woke up immediately and without being startled. She took the cap off her face and put it on her head as she brought her seat back to the upright position.

"It's them," she said, though she never looked directly at them. "They've picked up some friends. Let's see where they're headed."

"Maybe you should start the car."

Mireya looked at him in disbelief. "Relax. We'll follow them from a safe distance. Let's hope they take the van and not whatever their friends are driving. It's so easy to spot."

They watched as the group meandered through the parking lot, laughing and talking. At one point the biker and one of the new friends started pushing the small guy back and forth between them until he lost his balance and the biker had to catch him and set him back up on his feet. For some reason they all found this hilariously funny.

Their slow progress toward their vehicle was painful for Gary to watch. He clutched his knees with his hands, knuckles white, wanting to scream. He looked over at Mireya. She was dead calm.

"Oh no," she said. "They're turning one lane early." She reached into the back and grabbed her field glasses. "Maybe it's

OK…No…They're not cutting through to the van." She kept the glasses trained on the men until they stopped next to a car.

Gary was leaning so far forward his face was inches from the windshield.

"Gary, you're obstructing my view."

"Sorry." He leaned back reluctantly.

"Ok. They've opened the door. It's a light colored sedan. Nondescript…Like a Camry."

"Will you stop taking shots at my car?"

Mireya smiled. "They're taking something out of the trunk. Two of them are carrying it. I think it's a cooler."

"Are they going to have a tailgate party here on MacMillan Wharf?"

"Now they're taking something out of the back seat. I can't tell what it is. They don't seem to be getting into the car; in fact, I think they're walking away. They're going back to the van. Great!" She put down the glasses. "That'll make it easier to follow them."

The men took a long time to stow their gear in the van, but finally Gary and Mireya saw the roof racks move as the van backed slowly out of the parking space. Mireya waited until the van passed them, then she started the engine and pulled cautiously out of her space. She didn't turn on the headlights until they were out of the parking lot and almost to Commercial Street. The van had already crossed Commercial and was on its way to Bradford.

"Don't lose them, Mireya."

"No worries. For all intents and purposes, there's only one way into town and one way out."

As they crossed Commercial, they could see the van up ahead, turning right onto Bradford.

"See? I told you."

When they turned onto Bradford two cars were between them and the van. Perfect. Mireya relaxed and cruised along, exuding confidence.

Gary still had a white-knuckled grip on each knee.

Soon after they crossed the Truro town line, the van pulled over at a row of dilapidated cottages lining both sides of the road. The two new guys got out and ran into the rental office.

Mireya immediately pulled off to the other side of the road and turned off her lights. "I guess they're renting a cottage. What would you call that? A *ménage a quarte*?"

Gary just shook his head. "I thought college was a party. Our campus was like an Amish settlement compared to this town."

A few minutes later the new guys came out with a key and climbed back into the van. The van pulled back out onto the road and made its way down the row of cottages.

"Aren't you going to go?"

Mireya covered her eyes with one of her hands and leaned back against the headrest.

"Mireya?"

"They rented a cottage, Gary. Let's just wait here and see which one."

The van paused in front of a cottage and then pulled into the tiny driveway. All the doors of the van opened and the men piled out, laughing and shouting. They unloaded the cooler and some other gear and brought it into the cottage.

Mireya waited until she figured they were all permanently inside, then drove slowly past, making note of the number on the unit directly across the street. She went a little farther, turned around, and drove back to the rental office.

"Go inside and rent number eight. Say it has to be eight for sentimental reasons or something. We can watch them from across the street."

"You got it." Gary hopped out of the car, glad to have something to do.

He entered the rental office, which was just as shabby inside as it was outside.

The rental clerk, wearing a beer-stained T-shirt and sporting a three-day growth of beard, was nipping on a bottle of cheap bourbon and watching a small color TV with a built in VCR. Gary thought he got a glimpse of an X-rated movie before the clerk snapped the TV off. He stood up, turned in Gary's direction, and leaned heavily on the counter.

"Hello. I know it's late, but is it possible to rent number eight for the night?"

The clerk answered in a voice that was wheezy and labored. "You might not wan number eight. Bunch of gay boys jus rented the one cross the street. They looks like a noisy bunch."

"It has to be number eight. My wife and I happened to be on the Cape on business today, and we drove all the way up here because on our very first date we ended up in number eight. Know what I mean?"

The clerk stroked his chin a few times. "So eight's your lucky number, izzat what you're sayin?"

"Well, it sure was that night. Who knows?"

"Ezzackly. No problem." He handed Gary a form to fill out, and Gary paid for one night in cash. He handed Gary the key. "Hey, sweet dreams to you and the missus."

"Thanks." Gary smiled and left the office.

As he climbed into the Range Rover he held up the key for Mireya to see. "Number eight."

Mireya drove down to the cottage and backed into its parking space. Sounds of a party in progress emanated from the cottage across the street. They brought their overnight bags and photographic equipment into the cottage. There were two beds, one double and one twin, a pathetic excuse for a kitchenette along one wall, and a nasty spider-filled bathroom.

"Home sweet home," Mireya said. "You can have the big bed. I'll take the first watch."

Chapter 66

Mireya sat in a chair by the window, her feet up on the night table, eating a yogurt. Gary was sound asleep. She had kept the vigil until about four-thirty, when Gary relieved her. Because of the long nap she took in the car, she found herself wide-awake again at seven and convinced Gary to go back to bed. She knew he was exhausted and running on nervous adrenaline.

The cottage across the street had been rockin' and rollin' until about three-thirty in the morning. If none of them had jobs to go to, there was no telling how late they would sleep in. She looked at her watch. It was five minutes past eight.

She tilted the chair onto its two back legs and gazed out the window. A soft breeze carrying the smell of sea salt and the sound of waves lapping the shore filtered through the rusty screen. She closed her eyes and inhaled deeply, letting the salt air permeate her lungs. What in God's name was she doing here? How had she let herself get involved in this? What if she failed? Normally she would not give the loss or ruin of one human life the same level of importance as the loss of an entire species, therefore the consequences of her failure should be less in this case. She should feel *less* pressure. But it had become personal. Al Sullivan had retained her to find Connor. In his own way,

Connor had engaged her to find Sandra. She would entertain no more thoughts of failure.

Her sense of purpose remained strong. She was unwavering in her resolve. This was the day they would find Sandra.

As she imagined the perpetrators crawling from their beds in the cottage across the street, a dark shape began to take form in her mind. It took flight in her subconscious and winged its way into the forefront of her thoughts. She opened her eyes and raised her field glasses, scanning the skies for anything unusual.

After several minutes of observing nothing but gulls, she slowly lowered the glasses. She paused as they passed over a window in the cottage. She thought she saw a movement, but the curtains obscured her view. She focused and waited. Still nothing. She lowered the glasses a little more and a raptorous pair of eyes filled her field of vision.

"Ahhh!" Her feet fell off the night table, sending her chair forward onto all four legs. The field glasses clattered to the floor.

Gary sat bolt upright. "What is it?" he said, though he was not yet awake.

Mireya stared out the window at a large turkey buzzard that was perched on a bush just a few feet away.

"It's them!" Gary said, peeking over her shoulder.

Mireya snapped her attention back to the cottage. The two men were coming out the front door. Mireya grabbed her camera and took several shots of them as they climbed into their van.

Gary was across the room in two strides with his hand on the door.

"Wait! Not yet! They'll see you!"

Gary turned toward her and waited, his hand still on the knob.

Mireya watched as the van backed out of the driveway and turned south. "OK. Go."

Gary was out of the house in a shot. He loaded their bags into the Range Rover and they were in pursuit before the van got out of sight.

As she pulled out of the drive, she contemplated the empty bush outside the window of number eight and began to recite softly.

"Mountains loom upon the path we take;
Yonder peak now rises sharp and clear.
Behold! It stands with its head uplifted,
Thither we go since our way lies there."

"What do you call that?" Gary asked.

"A premonition."

Chapter 67

They followed the old van as it wandered down Route 6A and into Truro. Mireya kept her distance, piloting the Range Rover with relaxed confidence. Gary maintained a white-knuckled silence.

The van made a sharp left and parked in front of Dutra's Market, a small two-story wooden structure that housed the town's oldest deli/grocery store. While Mireya waited for several oncoming cars to pass, the two men left the van and entered the market. When traffic cleared, she made the left turn and squeezed the Range Rover into the last remaining spot in front of the store, just one car away from the van. She opened her door.

"What the hell are you doing?" Gary hissed through clenched teeth.

"Getting us some coffee."

"You can't go in there!"

"They don't know me. I'm just some tourist after a couple coffees. Put your sunglasses on and pretend to study this map. How do you want your coffee?"

"These guys are murderers! I should go in."

"No way. You're too twitchy. I'll interpret that comment as chivalrous rather than chauvinistic, but I'm still going to handle it."

"Twitchy?"

"Right. You're definitely not relaxed enough to pass for a guy on vacation…your coffee?"

"Black…Shit." He leaned back in his seat and flexed the fingers of both hands. "Be careful."

"No sweat." She donned her baseball cap, put on her sunglasses and climbed the steps to the entrance. Once inside the tiny market, she didn't have to look around to locate the two hung-over party boys. They were standing right in front of her, looking like they'd been rode hard and put away wet. She moved over one aisle and pretended to examine a display of Entenmann's pastries.

The big guy was leaning against the wall with his eyes shut. His partner turned toward him and waved a small well-manicured hand in front of his bearded face. No response. He began snapping his fingers a few inches from the big guy's nose. "R-i-i-i-c-k. Hel-l-o-o-o."

Without opening his eyes, Rick silenced the snapping by grabbing and enclosing the entire offending hand in the palm of his.

"Ow-ow-ow-ow-ow. Stop!"

Rick opened his eyes and relaxed his grip. "Paul, you snap your fingers at me one more time I'm gonna break your hand," he threatened, dropping Paul's hand.

"OK already!" Paul shook his squashed hand and flexed his fingers. "Get out the list."

Rick dug a crumpled piece of paper out of his pocket. "Teddy Grahams?"

"Got 'em. Two boxes: one honey, one chocolate. What else?" They began to move toward the back of the store. Mireya moved with them and went to the coffee machine in the corner. She poured two coffees.

"Decaf coffee, milk, orange juice, some of those Stouffer's frozen dinners, breakfast pastry…and Puppy Chow."

"More Puppy Chow? How much can a puppy eat?"

"That was just a sample bag we got with her. Maybe we should get some Milk Bones, too. She likes to give her treats."

"Good idea. God! I feel like my head is going to explode. I'll get us some coffee."

Mireya capped her coffees and turned away from the machine just as Paul arrived. She took her coffee and her box of pastries up to the cashier.

"Do you have the *Globe*?" she asked the young woman behind the register.

"Behind you," she replied.

Mireya turned and grabbed a *Boston Globe* and a copy of the *Cape Cod Times*. She paid the cashier and returned to the car. She handed the coffees to Gary through the open window and got into the car.

"What took you so long?"

"I think they're shopping for her. That probably means that they're going to her."

"You heard them say something? What?"

"They were buying Teddy Grahams and Puppy Chow. I think they got her a puppy. One of them said, 'Lets get some Milk Bones. *She* likes to feed her treats.'"

“Oh, God.” Gary covered his face with his hands, a gesture that accentuated rather than hid his anxiety.

“I know their names. The big guy is Rick, and the small guy is Paul.”

“I’m almost afraid to hope.” Gary wiped his eyes.

The door of the market opened.

“Quick! Show me something on that map.”

Gary spread the map out on the dashboard and pointed to something. Mireya sipped her coffee and pretended to be following what he was saying. Rick and Paul put their groceries in the van and backed out. Mireya followed.

The van turned down North Pamet Road on the east side of Truro, with Mireya following at an inconspicuous distance. After about a mile, the van entered a private drive on the left. Mireya drove past the entrance and pulled over.

“What are you doing? You’re losing them!”

“This is it. We can’t just drive down that private driveway. We have to stash the car and go in on foot. There’s a youth hostel down the road. I’m going to park the car in the lot below the hostel and run back here. Hang out here and pretend to be a hiker looking at a map. I’ll be right back. Turn on your radio, and let me know if anything happens.”

Gary jumped out of the car with his pack and the map. Mireya continued down the road and parked the car in a small lot designated for those who were hiking the Cranberry Bog Trail across the street.

She grabbed her pack and got out of the car, stopping to hide the keys in the rear wheel well.

Gary paced back and forth in front of the private drive and looked nervously up and down the road. He breathed a sigh of relief when he caught sight of Mireya running toward him. She slowed to a walk as she approached.

"I hid the key in the place I showed you."

Gary nodded. "Let's go."

They jogged up the long private drive, ready to jump for cover at any moment. They had gone at least a half-mile when they saw their destination. They both stopped, awestruck.

The house was spectacularly located on a cliff overlooking the Atlantic Ocean. The land on either side rose sharply to hilltops high above the level of the house, shielding it from view of any other beachfront properties. The house was an interesting blend of old and new styles. Each end of the side they could see had a contemporary octagonal-shaped extension. The roof and siding were cedar shingles, weathered in the traditional Cape Cod style, and the entire circumference had a wraparound covered porch. The land at the back of the house sloped down to an old cranberry bog, which was now conservation land.

"How are we going to get close enough for pictures? There's absolutely no cover on either of those hills."

Mireya pointed to the hill on the south side of the house. "I'm pretty sure that's Bearberry Overlook, which is public land. If we go up there, and we're seen, they'll think we're hikers photographing birds or something."

"You sure?"

"Yeah. Pretty sure. I don't want to go all the way back to the road, though. Let's see if we can cut through the cranberry bog."

She stepped off the drive and started down the hill toward the bog.

Gary took one last look at the house and followed.

Fifteen minutes later they were climbing a narrow path that took them to the top of the hill on the south side of the house. Mireya stopped when she reached a wooden observation platform at the summit.

"Let's stop here a while and pretend we're having a picnic while we wait for some activity at the house. I'm hoping they'll come out on the porch." Mireya dropped her pack on the platform and took out her camera and telephoto lens.

"Can we?"

"What?" Mireya looked confused.

"Have a picnic."

"Are you hungry?"

"Starving."

"You're always starving."

Mireya opened her pack and took out the box of pastries she bought that morning. She also had a Ziploc bag full of granola bars and another one full of dried fruit. Gary took out a two-liter bottle of water and an assortment of candy bars.

"Is that really what you carry for food when you hike?"

"When I'm prepared, I usually have Slim Jims and Pringles as well."

She shook her head and opened one of the granola bars. Gary dove into the box of pastry.

"Apple strudel. Love it."

Chapter 68

For the next three hours they waited on the observation platform, lying out of sight on their backs. They would have appeared to be a carefree couple daydreaming away a spring morning. Gary was wound so tight Mireya distracted him by ascribing shapes to the puffy white clouds that floated overhead, while staying alert to any movement in the house below.

"Unicorn." Gary pointed overhead.

"How did you come up with that?"

"See the horn?"

"Well, OK, but where is the rest of the head?"

"It's all kind of connected to the rest of it. It has a tail. See?"

It looks more like a teddy bear wearing a birthday hat. See the little round ears?"

"No way. Why don't you communicate with it and ask it what it is?"

"I can't."

"No?"

"No way."

"Why not?"

"Because a teddy bear is not a real animal."

"It's not a teddy bear. It's a unicorn."

"And so you're saying that a unicorn *is* a real animal?"

"OK. Fine. Nevermind. I still think it's a unicorn."

"Hey. Somebody's on the porch." Mireya picked up the binoculars and took a look.

"I see him," Gary said. "Is it one of our guys?"

"No. It's a new guy." She put down the glasses. "Let's get closer." Mireya handed the glasses to Gary, put on her pack, and picked up her camera. She carefully moved toward the north side of the hill.

"Gary. Stand with your back to the house and look around with the binoculars. I'm going to use you as a blind."

"That's brilliant."

Gary stood, seeming to look the other way.

Mireya knelt in front of him, ready to shoot pictures of the house and its occupants from between his knees.

"OK. There's one of our gay boys." She clicked off a couple of frames. "And there's the other one with the new guy." She took several more shots.

"Where's Sandra? Come on…where is she? A door is opening…There she is…No, Gary, don't turn around! She's carrying a puppy." Mireya's motor drive clicked off several shots.

The new guy took Sandra off the porch to an area near the southeast corner of the house where the land was a little more level and a better place for them to play. He took a couple of puppy toys out of his pocket and tossed them on the ground.

"What's happening?" Gary asked. "How does she look?"

“She looks beautiful. Just rotate to your right a little. Perfect. OK, Sandra. Look at me. Just once…There you are.” Mireya engaged the motor drive for several frames. “We’re golden.”

She took the roll of film out of her camera, popped it into a plastic container, and handed it to Gary. “Here’s our evidence. Now all we have to do is call the police. Those pictures will be all we need to send our bad boys down the river.”

Mireya stowed her camera in her pack, stood up, and shouldered it again. They stood side-by-side for a moment, looking down at the little girl and the puppy, barely discernable with the naked eye. Mireya took out her cell phone and held it up triumphantly. “May I have the honor, Gary?”

“By all means.” He tossed the film up in the air with his left hand, caught it with his right hand, and stuffed it in his pocket. As he did, he stepped back off the trail and onto a large black racer snake that was sunning itself just off the trail. The panicked snake thrashed its five-foot long body wildly, striking Gary in the knee. He leapt away from the snake and slammed into Mireya, sending them both over the edge of the hill.

Gary’s fall was broken about a third of the way down by some low-growing shrubs, but Mireya kept tumbling all the way to the bottom. As Gary watched, horrified, the two men Mireya identified as Rick and Paul ran off the porch and headed in her direction. His heart began to pound like a trip hammer when he saw the gun in Rick’s hand.

Chapter 69

Gary remained perfectly still as he watched the events unfold below him. Mireya immediately began to run for cover toward the cranberry bog. She must have sprained her ankle in the fall because she was limping badly. He fought back the urge to run to her rescue. He would be no help to either of them if he were captured, too. The new guy took Sandra and the puppy back into the house. When Gary was sure that nobody had seen him, he climbed back up to the top of the hill and ran for the other end of the cranberry bog.

Rick and Paul had been gaining on Mireya when she disappeared into the bog. Gary prayed that her resourcefulness would not fail her now. Even if he got to her before she was captured, how was he going to eliminate the guy with the gun?

Mireya hit the boardwalk that cut through the middle of the bog at a dead run in spite of the pain shooting up from her ankle with every step. She was sure they were getting close enough to see her. Even if she could outrun the men, she couldn't outrun the gun.

She stopped, contemplating the depth of the bog below her. She squatted down, dropped gently into the water so as not to make a splash, and submerged herself just enough to get underneath the boardwalk. If she floated on her back, there was just enough clearance for her face to be out of the water. Thank God for her camouflage clothing.

Moments later, Rick and Paul ran past her on the boardwalk. They got all the way to the other side of the bog and stopped, confused. Gary was approaching from the other side. He heard their footsteps on the boardwalk and melted back into the tall reeds growing on the embankment, praying that Mireya was well hidden.

"How the hell could she get away?" Rick asked, brandishing his gun. "She was limping, and we were so close."

"I don't know. If she went off to the side we would be able to tell." Paul rested his chin on one fist and turned slowly in a circle. He tapped his temple with his index finger. "*Maybe* she wasn't injured at all. *Maybe* she just wanted us to think that. Like one of those mother pheasants with the broken wing act." He dropped one shoulder and trailed his arm behind him, imitating a bird with a broken wing. "Maybe there was someone else she didn't want us to see back there." He raised his eyebrows to emphasize his point.

Rick looked at him with a mixture of skepticism and exasperation. "Mother pheasant? Get the fuck outta here. Let's go back."

"Well, it was just a thought. At least I have some ideas. Some imagination."

"Yeah? Well imagine this!" Rick thrust his fist in Paul's face, his middle finger pointing to the sky.

Paul slapped it aside. "Tease."

They started walking down the boardwalk in the direction of the house. When they were out of sight, Gary called Mireya on his radio.

"Mireya! Rey! Do you hear me?"

Suddenly Gary's voice came over Mireya's radio. The fall must have unplugged her earphone, and his voice was coming over the speaker. The wet radio emitted a garbled, screeching sound. She desperately tried to turn the radio off. Too late. Rick and Paul were running toward her.

The next thing she heard was the unmistakable click of someone pulling the hammer back on a revolver. She was looking down the barrel of a gun pointed through a crack in the boardwalk, directly at her head.

"You wanna come outta there, or just stay there, like, forever?" Rick waggled the gun in her face.

Mireya quietly unclipped the radio from her pocket and let it sink into the bog. She eased herself out from underneath the boardwalk and climbed back up on it. She stood up and turned to face Rick.

He pointed the gun in the direction of the house. "Start walking."

Mireya started limping down the boardwalk.

Rick looked at Paul. "Some mother fuckin pheasant."

Chapter 70

Inside the beach house, Rick gestured toward the kitchen. Mireya stopped in the center of the room. Rick came up behind her and shoved her roughly toward the table. Caught off balance, she put too much weight on her injured ankle and collapsed onto the floor. "Shit," she muttered through clenched teeth.

"Don't be such a caveman!" Paul rushed over to Mireya and extended his hand. "Here. Put your weight on your good foot." He pulled her up enough to get her onto one of the chairs. He dragged another chair over in front of her. "You know, with this kind of an injury you should really elevate that leg, and…"

Rick cuffed him on the side of his head.

"SIT!" Rick pointed at a chair. Paul sat down, but there was no mistaking the disapproval and anxiety in his expression. Mireya took off her pack and sat back in her chair, fairly certain that she had identified the weak link in this chain of command.

The third man entered the kitchen. Rick turned toward him, gun still in hand.

"Hey!" he shouted, sidestepping out of the path of the gun. "Put that gun away before you shoot one of us."

"But I thought…"

"You aren't paid to think, you're paid to do as you're told! Now put the gun away!" He picked up Mireya's pack, put it on the table, and unzipped the top.

"So, do you want to explain to me just exactly…who are you?"

"Mireya Richardson. I'm a wildlife photographer."

He pulled the field glasses out of her pack and held them up in front of her. "Are you sure you're not a spy?"

"Well, you do have to find them before you can photograph them. Who are you?"

"I'm Norman." He began unloading photographic equipment from her pack.

"I write articles for *National Wildlife* magazine."

"And just what were you doing on our hill?"

"Petrels."

Norman took a plastic sleeve out of the bottom of the pack, examined it, and tossed it on the table. It contained an article from *National Wildlife* magazine written by Mireya Richardson. "What?"

"I was looking at petrels. They're sea birds. Not exactly endangered, but interesting. And that's not your hill. It's conservation land, open to the public. And so's the cranberry bog."

"So if you weren't doing anything wrong, why did you run?"

"What would you do if a guy looking like *that,*" she pointed at Rick, "was chasing you with a gun? There are a lot of psychos in the world."

"I see your point, but I have a problem. You may very well be a legitimate private citizen making legal use of public land, but now that my scary friend here has assaulted you at gunpoint, I can't very well let you go. Can I?"

Mireya shrugged her shoulders. "No hard feelings."

Norman laughed and paced to the end of the room and back, considering his options. He turned toward Rick and Paul. "You boneheads made this mess, and now you're going to clean it up." He walked over to the cabinets, opened a drawer, and tossed Rick a set of keys. "These are the keys to the boat. Take her out on Cape Cod Bay after dark and drop her in the ocean. And all this stuff, too. I don't want any evidence laying around."

Paul jumped up from his chair, aghast. "That is *way* harsh, don't you think? I mean, what is she guilty of? Being a klutz?"

Rick pointed to Paul's chair. "SIT!...AND SHUT...THE FUCK...UP!"

Paul sat down, folded his arms across his chest, and turned his head away from Rick.

Norman reached into his pocket and tossed another set of keys to Rick. "I want you to take my rental car. That junky van attracts too much attention. I don't know why you didn't rent a vehicle like I asked you to. And lose the leather." Norman pointed to Rick's vest. "Cover up those tattoos and try to blend in for God's sake. Now get the hell out of here!"

Paul got up and carefully repacked Mireya's equipment.

Mireya made eye contact with him and smiled. She wondered where Gary was, but wasn't counting on outside intervention. If she were going to find a way out of this, she would have to rely on herself. Right now her instincts told her that Paul might not have the resolve to go through with this plan. She would have to do everything she could to get him on her side.

Chapter 71

"Where are you, Rey? Mireya!" Gary ripped the earpiece out of his ear and threw it on the ground. "Shit!" She must have lost her radio when she fell. He had heard the sound of running footsteps on the boardwalk and hoped it didn't mean they found her. He circled back toward the house, staying low on the hill.

His heart sank when he saw the two men taking Mireya up to the house at gunpoint. What he needed was a cell phone. His was dead. Mireya had kept hers hooked up to the charger in the car, and he hadn't thought to charge his in the cottage last night. Damn! Mireya's phone was probably at the bottom of the hill where she landed.

These guys knew what they were doing when they chose this place as a hideout. The house had a commanding view of the surrounding terrain, and he had no doubt that they would be watching everything now. It seemed like it took forever, but he crept as close as he could, using the low, scrubby bushes as cover. He took his compact field glasses out of his pack. They weren't nearly as good as Mireya's, and he was a lot farther away than they had been on the overlook, but at least he would be able to identify anyone who came out of the house.

He had been overjoyed to see his daughter, unharmed, playing with a puppy, and then horrified to see her captor chasing Mireya with a gun. What the hell was going on here? He wanted to go for the police, but was terrified that the men might move Sandra and Mireya to a new location after he left and he would lose them forever. His indecision determined his course of action. He waited.

With every moment that passed, his anxiety mounted. He thought of running to the youth hostel, which was the closest building to his location if he used the Cranberry Bog Trail, but his own experience with establishments of this type warned him that there may not be a phone, and it was off season so there might not be any occupants with a cell phone. He couldn't afford to waste time on something that wasn't a sure bet.

The rest of the houses on this street were large and secluded, and very possibly second residences for wealthy people who may not be living there in May. He had to think of some way to get help without losing track of the girls.

What were they doing to Mireya? He was sure she would play dumb, the innocent wildlife photographer taking pictures of birds. She stepped on a snake, lost her balance, and fell down the hill. She had all her photographic gear with her. The story would hold. They must be pretty *twitchy*, as Rey would say, or they wouldn't have chased her with a gun. They couldn't very well just let her go now.

He took his handkerchief out of his pocket and wiped the sweat off his face and hands. When he put his binoculars back up to his eyes, he saw people coming out onto the porch. It was Mireya, Paul, and Rick. Mireya limped down the porch stairs.. Paul seemed to be helping her.

They walked down the driveway to a flat area below the house where the cars were parked. Paul opened the door to the backseat of a white Lincoln Towncar, and Mireya got in after a few awkward maneuvers. Her hands were tied behind her back! So much for the possibility that they were taking her to the doctor or giving her a ride back to her car. They had already killed one woman who had seen Sandra. He was not about to let her be next.

He backpedaled out of his hiding place and crawled down the hill like a Marine on an obstacle course. When he felt he was safely out of sight, he made a run for it. Thank God he actually did study the maps Mireya had given him. He sprinted up the Cranberry Bog Trail and across the street to the parking lot.

Moments later he was driving up North Pamet Road. He slowed down as he passed the entrance to the private drive. Was he in time? Were they in front of him or still on the drive? His question was answered when just as he was about to move out of sight, a large white Lincoln pulled out onto the road behind him. This was an incredible stroke of luck.

He drove slowly, hoping that Mireya would recognize her car in front of them. He put on his sunglasses and her baseball cap. When he got close to the intersection of Route 6, he pulled over and opened his cell phone, pretending to make a call. As the Lincoln drove by, he turned and tried to look into the backseat of the big sedan. Its tinted windows made it impossible for him to see her, but if she were looking, she got a good look at him.

The Lincoln turned south onto Route 6, in the direction of Wellfleet. Gary followed, keeping his distance. About a mile past the town line, they made a right. Gary noticed a sign with an arrow indicating that this was the way to Wellfleet Harbor. Another mile and they had reached their destination, the parking lot for the town pier. The Lincoln continued to the end of the pier and parked in front of a slip where a large cabin cruiser was docked.

Gary parked near the entrance. He had no need to get closer as there were only about a half dozen other vehicles in a lot designed to hold a few hundred cars.

Now what? If they took off in that boat, there would be nothing he could do. He watched as Paul helped Mireya out of the car. They walked single file, keeping her between them, no doubt so that she couldn't make a run for it, and to hide the fact that her hands were bound behind her. They went down a narrow ramp to a long, floating dock to which all the boats were tied. They boarded the cabin cruiser and took Mireya below.

Gary scanned the businesses in the vicinity. There were two restaurants, The Harbor Grill and Captain Higgins Seafood, both closed. Another small building had four giant letters affixed to the roof: W.H.A.T. He had no idea *what* that was. A radio station? The building looked deserted. Wellfleet Marine Services was the only viable possibility. The boats were all stacked up and covered, so renting one was probably out of the question. The service end of the building was closed, but the small convenience store on the other end of the building appeared to be open for business.

There was no activity on the boat. Maybe they weren't in a hurry to go anywhere and were just hiding. He waited for a long time, praying that a police officer would cruise by, doing routine surveillance. When he couldn't wait any longer, he walked to the store. It was empty except for the teenage girl behind the cash register.

"Do you have a pay phone?" Gary asked.

"No. Sorry. No phone at all. I usually use the phone in the repair shop, but it's closed on Sundays and I forgot my cell phone."

"If I give you my phone and charger, could you plug it in for a while? I'll pay you for your trouble."

"Sure. No problem."

Gary went back to the car, dug his charger out of his duffle bag, and returned to the store. He connected it to his phone and set it on the counter. "Thanks. You have no idea how much I appreciate this."

"You're welcome."

"Maybe I can make a call while it's plugged in?"

"Maybe, but I usually have to go out in the parking lot in order to get a signal." She flipped open his phone and showed it to him. The no service indicator flashed on the screen.

"That figures. I'll be back in a little while."

Gary moved the car a little closer to the boat. He parked behind a small pick-up truck, which gave him some cover but didn't obstruct his view. He decided to wait another half hour, then retrieve his phone. He leaned back in his seat and tried to dredge up some of the patience that had seemed to come so easily to Mireya. He adjusted the back of her baseball cap so that it would fit him more comfortably. When he looked up again, Paul was out on the deck.

Chapter 72

Paul helped Mireya down the steep stairs into the boat's cabin. Her ankle was extremely swollen. She slid behind the cabin's table and put her foot up on the bench. Paul took a paring knife out of a drawer and cut the cord that bound Mireya's wrists, then went to the fridge and took a tray of ice cubes out of the freezer compartment.

"What the hell do you think you're doin?"

"I'm getting some ice for her ankle. It's very swollen, and she shouldn't have been walking on it."

"Forget her ankle."

"I will *not*. You know I'm opposed to suffering."

"In just a short while, her suffering will be over."

"This thing has gone *way* over the top. We never agreed to murder anybody."

"You were the one who wanted to take this job in the first place, not me."

"That's because the deal was that nobody was to be hurt. Remember we said '*no harm, no foul*?' And now we're considering a second murder?" Paul wrapped the ice cubes in a towel and handed it to Mireya.

"Yeah, well, the first one was accidental."

"Oh. And that makes it OK? What about the second one?"

"Who gives a shit? We're up to our dicks in it now. If we don't drop her in the bay, these people are going to drop both of us in it."

"OK, fine. So how do we do it?"

"What?"

"Do we just cruise out into the middle of Cape Cod Bay and throw her over the side?"

"Shit no! She's probably a good swimmer. We have to tie her up."

"What if she floats?"

"Floats?"

"That's right. The human body has buoyancy. It's a scientific fact."

"Fuckin flamboyancy in your case."

"So?"

"So we tie somethin heavy to her."

"Like what?"

"I don't know. There must be somethin heavy around here. How about the anchor?"

"We can't use anything that belongs to the boat. What if it can be traced?"

"Oh." Rick stroked his beard a few times, thinking. "We have some time before it gets dark. You'll have to go to a store and buy somethin heavy. Or get a bag and fill it with heavy stuff like rocks…or bricks or somethin. And while you're out get me some beer…and some rope."

"I have to do all this while you sit here on your butt and do nothing?"

"Shopping is your department. And besides, I don't trust you to be alone with her."

"Fine." Paul left the cabin.

After Paul left, Rick bound Mireya's wrists and ankles with duct tape, then taped her wrists to a brass railing at the end of the bench, above her head. He secured her ankles to the railing at the other end. After inspecting his work, he disappeared into the forward cabin. She was still wearing her backpack and shifted her weight around in an unsuccessful attempt to find a comfortable position. She was running out of time.

She constantly wiggled and worked her wrists and ankles in an attempt to get out of her bonds but wasn't making much progress. Tying her ankles to the other end of the bench made it impossible for her to get her teeth to the tape on her wrists. If she got the opportunity, she would dive overboard and take her chances in the bay. Rick was right on when he told Paul she was probably a good swimmer. A mile or even more in the water would be possible barring unforeseen complications.

Mireya's ankle was throbbing in spite of the ice. She struggled against the tape on her wrists and cursed her luck. If she'd been left alone with Paul she might have talked her way out of this.

Chapter 73

Gary slid down in his seat a little, his attention riveted on Paul. He reached into his duffle bag, took out a bottle of fruit-flavored Tums, and popped four in his mouth.

He would never again try to identify with the macho male heroes of action films. The calm bravado with which the likes of Bruce Willis, Mel Gibson, and Tom Cruise faced life and death situations involving family and loved ones was obviously not within the realm of his genetic make-up. He couldn't even spy on these criminals without feeling like his stomach resided just below his ears. Just once he'd like to go to a movie and see Bruce Willis jump out in front of a perpetrator, pull his gun out, and throw up. Now *that* would be reality.

Paul was walking briskly toward the little convenience store where Gary had left his phone; his face looked tense and angry. When he was well past the Range Rover, Gary got out, shrugged on his backpack, and followed. He had no idea what he was going to do but hoped a plan would come to him before Paul left the store.

Gary reached the entrance and had his hand on the doorknob when he changed his mind about going in. He walked to the back of the building and inspected the small lot behind it. It was basically a graveyard for boats that were beyond repair, tossed aside in the hopes that some day a use would be found for their parts. A fairly new aluminum skiff lay upside down with a huge breach in its hull, no doubt from losing a close encounter with a rock.

Gary turned a complete circle, amazed at the total lack of human beings in a place that would be thronged with them in another month. Other than himself, Paul, and the cashier, there appeared to be no one else on the whole pier. He walked back up toward the front of the building.

Paul came out of the store, letting the door slam behind him. He glanced over his shoulder at Gary, who reached for the door as if he was going in. Instead, he took two quick steps, clapped his left hand over Paul's mouth, picked him up off the ground with his right arm, and carried him to the back lot.

"You make a sound, and I'm going to break your scrawny neck with my bare hands."

Paul stopped struggling immediately. Gary found himself wishing the guy would give him a reason to hurt him. As if he didn't already have enough reasons. When they were around the corner of the building, Gary dropped Paul face down on the ground next to the skiff and pinned him there with a well-placed knee in the center of his back.

"The little girl you kidnapped is my daughter. If you want to live through the rest of this day, you'd better not make a sound." Gary took his hand away from Paul's mouth and took off his backpack. He pulled out his roll of duct tape, put a strip over Paul's mouth, and began tying him up with the coil of rope he always carried.

"My friends frequently make fun of the fact that I was a Boy Scout. But what we Eagle Scouts learn, *besides* how to help old ladies across the street, is how to tie about a hundred different knots.

"What you need to know about my *knots du jour*, is the more you struggle, the tighter they get. So, if you want to avoid a few hours of excruciating pain, just lie still, and when I get *both* of my girls back, I'll let someone know where to find you."

Gary stood up and inspected his work. Paul's wrists were tied behind his back and his ankles were tied together. A short length of rope connected his wrists and ankles, requiring that his knees remain bent. Gary added a few more strips of duct tape to Paul's mouth for good measure, picked up the transom of the skiff, rotated it a few feet, and put it back down on top of Paul.

Gary stopped to inspect the plastic bag that Paul dropped: a six-pack of beer, a bag of pretzels, and a hundred feet of lightweight cotton rope. He took the rope out, stuffed it in his pack, picked up both the pack and the bag, and entered the store.

"So how are we doing?" he asked the cashier.

She smiled, picked up the phone, and examined the display. "It's not fully charged, but you've got enough juice for a few calls."

"Great! You're a lifesaver." He took the phone and charger from her and left a five-dollar bill on the counter.

"Hey! You don't have to do that! Please!"

Gary waved at her on his way out the door. As he jogged back across the lot, he zipped the charger into a side pocket on his pack and put the pack back on. There was only one guy on the boat with Mireya now. Unfortunately he was the one with the gun.

He was just about to open his phone, when it rang. *Please don't let this be my family.*

"Hello."

"Gary. It's Blake. I just wanted to find out how you're doing. Any news on your daughter?"

"Actually, the police have a pretty good lead they're working on."

"Great! I just heard from Jim. He finished the visual on-site for you and says everything is good to go."

"How can that be? What did he say about the dumping?"

"What dumping?"

"I heard a rumor that the old Pine Point Power Company dumped coal ash on that land, and I suspect the lake and who knows what else may be contaminated. I'm sure Joan gave him all my notes about it. I was going to stay a few extra days and interview some former employees still in the area, but then Sandra disappeared. Whatever you do, don't green light this to Sund Oil without checking it out."

"What could he be thinking? We can't afford to be wrong about a twenty million dollar land purchase. Don't you worry about it though; I'll get to the bottom of it. I just wanted to wish you luck on finding your daughter."

"Thanks, Blake. I'm very optimistic."

"That's great. I'll call you after I straighten this out with Jim."

Gary snapped the phone shut.

"A twenty million dollar land deal. Twenty million dollars…Oh, shit!"

Gary opened his cell phone again and dialed. While it was ringing he saw Rick come out on the deck and look around. Gary crossed his fingers and silently prayed that Rick would leave the boat and search for Paul.

"Murphy."

"John. It's Gary."

"Where the hell have you been? We were about to report *you* missing."

"Look, John, I may not have much time so listen carefully. I think I know who took my daughter. I was doing an environmental site assessment on a piece of land in Minnesota owned by Nelson Paquette, Paquette Investments, Manhattan. I discovered evidence of some past toxic dumping that might kill the deal, and it's a twenty million dollar deal for Paquette.

Sandra disappeared just as I was about to investigate it, and the engineer who replaced me immediately made a positive report without following up on any of my findings. I believe Paquette is responsible for Sandra's disappearance. I think he's holding her at a beach house on North Pamet Road in Truro, on Cape Cod. Its land abuts a cranberry bog and Ballston Beach."

"You're sure she's there?"

"I've seen her."

"Jesus, Gary. How did you come up with all this?"

Shifting his gaze back to the boat, Gary noticed that Rick was out on the deck again looking nervous.

"I don't have time for details now. Can you get her out of there?"

"I'll have a perimeter set up by local police inside fifteen minutes and State Police and SWAT on the scene in a half hour. If she's there we'll get her out safe."

From behind Mireya's car Gary thought he could see Rick untying one of the mooring lines. *He's leaving without Paul!*

"Shit! I have to go. Call me when you have her!"

He shoved his phone in his pocket and for a moment was frozen with indecision. He opened the back of Mireya's car. He had a life raft. A lot of good that would do. He needed a boat. Maybe he could steal one. On impulse he grabbed the case containing the flare gun, slammed the door, and ran for the dock.

Chapter 74

Gary didn't want to attract Rick's attention, so he took the ramp in the opposite direction of the one that led to the cabin cruiser. Most of the smaller boats were docked down there, and in his mind, smaller equaled easier to steal.

The first boat had no motor, the next two were padlocked, and the fourth was completely encased in a custom cover. He looked to the end of the dock and saw an elderly man untying a boat. A second man was approaching with a small cooler. A pile of fishing gear on the dock awaited stowing.

Gary accelerated in their direction and pulled his wallet out of his back pocket. He held it up, flashing his driver's license. Without slowing down he shouted, "Federal officer! I need your boat! Kidnapping in progress!" He grabbed the rope from the first man and leapt from the dock to the center of the boat, landing in a crouched position. Miraculously, he didn't lose his balance. His momentum pushed the boat several feet from the dock. He realized that he was still carrying Paul's bag of beer and pretzels and dropped it, the flare gun, and his wallet in the center of the boat. He fired up the little outboard with one pull, opened the throttle, made a 180-degree reverse, and powered away from the dock while the two men looked on in shocked disbelief.

The cabin cruiser was already away from the pier and heading out into Wellfleet Harbor. It was at this moment that he realized his error: He had commandeered a sixteen-foot aluminum rowboat with an eight-horsepower outboard motor to pursue a thirty-foot cabin cruiser that probably had a big three or four hundred-horsepower inboard motor. What could he have been thinking?

He could see Rick at the wheel. He was taking his time while in harbor waters, driving conservatively to avoid attracting any attention. Gary was running his little motor at full throttle and was almost able to keep pace with the big boat. But Gary knew that as soon as they left the harbor, the cruiser would accelerate and disappear into the horizon. And if the ocean was rough, he wasn't even sure he could keep the little boat from capsizing. His impulsively conceived plan was falling apart.

Wellfleet's harbor is deep and well protected from the open waters of Cape Cod Bay by a four-mile-long sandbar known as Great Island. The cabin cruiser would have to travel the entire length of Great Island and around Jeremy Point to reach the bay. The outermost mile of the sandbar is extremely narrow, and at high tide parts of it are partially submerged. Gary angled his boat toward the sandbar. It was close to high tide, and if he could find a place that was narrow enough, maybe he could get into the bay ahead of Rick. If Rick turned north after entering the bay, Gary could choose a course to intercept. If Rick turned south, or headed west, Gary would gain nothing, but this was his only chance.

He aimed the boat at the narrowest place he could see and made a run for it. At the last minute he shut off the motor and flipped it forward so that the propeller was out of the water. When the boat beached itself, Gary jumped out, grabbed the bow line, and began to haul the boat across about fifty feet of sand.

He made good progress until he hit a small ridge in the center of the sandbar. He threw all of his weight against the rope to no avail. He dropped the rope, ran to the back, lifted one side of the transom, and dragged the back of the boat up and over the ridge. He grabbed the rope again and started hauling it the final twenty feet to the water.

He leaned as far forward onto the rope as he could and drove himself forward. This was taking too much time! He let out a primal scream and lunged against the rope, his tired legs pumping double-time until he hit the water. He pushed the boat as far out into the surf as he could, then jumped in and fired up the motor.

He headed due west and scanned the water for the cruiser. Daylight was fading, and Rick had turned on the running lights. Gary could just make out the boat clearing Jeremy Point. "Go north, you sonofabitch, NORTH! You know there's way more traffic to the south so go north, you moron. NORTH!"

Gary kept the little boat heading west, running the motor wide open. The chop was much bigger out in the bay, and he and his boat were both taking a pounding. Within minutes Gary was soaked. He was fighting against the waves and trying to watch the cabin cruiser through his binoculars at the same time. The big boat began a gradual curve to the north. "YES!"

Gary turned the little boat slightly north, on a course to intercept. It was almost dark now, but that only made it easier to keep track of the cabin cruiser's lights. He was finally close enough that he didn't need to use the glasses. His phone rang. Sandra!

It was John Murphy. "Gary! Everyone is in place. We should have your little girl out of there very soon."

Gary had the phone pressed tightly to his ear to block out some of the noise. "THAT'S GREAT, JOHN! I NEED HELP!"

"Where the hell are you? I can hardly hear you!"

"I'M OUT ON CAPE COD BAY. IN A BOAT. A FRIEND WHO HELPED ME FIND SANDRA HAS BEEN TAKEN HOSTAGE BY ONE OF THE KIDNAPPERS. HE HAS A GUN. HE'S IN A BIG WHITE CABIN CRUISER WITH A BLUE CANOPY ON TOP. HE JUST TURNED NORTH OUT OF WELLFLEET HARBOR. I NEED THE COAST GUARD!"

"But where are *you*?"

"I BORROWED A BOAT, BUT IT'S TOO SMALL. I CAN'T KEEP UP. CALL THE COAST GUARD!

"JOHN?...JOHN!...SHIT!" Just as Gary threw the phone in the bottom of the boat, the motor began to sputter. A few seconds later it died. Gary pulled the cord a few times then picked up the gas tank. Empty. "SHIT! SHIT! THIS **CANNOT** BE HAPPENING!"

He shifted to the center of the boat and pulled the oars out from underneath the seats. He snapped them into the oarlocks and began to row. This was not a sleek racing shell on the mirror-like surface of the Charles. This was a clumsy rowboat, and he was fighting against three-foot waves in the open ocean. He didn't care. He would not give up! He pulled against the oars until his shoulders screamed for relief.

He suddenly realized that he could no longer hear the drone of the cabin cruiser's big engine. He glanced over his shoulder. The boat had stopped.

Chapter 75

Mireya heard the boat's powerful engine throttle back until it was idling. The boat quickly came to a stop. The waves were hitting the boat broadside, causing it to rock violently from side to side. If she weren't so focused on her dwindling chances for escape, she might have been nauseous.

She could hear Rick walking around on the deck. Before long he came down the cabin stairs. He was wearing his roll of duct tape like a bracelet and carrying the paring knife Paul had used in his teeth. It was a biker-turned-pirate look. He cut the tape that secured her ankles and wrists to the railings, put one arm around her waist and dragged her up the stairs to the deck.

As soon as Rick released her, Mireya locked both of her hands to form a fist and swung as hard as she could, hitting him solidly in the midsection. She lunged for the railing, but before she could haul herself overboard, he grabbed her pack and yanked her backward, slamming her up against the bulkhead. She blacked out for a moment. As she regained consciousness, the boat and Rick swimming in and out of focus, she closed her eyes and concentrated on a dark shape that hovered in the forefront of her mind. She opened her eyes, and the same image appeared before her. She inhaled sharply and slowly raised her hands, pointing at the starboard railing.

Rick turned and looked in that direction. "What the hell is that?"

"It's a turkey buzzard. They *never* fly at night and *never* over the water."

"So what the fuck's it doing here?"

"It's a warning."

"Of what?"

"I will sing a song of the sky.
Now this is the owl flying downward, circling, tired of all songs.
The salmon where the swift current moves circling, runs circling.
Their call is urgent.
The sky turns over.
They are calling for you."

"What the fuck does that mean?"

"It's a warning that you should not commit this sin that you are contemplating. You will suffer dire consequences."

"What are you, some kinda witch?"

"I'm a Navaho. This is a very powerful sign."

"Yeah, well, fuck your signs, and while you're at it, shut the fuck up or I'll tape your mouth shut!" He grabbed a wrench out of the open toolbox on the deck next to him and flung it at the bird. It was a narrow miss, but the buzzard flew off the railing and disappeared into the night.

Rick snapped the lid shut on the toolbox, took the roll of duct tape off his arm, and began to wrap strips of tape from the handle of the toolbox around the tape that already bound Mireya's ankles. When he'd attached several layers, he sat back to inspect his work. Unsatisfied, he took one of her bootlaces and wrapped that around the handle and between her ankles, tying it in a triple knot.

He stared down at the toolbox, conflict raging across his face. "I just want you to know I got nothin against you personally. If it were up to me I'd just let you go. I got no choice."

Mireya waited, hoping he would look at her. Finally, he lifted his head and his eyes met hers. "You *do* have a choice. There's *always* a choice."

Chapter 76

Gary pulled on the oars with every ounce of strength he could dredge up. He was roughly a hundred yards from the cabin cruiser. Every few strokes he glanced over his shoulder. He had seen Mireya lunge for the rail, and he had seen Rick grab her, preventing her escape. Mireya was sitting on the deck, slumped against the bulkhead. Had Rick injured her? He seemed preoccupied with her feet, but Gary couldn't make out what he was doing without dropping the oars and using his field glasses. He had to get there in time. He had no idea what he was going to do, but he had to get there.

He groaned with every pull on the oars. His back and shoulders screamed for mercy. Tears of anger, frustration, and exhaustion left their tracks on both cheeks. *She* was the reason that Sandra was safe. He could *not* let her down.

He glanced over his shoulder again. They were still sitting on the deck. Was she trying to talk him out of whatever he was planning? She was on a mission. She could be convincing. *Please buy us some time!*

He had closed the distance to about fifty yards. The incoming tide helped him by pushing the big boat in his direction. Rick still hadn't seen his little boat, thanks to the cloak of darkness. Rick had turned on all the exterior lights, illuminating them both clearly against the dark horizon. They were sitting right over the idling engine, and there was a strong onshore breeze so they probably wouldn't hear him as he approached. Just when he was beginning to think that he could pull alongside unnoticed, he saw Rick pick up Mireya and throw her over the side.

"YOU BASTARD!" he screamed as he watched Mireya disappear into the black waters of the bay.

Rick had already run to the wheel and jammed the throttle wide open. The big boat shot forward like a scared rabbit and in moments was gone from the scene.

"YOU STINKING SONOFABITCH!" Gary screamed at the disappearing boat as it pounded through the waves. It was already so far away Gary could barely make out Rick at the wheel. Without the big boat as a reference point, Gary was lost in the dark. He would never find the exact place where Mireya went over the side.

He rowed furiously for another minute and then stopped. He stood up, shucked his pack, and took out his flashlight, shining it into the water around the little boat. The futility of this action embarrassed him. Mireya had hit the water with something heavy tied to her feet and disappeared immediately. How deep was the water? Fifty feet? A hundred feet? As if it mattered.

He had failed her. She had given him back his world, his life, at the cost of her own. How would he ever come to terms with that? How would he ever forgive himself for this inadequate, ineffective excuse for a rescue?

Legs braced in a wide stance in the center of the rowboat as it rocked wildly in the surf, he turned his face to the starless sky. He screamed until he lost his voice.

"M – I – I – R – E – E – Y – A – A – A !!!"

Chapter 77

Mireya cried out when Rick picked her up and the weight of the toolbox against her restraints intensified the excruciating pain in her ankle. This could have been a fatal mistake. She might have been able to take two more deep breaths before hitting the water, which was shockingly cold. She tried to lay out horizontally, hitting the water in a reverse belly flop, hoping that it would delay the inevitable, but the toolbox was too heavy and yanked her under the surface immediately.

She began a rapid descent. It was cold and *so* dark. She immediately curled into a ball, bringing her knees to her chest. She felt for the clasps that secured the toolbox cover and unsnapped all three. She grabbed the bottom of the toolbox and pulled it wide open, jettisoning the tools. Her rate of descent slowed immediately. The pressure in her eardrums was so intense she thought they would burst.

How deep was she? She might be able to kick her way up to the surface with the empty toolbox still attached, but which way was up? She had been taught to follow her bubbles up, but it was so dark she couldn't see them. She would have to rely on the anchor effect of the toolbox to tell her which way was down. She straightened herself out and when she started moving downward, she kicked in the opposite direction.

She kicked with both legs together, mermaid fashion, and hoped that the open dangling toolbox would act a little more like a fin than an anchor. Every time she kicked she made a downward scooping motion with both hands. It was so dark she had no idea if she was making much progress, but vowed to keep it up until she ran out of air. It wouldn't be long.

She tilted her head up, hoping to see anything…the moon, a searchlight…anything that would show her the surface of the water. She was enveloped in utter and absolute darkness. She thought her head would split open from the pain in her ears. Still, she kicked.

She knew she was building up an oxygen deficit. Fatigue was setting in, and she was feeling lightheaded. She kicked on. The pain in her ears lessened. She was making progress, but her legs were beginning to weaken, and she had the overwhelming desire to inhale. She kept this desire at bay by letting out a few bubbles every so often, and kept kicking.

How much farther to the surface? No way to tell. She was on the verge of a blackout. She had emptied her lungs of every molecule of air, and she needed to breathe! Her arms were still working, but her legs had lost most of their strength. She had to breathe! She could no longer override her autonomic systems. She felt the salt water stinging her nasal passages.

Except for the temperature, she could be returning to the womb. This wasn't so bad. She was enveloped in a shroud of darkness, floating weightless, helpless, her arms and legs still trying to pump and kick like some involuntary reflex. She could allow her spirit to go. She could yield to the cosmos with no regrets, but her body stubbornly continued its feeble quest for survival.

Her head broke the surface of the water and she was immediately slapped back under by a breaking wave. She gave one last valiant kick and broke the surface again. She gasped for air, then immediately began to choke. She sunk back under the water, gathered her strength and broke the surface again, gasping and choking. She repeated this cycle at least a dozen times until she felt as though she had regained some of her mental and motor control.

She only had one chance. She had to rid herself of the toolbox that threatened to drag her back into the darkness. She curled herself up into a ball again, unsnapped a pocket on the right leg of her cargo pants and took out her survival tool. She kicked back up to the surface for another breath. Her hands were so cold she could barely close her fingers around the slender metal key to her survival, but she could not afford to drop it.

With great difficulty and much concentration she succeeded in prying open one of the attachments. It was the saw, not the knife blade, but it should work. She curled into a ball and went to work on the duct tape. The saw was sharp, and in a few moments her good ankle was free. She tried to kick to the surface, but her injured ankle was so damaged she didn't have the strength to move the toolbox through the water. She kicked hard with her good leg but only succeeded in sending her laceless boot to a watery grave.

She had to free herself of the toolbox. She curled up again and worked on the tape as she drifted slowly downward. She didn't know whether to damn that moron for using so many layers of tape or bless him for being so stupid as to tape only the handle to her legs. If he had put tape around the whole box, she would have been dead.

She sawed blindly in the dark, her bound wrists making the job cumbersome almost to the point of impossibility. Suddenly she felt the box break loose. She was free! She had drifted deeper than she thought and was almost out of air when she broke the surface again. Without the toolbox and bound ankles, she was able to tread water and keep her head above the surface. Cutting the tape around her wrists wasn't possible. They were bound together too tightly, and she was too weak to hold the saw in her teeth.

She concentrated on the shoulder straps that secured her backpack. If she could cut both of them, she could eliminate the weight of the pack. She had just begun working on the first one when she heard someone screaming her name.

Chapter 78

It was a primal scream, venting unbridled rage. She waited and listened. There it was again. She swam toward the sound in a kind of dogpaddle/sidestroke that was the most efficient technique she could manage with her bound wrists. The buoyant feeling she had experienced when first free of the toolbox was disappearing as the weight of the pack began to drag against her.

She heard the scream again. It was definitely her name, but the scream was losing strength, the rage trailing into grief-riddled anguish. It had to be Gary. He was the only one who would be out here looking for her, but she could not imagine such a sound emanating from the mild-mannered Boy Scout.

She continued to struggle in the direction of his voice. On the crest of a wave she caught sight of him, straddling the center seat of a tiny boat, illuminated only by the flashlight in his hand. She was amazed that he could remain standing as the boat pitched and rocked in the choppy seas. She tried to call out his name, but could summon only enough air from her lungs for a croaking whisper.

She had to reach the boat. She was too weak and had taken in too much seawater to make it to shore. The probability that hypothermia would play a negative role in her survival became more likely the longer she stayed in the water. She put her head down and kicked as hard as she could in Gary's direction, looking up only when she rode the crest of a wave so that she could check her progress and correct her course. Her progress was slow, but at least she was swimming parallel to the waves and not into them. She was closer now. Gary was silent, his head down, shoulders slumped, arms and flashlight hanging by his sides. She prayed she would get there before he decided to leave.

She could no longer hold her breath and kick, needing to gulp for air with almost every stroke. The weight of her pack was like an anchor on her back. She struggled along, only about twenty feet from the boat. She tried again to call his name. No sound passed her lips. A wave broke over her head and she swallowed more water, making her gag. She slipped below the surface. For a moment she drifted, summoning the strength to kick her way up again.

Gary was so close, but even if he had been facing in her direction she was enveloped in total darkness. Invisible. It took all of her concentration to keep her head above water. Her breath came in shallow, raspy, ineffective gasps that felt more like hiccups than inhalations. Gary reached down and picked up an oar. *No! You can't leave me!*

Mireya kicked and paddled and fought for air, so weak she could barely keep her face out of the water as she inched herself along. Gary was still holding the oar, leaning against it like a crutch. She was close now. Gary still had his back to her. She extended her arms as far as she could. Her fingertips brushed against cold metal. The next wave pushed her into the boat, her face and hands pressed up against the curve of the bow. She could no longer see Gary. When she reached up to grab the gunwale, she immediately sunk below the surface. Her legs were so weak that if she stopped paddling, she couldn't stay above water.

She was touching the side of the boat, three feet from Gary, and she was drowning. She had read that drowning was a quiet death. Now she understood why. She was an arm's length from safety, and she couldn't make a sound. The wind and the waves obscured whatever feeble noises she made as she struggled to keep her nose and mouth out of the water.

She made another desperate attempt to reach up over the gunwale. She felt her palms against the smooth metal, slowly sliding down the side of the boat as her head slipped under the water. She could no longer will her legs to move. Her arms were stretched above her head, her fingers unwilling to lose contact with the boat until the last possible moment. If Gary couldn't save her, she was at least glad that he would never know how close she was, that if he had just turned around, if his flashlight had just shone in her direction…

A large swell, much bigger than the others, lifted her upward. Her arms were still stretched above her head. She felt her hands sliding back up the metal side of the boat until her fingers curled around the gunwale. She had to hold on! The boat rocked back in the other direction and her head came out of the water. She gasped for air. She focused what little resources she had left on breathing and hanging on to the boat.

The wind had picked up, and the little boat was rocking wildly. She waited until it rocked toward her and lifted herself up so that her chin rested on her hands. Gary was now sitting with his back to her. She opened her mouth to call his name and succeeded only in vomiting seawater into the boat. He stood up and spun around at the sound. For a moment she was blinded as his flashlight shone directly in her eyes, then the light disappeared as Gary lost his balance and fell backward over the side.

Chapter 79

She would have smiled, had she been able, at the klutz who fell out of the boat. The important thing was that he had seen her. She was saved, if she could just hang on. She channeled all her determination to her fingers, willing them to keep their grip on the boat as it rocked wildly.

Moments later she felt a strong arm encircle her waist. Her fingers relinquished their grip on the boat as she slipped away from the conscious world.

Gary was simultaneously ecstatic and terrified. Mireya had not only survived, but had found him. She found him in this ridiculous excuse for a boat, on this vast bay, on a moonless, starless, pitch black night. She was unconscious, hypothermic, and from the tortured sound of her breath, he surmised that her grip on the world of the living was tenuous at best.

His immediate problem was how to get her into the boat. It would be impossible to lift her dead weight into the boat while he was still in the water, but how would he get back into the boat without letting her go? He understood why she was unable to shed the heavy pack. His knife was in his pack in the bottom of the boat, so he couldn't get it off her either. He had to secure her in some way so that he could climb into the boat. He considered the bow line, but was afraid that if he tied her to it she might slam her head into the bow when the boat rocked.

Her wrists were bound with several layers of duct tape. He lifted her arms and gently hooked that tape over the oarlock, then slowly let go of her. She was hanging by her wrists with her head well above water. When the boat rocked, her arms acted as a cushion between the side of the boat and her head.

He quickly moved to the opposite side of the boat. Her weight against the oarlock helped to stabilize the boat as he climbed in. He grabbed her backpack and her belt and hoisted her into the boat, setting her down in the section between the center seat and the bow. He propped her head up and slapped her cheeks.

"Mireya! Come on, Mireya. Wake up!"

Her eyelids fluttered, and as soon as her eyes opened, she grabbed the side of the boat and began to wretch, bringing up all the seawater she had swallowed. She leaned back into Gary's arms. She was shaking uncontrollably.

"Stay with me, Rey. We gotta get you out of here." He found his knife and cut the tape off her wrists. He removed her pack and propped it up behind her head. She was so cold and had lapsed back into unconsciousness. He had to find some way to warm her. He went through his pack, looking for anything that could provide or help retain heat. He found two pairs of dry socks in a large Ziploc bag, his plastic rain poncho, four chemical hand and foot warmer packets, and a towel, also enclosed in a Ziploc bag.

It wasn't much, but it was better than nothing. He carefully removed the boot from her injured foot and ankle. It was horribly swollen. He peeled off her wet socks and replaced them with a pair of his dry ones. Next he applied the adhesive strip on a foot warmer packet to the bottom of each foot and then covered them with his second pair of socks. He put each foot into a Ziploc bag, and closed it as tightly as possible.

Now what? What would a hospital do for a severely hypothermic patient? Probably wrap her in an electric blanket and warm her blood with a transfusion of heated saline or with a heart-lung machine. He thought he remembered seeing something like that on one of the many TV medical dramas. A lot of good that did him. His resources consisted of one dry towel and two chemical hand warmer packets. He shook the hand warmers until they started to produce heat, and then taped one to each side of her throat, over her jugular veins. He wrapped the dry towel around her neck and covered her with his rain poncho.

As he turned around to get into position for rowing, his foot kicked something out from under the seat. It was the flare gun. He opened the case to find a gun and four cartridges. What the hell. He took out the gun, inserted a cartridge and fired it straight up in the air, trying to be hopeful as he watched it light up the night sky. Maybe John had understood what he was saying and sent somebody out looking for them. Fat chance. He picked up the oars and started to row for shore.

Chapter 80

Gary was sure that he was making much faster progress rowing with the waves than he had against them, but he was too tired to turn around and search for landmarks. As long as he was headed for shore, he was satisfied. He would figure out where he was when he landed. His arms and shoulders were numb with pain, but he kept rowing stubbornly, woodenly, as if he were a machine rather than a man. Pain and exhaustion had sucked dry the passion and fury that had carried him across the Great Island sandbar and against the open ocean currents.

Gary had been unable to save Mireya from the bastard who threw her overboard, but somehow she had saved herself from drowning and in doing so had given him a second chance to help her. She was in desperate need of medical attention.

He stopped rowing long enough to shoot another flare into the air. While the burst of light momentarily vanquished the night, he pulled back the poncho and checked on Mireya. The phosphorescent illumination endowed her face with the pallor of a wax museum figure. Though her skin was warm under the towel, she was like ice everywhere else. Her lips and fingertips had a bluish cast. Her pulse was weak and slow; in fact, he couldn't even find a pulse on her wrist. Her chest rattled when she tried to breathe; her respirations were short, shallow, and infrequent. She had stopped the violent shivering, but her stillness scared him more. The flare could no longer restrain the night, and darkness enveloped them once again.

As Gary turned back to pick up his oars, a faint sound carried on the wind made him stop and listen. He turned his head slowly like a satellite seeking a weak signal. There it was again, louder now. He focused in the direction of the sound. Helicopter! He could just see its lights on the horizon. He grabbed the flare gun and launched another missile of light into the sky with a silent plea: *Please let this be the Coast Guard.*

The chopper was definitely coming in his direction. He pulled out his flashlight and began waving it. The sooner they located him, the faster he could get Mireya airlifted to the nearest hospital, and the sooner he would be reunited with his daughter.

What were only minutes seemed like hours, but finally the chopper was hovering directly overhead. A voice came over a loudspeaker. "This is the United States Coast Guard. Are you Gary Coakley?"

Gary nodded and waved. A man in a wet suit descended on a cable from the helicopter. When he was within reach, Gary grabbed his legs and guided him down into the boat. He immediately extended his hand. "Gary, I'm Tom Harper. We're going to get you out of here."

Gary shook Tom's hand. "I'm fine. You need to get *her* out of here." He pointed to Mireya. "She's severely hypothermic. She almost drowned."

"OK. Let's take a look." He moved to the middle of the boat and opened a medical kit. Gary held his flashlight on Mireya so Tom could check her vital signs.

He began to speak over his wireless headset. "We have a severely hypothermic female. Core temperature is eighty-six degrees, no radial pulse, carotid pulse is forty-five and weak. Send the basket down."

He turned to Gary. "We have everything we need to begin her rewarming in the chopper. We'll wrap her in a special blanket, start her on warm, humidified oxygen, and warm IV fluids. I'm very concerned about the seawater in her lungs. She needs to go straight to the hospital."

Gary nodded as he watched a large basket descend from the helicopter. "Do you know anything about my daughter?"

Tom spoke into his microphone again. "Do we have an update on the kidnapped girl?" He paused to listen. "They're going to check with the State Police." He stood up and grabbed the basket, setting it down across the center of the boat. "You steady the basket. I'll lift her in."

When Mireya was belted into the basket, Tom put his hand to his ear, listening. A smile stretched its way across his face. "The State Police have your daughter. They took her to the barracks in Yarmouth. She's eating ice cream, and she has a golden retriever puppy."

Gary collapsed onto the rear seat of the boat. Sandra was safe, and the responsibility for Mireya's rescue had been taken from him. He was immediately hit by a wave of exhaustion as he pulled the plug on the reservoir of adrenaline and fear that had been sustaining him for the last twenty-four hours. Tom was talking to him, but he could barely lift his head to respond. Tom was taking his pulse and his temperature. He was too tired to resist.

"Gary! You're soaking wet and slightly hypothermic yourself. Your core temperature is ninety-five. You should go to the hospital, too."

Gary shook his head slowly as he watched the basket carrying Mireya disappear into the helicopter. "No way. I need to see my daughter. I'll be fine."

Tom stared at him a moment, then talked into his microphone. "Where's the cutter?" He pressed his hand to his ear as he listened to the response. "OK. Send down a blanket." He turned to Gary. "A Coast Guard cutter is on its way. Be here in about five or ten minutes. They picked up a guy in a boat that matched the description you gave. They're going to pick us up and bring us into Wellfleet Harbor. They'll have dry clothes for you, and as soon as you warm up we'll take you to your daughter."

Gary nodded, too tired even to say thanks.

Chapter 81

Gary sat wrapped in a shiny space blanket on the rear seat of the boat. Tom sat in the center seat facing him, engaging him in conversation and making him drink warm, slightly fruity tasting liquid out of a thermos bottle. With Mireya safely on her way to the hospital, Gary wanted only two things: to see his daughter and to sleep.

He sat with his chin on his chest and mumbled answers to Tom's questions, too tired to lift his head. He drifted off, unable to focus on Tom's voice any longer. He was imagining Sandra eating ice cream and chattering on to a benevolent police officer who was holding her fluffy golden puppy. Suddenly, he joined them in the room. The police officer turned to look at him, put the puppy down, and started slapping his cheeks.

"Gary! Gary! Come on, buddy. Wake up." The police officer's face faded, and he was looking at Tom Harper. Next to the rowboat was a Coast Guard cutter, which from his low perspective could have been the Queen Mary. "Let's go, Gary. Can you stand up?"

Gary nodded. As much as he hated abandoning his daydream of Sandra, he knew that if he wanted to see her for real he had to get moving. He stood up, shrugged off the blanket, grabbed a rung on the ladder that the cutter had lowered for them, and slowly made his way up the side. At least two sets of hands pulled him up over the railing and steadied him as he stood on the deck. Tom was right behind him, wrapping the blanket around his shoulders again.

"OK, Gary. Let's get you below and into some dry clothes." Tom steered him toward a narrow stairway that led to the lower deck. One of the guardsmen went down in front of him, and Tom steadied him from behind. When he reached the floor, he was in a moderate-sized room that was obviously used as a dining and/or meeting room. There was a long table on one side and upholstered benches on the other. One wall held a large bulletin board and maps that could be pulled down. The warmth of the air in the room made him feel a little lightheaded.

The guardsman was motioning him toward a passageway behind the stairs. He felt Tom's hand on his shoulder. He was about to turn in the direction of the passageway when a door opened on the opposite end of the room. Through it walked Rick, in handcuffs, followed by another guardsman.

The sight of the man who had stolen his child and thrown Mireya to death's door sent a white-hot bolt of adrenaline surging through Gary. Moving so quickly the guardsmen were momentarily stunned, Gary crossed the room in three strides and landed a fist across Rick's nose that had all his strength, weight, momentum, and rage behind it. The sound of Rick's nose breaking reverberated through the room like a rifle shot. The strength of the blow sent Rick and the guardsman behind him sprawling back through the door and onto the floor.

Tom and the other guardsman sprang into action and pulled Gary back before he could do any more damage.

"LET ME GO! THAT'S THE SONOFABITCH THAT TOOK MY LITTLE GIRL!"

"Easy, Gary. You recognize the guy?"

Gary nodded. "It's him. Him and his wimpy friend. And he tried to kill Mireya."

Rick had struggled to his feet and held a bloodstained towel to his nose. "You're crazy! I'm charging you with assault."

"You're a kidnapper and a murderer!"

"I never kidnapped nobody. You got no proof."

"Really?" Gary reached into his pocket and pulled out one of the rolls of film Mireya took. He held it aloft in its little airtight case. We've been following you for days. We have pictures of you and your little friend at the house in Truro *with* my daughter. *And*, I saw you throw Mireya off the boat."

"That's bullshit. You didn't see nothing."

Tom interceded. "I'm sure we can get Mireya to identify him.

Rick glanced furtively back and forth between Gary and Tom. "I don't know anyone with that name."

"Whatever you say, pal. I'm sure she remembers you." Gary looked smug.

"I'm still filing assault charges against *you*!" Rick pointed at Gary.

"Why?" Tom asked.

"*Why?*... *Why?*... HE BROKE MY FUCKIN NOSE!"

"Really?" Tom asked. "Did anyone else see that?" He looked around the room. "Because I thought you did that resisting arrest. You know, when you fell down the stairs."

The other guardsmen nodded in agreement.

"THIS IS BULLSHIT! I DIDN'T FALL DOWN NO FUCKIN STAIRS!"

"Well, that's what the report is going to say. Let's go, Gary." Tom led Gary down the passageway to a small cabin. A sweatshirt, sweatpants, and socks were on the bed. "Do you need help getting into these dry clothes?"

Gary shook his head. "This guy has a partner."

"Partner?"

Gary nodded. "I tied him up and left him underneath a little aluminum skiff behind Wellfleet Marine Services garage. It's right on the town pier."

"You've had a busy night."

Gary nodded again. He dropped his wet shirt and jacket on the floor and pulled on the sweatshirt.

"I'll have someone pick him up. Climb into that rack when you're changed. It'll take about forty-five minutes for us to get back into Wellfleet Harbor towing your boat. You may as well catch a nap."

Gary had no recollection of the guardsman helping him change into the sweatpants and socks, bundling him into the bunk, and covering him with a pile of blankets.

Chapter 82

Gary may as well have been lifeless, soulless, his conscious mind extinguished and floating in a black hole of exhaustion. As an act of self-preservation, his brain put his body on standby as it attempted to recharge and repair the damages wrought by an extended period of extreme overexertion.

Slowly, and by the smallest increments, he became aware of something outside of the void. Dulled by inactivity, his thought processes wandered aimlessly, searching for the source of the stimulus that impinged on his perfect and absolute repose. Something was touching him. Something was touching his face. Tap. Tap. Tap. Both cheeks. Tap. Tap. Tap.

Unwilling to allow the outside world to intrude into his recuperative abyss until he could at least recall his current surroundings, he lay perfectly still. The persistent tapping continued. What was that sound?

He reacquired control of his eyelids. Raising them a crack, he peeked through the curtain of his eyelashes. He could see small arms. A child's arms attached to tiny hands that were lightly slapping his cheeks. He turned his head to the right and beheld the face he'd been longing to see since Wednesday.

"Time to wake up, Gary!"

"Sandra!" Gary sat up and drew her into his arms. "I missed you so much! Are you OK?"

"Now I am." She hugged his neck so tightly she was choking him.

He pulled her arms away and looked at her face. "You got prettier. How can that be?"

She shrugged and put one hand on each side of his face. "I don't know, but your face got prickly, Gary."

"What did you call me?"

"Your face is prickly, D-A-A-A-A-D."

"That's better." He cuddled her to his chest and kissed the top of her head. He caught the eye of the police officer who was standing in the doorway.

"Thanks for bringing her."

"No problem."

"How long have I been sleeping?"

"According to them," he gestured toward the rest of the crew, "about two and a half hours."

"I feel like I could stretch that to two and a half days."

Tom squeezed through the doorway and joined them. "Welcome back, Gary."

"Thanks."

"You're all warmed up, and all you need is a good night's sleep."

"What about Mireya?"

"They took her to Mass. General and got her warmed up too. She took in too much seawater and has a bacterial infection in her lungs.

She's on oxygen and IV antibiotics. She'll be in the hospital for a few more days, but she should be OK."

Gary sighed and leaned back against the wall with Sandra curled up in his lap. "So now what?"

"The State Police picked up the guy you left under the boat, and he hasn't stopped talking since they peeled off the duct tape. They're going to arrest Nelson Paquette first thing in the morning. We got you a room at a local inn, and we'll need to take your statement tomorrow."

Gary nodded. His eyelids were getting heavy again.

"Let's get you to your room. One of the local officers is going to drive your car over there so you'll have it in the morning."

Gary swung his legs off the bed and stood up, still cradling Sandra in his arms. He staggered as he took his first few steps toward the door, shaking off the last remaining tentacles of deep slumber. The police officer held out his arms, offering to carry Sandra.

Gary smiled and shook his head. The officer, a dedicated family man, nodded his understanding, gently picked up a crate containing a sleeping puppy, and led the way down the passageway and off the cutter.

Chapter 83

After a morning of giving statements and answering questions at the Yarmouth State Police Barracks, Gary put his daughter and her new puppy into Mireya's car and drove home. The drive afforded him the opportunity to have a long telephone conversation with Mireya without any police around. It was important that their versions of the story match, as she would be making her statement to the police the next morning from her hospital bed.

Mireya asked him to call Connor's owner, Al Sullivan, and fill him in on his courageous dog's enormous contribution. Gary voiced his strong opinion that she should be the one to tell the story, but she insisted that he do it. In the end, he couldn't refuse.

When they arrived home, Gina had already called and left Al's number on their machine, but Gary knew he and Sandra would be on the phone with family all night. It was only Monday. Tomorrow morning would be soon enough…

"That's quite a story," Al said, shaking his head in disbelief.

"All true," Gary replied. "Connor was the key to finding my daughter, solving a murder, uncovering a huge, fraudulent real estate deal, and putting all those responsible behind bars."

"Imagine that." Al sat down at his kitchen table. He untangled himself from the long telephone cord that had allowed him to pace up and down the kitchen floor as he listened to Gary's account of the week's events. "I think you gotta give most of the credit to our psychic friend. She's got *some* talent. Never thought I'd live to see the day when I'd admit *that.* What I want to know is, how come I ain't seen her face all over the news? Everything you said is in the paper, but nothing about Connor or Mireya."

"Mireya is…somewhat reclusive. She wants to be left out of this if possible. We told the police that we went to Provincetown, and I got lucky when I overheard an incriminating conversation in one of the bars at the Atlantic House. We followed the guys and the rest is, as they say, history. My daughter was able to give the police enough details about the murder that Mireya's part in it was unnecessary. They found the murder weapon in the old van. The woman's body was in the back of her car, parked out of sight at somebody's vacant vacation house in P-town."

"So why do you suppose she does it?"

"Does what?"

"Finds all the lost pets."

"She does it for the animals."

"Not the money? I guess it's not really much money."

"She doesn't need the money. She doesn't charge much because she doesn't want to discourage anyone from trying to find their pet. The money that she does collect goes into an account that helps to support a number of animal shelters."

"An animal philanthropist."

"Something like that."

"Well I'll be." Al stood up and resumed walking up and down the kitchen floor. "I thank you for taking the time to fill me in on all this. It makes Connor's death seem like less of a waste, if you know what I mean."

"I do. My daughter wanted me to ask what you did with Connor."

"You mean…after I found him?"

"Yeah."

"I buried him in my back yard. I just finished making a little garden there. My granddaughter helped me. Planted a bunch of stuff that's supposed to attract butterflies. Her idea. I just have to keep it watered."

"Could we come for a visit? I mean, if it wouldn't be too much trouble. Sandra formed quite an attachment to Connor in the short time they were together, and I think she needs to say good-bye."

"She needs closure." Al covered his eyes with his free hand, not believing those words had come out of his mouth.

"Exactly."

"No problem. How about tomorrow afternoon? Let's say two o'clock. Unless she's still in school."

"I'm keeping her out of school for the rest of the week. Her pediatrician wants her to talk to a counselor a few times, and I can't bear to have her out of my sight."

"Understandable. I'll see you tomorrow." Al hung up the phone. He walked into the living room, sat in his favorite La-Z-Boy, stared at the empty couch that was still flecked with golden dog hair, and tried to imagine if a more perfect dog could ever exist.

"Not in this lifetime. No way."

Chapter 84

Gary pushed the off button on his phone and leaned back in his chair. They were coming to the end of this episode in their life. Sandra had more to deal with than a girl her age should, but her counselor said she was in pretty good shape, considering what she'd been through. It was fortunate that her captors had made an effort to minimize the trauma to her, may they roast in hell just the same.

This afternoon they would visit Mireya in the hospital, and tomorrow they would go to the cemetery where Mrs. Matthews was buried, followed by a visit to Al Sullivan's. After that they would take it one day at a time, just like they did after Karen died. Tie up the loose ends and move on. Survive.

But what about Mireya? In many ways she was the most extraordinary person he'd ever met. He was indebted. He was in awe. He was mystified and enchanted. Could *he* move on?

"SANDRA! WE HAVE TO GO PRETTY SOON! ARE YOU READY?"

No answer.

"SANDRA?"

The house was quiet.

"SANDRA!"

He was running, taking the stairs three at a time. She was supposed to be in her room.

"SANDRA!"

He burst through the door and into her room. She was sitting in the middle of the floor surrounded by her huge collection of stuffed Snoopy dogs. She was wearing the headset to her Walkman, her head bobbing to whatever tune was playing.

"SANDRA!"

She pulled off the headset. "Chill, Gar…Dad."

"I'm sorry, honey. Didn't you hear me call?"

She shook her head.

"What are you doing? You're supposed to be getting ready to leave."

"I am. I want to bring her a present. Which one of my Snoopies do you think she'd like best?"

Gary smiled. "Oh, I don't think she'd want you to part with any of your Snoopies. Why don't we stop and buy her some pretty flowers?"

"She likes flowers?"

"She's a girl. All girls like flowers."

"I'm a girl, and I'd rather have a Snoopy."

"Good point. I still think she'd like flowers."

"OK. Can I bring my new Snoopy in the car?"

"Sure thing."

They drove Mireya's car to her house. As Mireya promised when they talked on the phone, Gina had moved Gary's car out onto the street. He pulled the Range Rover into the driveway, used the remote control to open the garage door, and parked it inside. He locked it up and left the keys on a shelf behind a can of paint.

They transferred their stuff into the old Toyota sedan. Sandra had picked out a flower arrangement that was a large stuffed bear with his arms around a vase of flowers. Gary carefully propped it up on the seat in the hope that it wouldn't tip over. Sandra wasn't satisfied until he had the bear safely belted into the center position of the back seat.

From Mireya's house he followed the Charles River up Memorial Drive, crossing over to Boston via the Longfellow Bridge. Massachusetts General Hospital was just a few blocks north. Gary worried about Sandra's reaction to the hospital environment. His wife had lingered on life support for four days before dying. Though very young, that was Sandra's only experience with a hospital.

Though she had been characteristically uncommunicative on the phone, Mireya assured him that she was doing well and would be going home in a few days. He kept telling himself that this would be a positive experience for them both.

When they entered Mireya's private room, she was sleeping. She was connected to oxygen, at least two different IVs, and some kind of monitor. Gary touched Sandra on the shoulder and raised his index finger to his lips, signaling her to be quiet. She tiptoed over to the bed, and as if on cue Mireya opened her eyes. She was staring at a bear bearing flowers.

"What a surprise! I wasn't expecting any bears today."

Sandra peeked out from behind the flowers.

"Oh! And the bear brought a friend!"

"I'm Sandra. My dad says you're very brave."

"I'm glad to finally meet you, Sandra. Your father is the one who's brave. He wouldn't let anything stop him from finding you." Mireya pushed the button that raised her to a sitting position.

"My dad says he couldn't have done it without you."

"Well, we made a good team. These are beautiful flowers, and I really like the bear. What's his name?"

"He's a Get Well Bear. He didn't really come with a name, but I think I would call him…Jeff."

Mireya made a closer inspection of the bear. "I agree. I think he looks just like a bear that would be named Jeff."

Gary took the flower arrangement from Sandra and put it on the table next to the bed. "Sandra picked out the bear…"

"Jeff!" Sandra and Mireya both chimed in.

"Right. Jeff. But I got something for you, too." He held up a small bag from Starbucks.

"Coffee! You brought me real coffee? The stuff they call coffee in here tastes like dishwater." She reached for the bag.

"I hope this isn't against the rules."

Mireya took her attention away from the coffee and looked back at him. "Back to being a law abiding citizen so soon?"

Gary blushed. "It's French Roast."

"My favorite."

"I know."

Mireya took a sip of the coffee and sighed. "Heaven. Now, are you going to tell me what happened to your hand?" She pointed to his right hand, which was sporting a gauze bandage across the knuckles.

"Dad punched Rick in the face and *splattered* his nose. The police officer said his nose is going to look like an Idaho potato."

"Interesting. Was Rick in custody at the time?"

"Well…"

Sandra held up her hand to silence her father. "Tom says the police report is gonna say that Rick fell down the stairs."

"Who's Tom?"

"The National Guardsman who got you onto the helicopter. Where did you hear all this, Sandra?"

"Tom and another guy were talking to Roger in the parking lot before they took me onto the boat. They thought I was sleeping in the back of the car."

"Roger?"

"He's the policeman who took care of me that night."

"Oh, right. And remind me to watch what I say around you."

Sandra smiled. "Tom said it was a *righteous* shot to the nose!" She thrust her little fist in the air triumphantly.

"OK. Enough about that."

"Gary Coakley, superhero." Mireya raised her eyebrows.

"Not you, too?"

"Gary Coakley, super-D-A-D."

"OK. Both of you. Quit."

The girls were smiling and staring into each other's eyes. Sandra got quiet. "Dad and I are going to visit Connor tomorrow. Do you want to come?"

"I would, Sandra, but I can't leave the hospital yet. Tomorrow morning I get fitted for a cast for my fractured ankle."

Sandra seemed to consider this, running her fingers lightly along the bed next to Mireya's lower leg. "Do you know Connor?"

"Very well, in fact."

Sandra made eye contact with Mireya again. "Connor told me everything would be all right."

"He did, did he?"

Sandra nodded, still staring into Mireya's eyes.

"That was true, wasn't it?"

"Maybe," Sandra replied, "but Connor died, and that's not all right."

"Do you want to know what Connor told me?"

Sandra nodded.

"He showed me how to find you. He told me he was sorry that he couldn't stay and watch over you. But he said that it's going to be your puppy Scooby's job from now on. He knows that Scooby is young, but says he'll be really good at the job when he grows up a little."

Sandra smiled. "Is he OK now?"

"Connor?"

Sandra nodded.

"He's fine. He misses Al, his owner, but he's fine."

"He's in heaven?"

Mireya hesitated a moment, then nodded. "Yeah. He is."

"Is Mrs. Matthews there?"

"Mrs. Matthews?"

"Our housekeeper. She died, too."

"Right. If you concentrate, can you get a picture of Mrs. Matthews in your mind?"

Sandra nodded. She looked mesmerized.

"Tell me what you see."

"She's in the kitchen, and she's making our dinner. She has the green apron with the Irish thing on the front. She's laughing and shaking a spoon at Scooby."

"Sounds like she's happy."

Sandra nodded.

"Well, there's your answer."

Sandra nodded again. She reached out and touched Mireya's cheek. "When are we going to see you again?"

"I don't know."

"Why not?"

"Nobody can predict the future."

"Not even you?"

"No." Mireya's expression was melancholy.

> *"Mountains loom upon the path we take;*
> *Yonder peak that rose so sharp and clear;*
> *Behold us now on its head uplifted;*
> *Resting there at last we sing our song."*

"What does that mean?"

"It means that our paths crossed because the great spirits gave us a difficult task to accomplish."

"You mean, God?"

"If you like. We were given the task of finding you. It was like climbing a steep mountain. Now that you're safe, and we're on top of the mountain, we should be happy and celebrate, and not worry about the future."

Sandra climbed up on the bed and gave Mireya a hug. Gary stood behind her. "We should go, Rey. You look tired." He leaned over and kissed Mireya on the forehead.

Gary and Sandra walked hand-in-hand down the hospital corridor. When they were in sight of the elevators, Sandra ran forward, pushed the down button, and then turned and looked up at Gary. "You really like her don't you, Dad?"

Gary nodded.

"Her eyes are…are…"

"I know what you mean. Yes, they are." He took his daughter's hand as they stepped onto the elevator.

Chapter 85

Gina entered the room and found Mireya sleeping. She quietly walked over and looked at the card that accompanied the cute flower arrangement and stuffed bear on her table. Mireya woke up.

"Gina."

"How are you feeling, Rey?"

"Fine. Just tired."

"When were they here?" Gina pointed to the flowers.

"Just a little while ago."

"How is the little girl doing?"

"Really well. Gary says her counselor is very encouraged. They're visiting the graves of the housekeeper and Connor tomorrow. She has a lot of good-byes to deal with."

"And did she say good-bye to you today?"

"In a manner of speaking."

"And did she *know* it was good-bye?"

Mireya was silent.

"I wish you wouldn't do this, Rey. You should come home and rest and write your articles. You're too weak to be running off on a new assignment."

"Give it up, Gina. The arrangements are all made. I'm not going on assignment. I'll be at Vernie's for two weeks. I'll be recuperating and writing; I'll just be doing it in Palm Beach instead of Cambridge. Did you get my new phone?"

"Yes. I left it home. You can't use it in here anyway. What about the mouse?"

"I'll go after the mouse only when I'm able to walk comfortably, not before."

"I still think you're running away."

"You can think that if you want, Gina. It's not going to change anything."

Gina put a paper shopping bag on the tray table. "I brought your dinner."

"I'll eat it later. What about my equipment? Did you drop it off?"

"Yes."

"Well? What did they say?"

"It will be a few days before they know if they can salvage it."

"I'll have to go without it. If they can't save it, I'll just have to buy some new stuff."

"You need to sleep, Rey, and not worry about this right now. I'll be sitting right over here saying prayers for you."

"Don't forget to say one for my camera."

"Shhhh!" Gina put her hand on Mireya's forehead and slowly passed it down over her eyes. When she removed her hand, Mireya's eyes remained shut. She placed two long feathers on Mireya's chest, sat down in her chair, and bowed her head.

Chapter 86

Gary and Sandra left the jewelry store with a large, beautifully wrapped package. This and the large pot of flowers they bought seemed to cheer Sandra up a little. The visit to Mrs. Matthew's gravesite was difficult. She had been a tremendously stabilizing and comforting influence on Sandra's life. She was like a grandmother. Not the same as a mother, but a maternal family member, and they both had loved her. Sandra cried the entire time they were there and all the way home.

Now they were on their way to Al Sullivan's house in Dorchester to visit Connor's grave. Gary hoped that Sandra would hold on to Mireya's words and not be as devastated as she was this morning. Sandra had insisted that they bring both puppies because she thought Al sounded lonely on the phone. "Don't puppies always cheer you up?" she had asked Gary. "That's what I have you for," had been his reply.

Gary pulled into Al's driveway just a few minutes before two o'clock. Al greeted them on the front step. He bent low to shake Sandra's hand in a way that was grandfatherly and genuinely kind. When he took Gary's hand, Gary was struck by the odd combination of curiosity and nervousness in his demeanor.

Al led them to the backyard, where in a quiet corner a small but pretty garden marked Connor's resting place. Al had fashioned a cross out of wood and had lettered it simply with "Connor." Sandra placed the potted flowers next to the cross. As she stood up, her shoulders began to shake, and Gary knew she was crying again. He put his hands on her shoulders, feeling completely helpless.

Al knelt down next to Sandra. She turned to look at him and immediately reached out and tried to wipe the tears from his cheeks. He took her little hand in his and kissed it in an effort to comfort her.

She tried valiantly to compose herself, without success. Her voice was shaking as she asked Al, "Did you know that my mother died? And Mrs. Matthews died, too?"

Al blinked hard, and a fresh wave of tears surged down his cheeks. "I'm awful sorry to hear that."

"I think Mrs. Matthews died because she was looking for me, and the men stole Connor to keep me company, and then he died. Then they killed the woman who hit Connor. It's all my fault. I'm sorry." She began to sob uncontrollably.

Gary knelt down and put his arm around Sandra. This was his and her counselor's worst fear.

Al reached out and turned Sandra's chin toward him. "Now you listen to me, Sandra. None of this is your fault. There are very bad men in the world, and they do very bad things. You have no control over that. These bad men kidnapped you because an even worse man paid them to do it. And you know what? I'm glad those guys stole Connor. Yes, I am."

"You are?" Her sobs subsided.

"Absolutely. Do you realize that if they hadn't taken Connor, Mireya could never have found you? I think that was Connor's purpose. To help save you."

"Mireya said that great spirits gave her and my dad a task, and it was to find me. Do you think they gave Connor the task, too?"

"I'm sure of it. And you know what else?"

Sandra shook her head.

"I would have never met you. A lonely old guy like me needs all the friends he can get."

"And you got to meet Mireya, too, right?"

"Right. Although I haven't seen her face-to-face yet. Have you?"

Sandra nodded. "At the hospital. She has beautiful eyes. And she *knows* things."

"That she does."

"Do you have a family?"

"My children have grown up and moved away, and my wife died several years ago. I do have a granddaughter that goes to school in Boston. I get to see her every so often. Pretty much it was just me and Connor."

Sandra was quiet, and looked reflectively at the cross. As Gary stood up, Al held his hand out to him. "Give me a hand, young fella. My knees ain't what they used to be."

Al looked down at Sandra. "I just happen to have a hand-packed quart of Friendly's ice cream in my freezer. What do you say we all have an afternoon snack?"

Sandra looked up at him. “What flavor?”

“Mint chocolate chip.”

Sandra looked at her father. When he nodded, she replied, “OK.”

Gary leaned down and whispered in her ear. “Why don’t you go to the car and get the present?”

Sandra trotted off toward the car.

“Thanks for your help with her,” he said to Al. “This has been unbelievably hard.”

“Who’s Mrs. Matthews?”

“Our housekeeper and Sandra’s nanny. She had a heart attack the day Sandra was taken.”

“Poor kid.”

Sandra came running back, carrying the beautifully wrapped box they had picked up at the jewelry store. She handed it to Al. “This is for you, from me and my dad.”

“Oh my. This looks too pretty to open.”

“You *have* to open it.”

“OK. Al removed the wrapping. Inside the box was a handsome picture frame made from some exotic wood. At the base was an engraved brass plate.

CONNOR

Kindness and Courage

In Life

And After Life

"We thought you could put your favorite picture of Connor in there and hang it in your house."

"That's a great idea, and this is one of the best presents I ever got. Thank you both."

Sandra handed Al a card. "This is for you, too."

"Uh oh. Should I have opened this first? You know, my wife always used to yell at me for opening the present before the card."

"No. It's from Mireya."

"Really?"

Sandra nodded.

He turned the envelope over in his hands. It was made of the same heavyweight paper that wedding invitations were sent in. This was definitely not a store-bought card. He opened it and realized it was Mireya's personal stationery. Her monogram was printed on the front of the note card with a delicate drawing of a feather underneath it.

He looked inside:

A message from Connor:

"Don't let the turkeys get you down."

Mireya

Al stared down at Connor's grave and shook his head. Sandra looked up at him. Until that moment, she couldn't believe that anyone else could match the depth of sadness that she felt. She took the card from his hand and read it. "Does this mean something to you?"

"Yes. It does." Al took out his handkerchief and wiped his eyes.

Sandra tugged on Al's hand and actually managed a smile. "Would you like to meet my puppies?"

"You brought them with you?"

"They're in the car."

"That's great! Let's see 'em."

Sandra grabbed Gary's hand and dragged him to the car. They each returned with a puppy.

"This one," she pointed to Scooby "is my puppy, and his name is Scooby-Don't."

"Don't?"

Sandra nodded. "And this one," she pointed to the puppy she was leading, "is the puppy they got me after Connor died. I named her Connie because she's a girl."

"What a beautiful puppy."

"I think she has a purpose, too."

"Really? What's that?"

"To keep you from being lonely." Sandra handed Al the leash.

"You don't want to give up your beautiful puppy!"

"I don't think she's really mine."

"Why not?"

"First they gave me Connor, and he wasn't really mine. His purpose was to lead Mireya to me. Then they gave me Connie, and I don't think she's really mine either. Maybe my purpose was to lead her back to you. Like a circle." She traced a circle in the air with her index finger.

"That's a beautiful thought, Sandra." Gary looked at his daughter, amazed.

"Mireya explained it to me."

"She did? I don't remember her talking about that."

Sandra nodded, then turned and looked up at her father. "Can someone my age have a purpose, Dad?"

Gary nodded. "Sure."

"We should ask Mireya. She knows things. Can we call her?"

"I don't think we need to, honey. I think you're absolutely right."

"Can we call her anyway?"

"I think we should let her rest."

"Please, Dad. Please?"

"OK." Gary took out his cell phone and a business card on the back of which he had written Mireya's hospital room phone number. He punched the numbers in and waited. After several rings, the hospital information operator answered.

"I'm trying to reach Mireya Richardson's room."

"What room number?"

"Four fifteen."

"One moment." He waited for a minute and the operator came back on the line. "She's been discharged."

"Excuse me?"

"The patient. M. Richardson. She was discharged at noon."

"Discharged?"

"That's correct."

"Thank you." Gary terminated the call and looked at Sandra and Al. "They discharged her. I thought she was supposed to be in there for a few more days."

"That's good though, right?" Al asked. "That means she must be feeling much better."

"Call her at home, Dad."

"The police found her cell phone and returned it to her, so I could try that." He looked at his daughter's face, brimming with anticipation, and dialed the number. It rang a few times and then connected him to her voice mail.

> *"Rey, it's Gary. We called the hospital and heard that you were discharged. We hope that means you're feeling much better. Sandra wanted to ask you a question..."*

Chapter 87

Mireya took a seat at the gate and waited for her flight to begin boarding. She reached into her backpack and pulled out a file labeled *Peromyscus gossypinus allapaticola* (Key Largo Cotton Mouse). She had downloaded several research articles about a month ago and would finally have some time to catch up on her reading. Photographing this elusive little rodent would no doubt take a great deal of time and patience, but at least she wouldn't be hanging off a cliff while she was doing it.

Her plan was to spend as much time as she could tolerate with her college friend, Veronique Almay. Vernie had sounded positively stunned when Mireya called and finally accepted her open invitation to visit. She was horrified to hear about Mireya's brush with death, but the lawyer in her was automatically plotting lawsuit strategies. To Vernie's extreme disappointment, Mireya insisted that the entire experience was behind her and was going to stay that way.

Vernie was delighted to have Mireya recuperate at her home for an indefinite period of time, but she was in the middle of two high-profile divorce proceedings and her workload wouldn't allow her to stay home and entertain. Mireya assured her that this would work out better because of the backlog of writing she simply could not postpone any longer. Mireya would have her own room with a private bath and doors leading directly to the pool. She wouldn't need to be entertained.

When her ankle improved, she would rent a car and move her base of operation down to Key Largo. During the off-season she would have no trouble renting a cottage.

Gina insisted that she was running away. She thought about it as she took a sip from the cup of coffee she bought at the Dunkin' Donuts counter on her way to the gate. Maybe Gina was right, but what did it matter? She didn't fit in with people. Gina didn't want her to be alone, but she didn't *feel* alone. She was surrounded by the souls of animals. She had only to open her mind and her heart and she was filled to the brim.

The flight attendant announced that first class passengers and those with special needs or small children could begin boarding. As she stuffed her folder back into her pack, she heard her phone ring. It was her old phone. She unzipped a side pocket on her pack and took it out. No doubt Gina was responsible for putting it in there. She looked at the caller ID. It said "WIRELESS CALLER – BROOKLINE." Gary. She listened to it ring a few more times and then shut the power off. She dropped the phone in the bag that her coffee had come in, crumpled it up, and threw it in the trash. She paused a moment, staring at the trash receptacle, then picked up her pack and crutches and made her way to the gate.

She stretched out in her seat and thanked her lucky stars that she was able to afford first class. She couldn't imagine being crammed into coach with her ankle throbbing as the pain medications wore off.

The flight attendant arrived with a bottle of water for her so she could take her next round of vicodin and antibiotics. The pilot announced that their departure would be delayed for a half hour because of a security problem with another plane.

If they weren't going to leave the gate for a while, she could turn her new cell phone back on and check her messages. Her machine announced that there was one new message.

> *"Hi, Rey. Sorry to call on your Lost Friends line, but it's the only number I have for you besides your old cell phone, and I'm not sure you're even using that anymore. We were surprised to hear that you were discharged from the hospital so soon, but we hope that means you are feeling like your old self again. Sandra wanted to ask you a question so I'm giving the phone to her."*
>
> *"Hi. This is Sandra. I wanted to ask you if you told me about the circle. I think you did, but Dad doesn't remember us talking about that. I was thinking that Connor leading you and Dad to me and then me leading Connie back to Mr. Sullivan is like one of those circles. If I keep Connie then it won't be finished and nothing will connect. And maybe a great spirit gave me the task if I'm not too little to have a purpose. Will I get another purpose some day? I have a lot of questions, so I hope now that you're out of the hospital you can come*

over for dinner. Dad just made a funny face at me. I think it's because he can't cook. Bye."

Mireya smiled and turned the phone off again. What could she say to a child as bright and endearing as that? She dragged her pack out from under the seat and fished around in the main compartment until she found a slim packet of note cards engraved with her name. She searched some more until she found a calligraphy pen. She had the pen poised on the page for at least a minute; still she was undecided. She procrastinated further by addressing the envelope to Sandra. She reached into the inside breast pocket of her jacket, pulled out one of the feathers Gina had given her, and placed it inside the envelope. Mireya smiled. It was suddenly clear to her what she should write. Sandra would come to understand it as she had understood the circle:

In beauty it is done,

In harmony it is written.

In beauty and harmony it shall so be finished.

Mireya

About the Author

Barbara Davidson-Miles grew up in Windsor Locks, Connecticut, and graduated from Russell Sage College. She and her husband, Steve, share Mile's End Farm in Sterling, Massachusetts, and Mile's End Farm South in Loxahatchee, Florida, with thirteen horses, five dogs, three cats, three parakeets, two lovebirds, and their African Grey Parrot, Kibo. Barbara is currently working on her next novel.

Printed in the United States
1081100001B/109-123

9 781410 710963